Feeling much better, Kate returned to the dim bunker of the *Beacon* office. Barry was now at his desk, pulling his notebooks out of his backpack, a large cup from Port City Java balanced precariously on the corner of his desk.

"Hey, there, Kate. What's up?"

"My blood pressure, for one thing. Had to listen to thirty people ranting and raving about that Timmy Kessler story. I'm sure there's more piling up in my inbox, if you care to listen."

"Comes with the territory, my friend. Just get used to it. I don't even notice them anymore."

"Even when they say things about your mother?"

"Well, that does sting a bit, but I try not to take it personally." He smiled and took a swig of coffee. "What's that you got there? Fan mail from some flounder?"

"No, it's from the kids at Holly Tree Elementary School. Guess they sent me some handmade notes or something. Let's see what I've got."

She undid the string that held the envelope shut and dumped the contents onto her desk.

Suddenly, the room was filled with her screams.

ALSO BY JUDY NICHOLS

Caviar Dreams

TREE HUGGERS

BY

JUDY NICHOLS

ZUMAYA ENIGMA   AUSTIN TX

2008

TREE HUGGERS

© 2008 by Judy Nichols

ISBN 13: 978-1-934135-23-5

ISBN 10: 1-934135-23-2

Cover art and design by April Martinez

Look for us online at http:www.zumayapublications.com

Library of Congress Cataloging-in-Publication Data

Nichols, Judy, 1956-
Tree huggers / by Judy Nichols.
    p. cm.
ISBN-13: 978-1-934135-23-5 (alk. paper)
ISBN-10: 1-934135-23-2 (alk. paper)
1. Women journalists – Fiction. 2. Murder – Investigation – Fiction. 3. Green movement – Fiction. I. Title.
PS3614.I343T74 2007
813'.6 – dc22
              2007037173

For Alysoun, the best kid in the whole world.

ACKNOWLEDGMENTS

I'd like to thank Nancy Nichols, Amy Kisner and Kathy Wendorf for their help and encouragement during the final edits. Thanks also to the Christian Insights Adult Sunday School Class of Pearsall Memorial Presbyterian Church, whose ideas have inspired me both on my literary and spiritual journeys.

Although Abigail's Attic and the Nature Trust are fictional, they are based on two very real organizations: The Phoenix Employment Ministry of Wilmington, NC (www.phoenixwork.org), which has helped many Wilmington residents find meaningful work, and the Nature Conservancy (www.nature.org).

Thanks especially to Liz Burton, who helped me make this story the best it could be.

And finally, thank you, Nigel, for your love, support and the pleasure of your company for all these years.

What's New in Real Estate

Sept. 3 — Edward Kominsky of Kominsky Builders, Inc., is pleased to announce the completion of the first luxury home in Normandy Sands.

"This house is absolutely gorgeous," said Warren Owens, a spokesman for Kominsky Builders. "We used quality materials like Italian marble, mahogany and redwood. The craftsmanship is exquisite. And the view of the beach is breathtaking. You have to see it to believe it."

This fine home is shown by appointment only. Contact Warren Owens at Kominsky Builders for more information.

Winslow Beach Beacon

1. BURNING DOWN THE HOUSE

IT WAS A TRAVESTY OF A HOUSE, A SPRAWLING HULK OF GLASS AND freshly painted cedar siding with redwood decks jutting out at all different angles. The real estate agency handout stated it was six thousand square feet of pure luxury. It had five bedrooms, seven bathrooms, four wood-burning fireplaces, a great room, a home office, a gourmet kitchen, a wine cellar, a music room, a den and a few extra rooms with no particular purpose whatsoever.

And then there were the breathtaking views of the North Carolina coastline, visible from virtually every window on the east side of the house.

It was perfect for the discerning homeowner who could afford the multi-million-dollar price tag, as well as the army of maids required to keep it clean.

John Cochran surveyed the building with disgust. He knew his beat-up old Volvo looked out of place, parked here next to the huge six-car garage. He was also aware that *he* looked out of place at this obscene display of conspicuous consumption. Wearing a pair of old blue jeans and an even older "Save the Whales" T-shirt, his hair graying and his face weathered, Cochran appeared to be a tramp. All he needed was a "WILL WORK FOR FOOD" sign.

In reality, he had enough money to buy this piece of property and several others like it if he chose.

He leaned against the car and worked on a crossword puzzle while he waited for Warren Owens to show up. Owens was a representative from the development company that was intent on buying up Cochran's beloved stretch of Carolina pine savannah and building houses on it.

"Over my dead body," he muttered.

A shiny new Mercedes sedan pulled into the driveway, and Warren

Owens hopped out. He was a man who'd done well for himself. His designer suit fit him perfectly, and it looked great with the French linen shirt, the Italian silk tie and matching handkerchief. Though he was not yet forty, his brown hair was already starting to thin, and he had developed a noticeable paunch. Still, he exuded an air of affable self-confidence.

He was the perfect salesman.

"John, John, great to see you again, my friend," he said, extending his hand and grabbing John's in a well-practiced firm handshake. "Glad you could make it."

"Yeah, right. Let's get on with it," Cochran said, sneering. "Already I can tell you this building is a waste of good wood. You could have built ten houses for people who really need them instead of this castle for spoiled yuppies with more money than sense."

"Now, John, there's nothing wrong with having a little bit of luxury in your life. You should try it. Spend some of that money you've got on yourself. Shane tells me you never have any fun."

"Now, that's something my son does know plenty about – having fun. Twenty-seven years old, never had to work for anything. By the way, isn't he supposed to be joining us?"

"Yes, he and Mr. Kominsky will be driving in together." Owens glanced at his watch, and Cochran noted its prestigious brand name. "They should be here in about twenty minutes."

"If Mr. Kominsky can get my son to arrive anywhere on time, my hat's off to him. Nice watch, by the way."

"Thank you. My wife gave it to me last Christmas. I'm a Timex man myself, but I have to admit, it sure is a fine way to tell time. Come on, let me show you around."

He placed a hand on Cochran's shoulder and steered him to the huge slab of ornately carved dark wood that served as the front door.

"Lovely door, isn't it?" Owens gave it a proprietary slap. "Solid teak. It'll stand up to wind, rain and salt, whatever the Atlantic Ocean dishes out. They used this stuff to cover the decks of the *USS North Carolina*."

Pausing from his spiel, he opened a small gray plastic box by the door, revealing a security keypad. He punched in a series of numbers and opened the door.

"State of the art security system," he continued. "Keyless entry, twenty-four-hour surveillance cameras, the works. If anyone breaks in, the local police are notified right away. And of course, there's a whole slew of smoke detectors hooked up directly to the security command center. No need to call nine-one-one – the fire department is dispatched immediately."

"Doesn't it take a while for them to get here? It's pretty out-of-the-way," Cochran observed as they crossed the marble floors of the foyer. "The Winslow Beach firehouse is twenty miles away and it's run by volunteers. They'd all have to be paged. And there's not a fire hydrant in sight. Where's the water going to come from? A good-sized fire could burn this place to the ground."

Owens laughed nervously and smiled.

"Oh, John, don't be such a worry-wart. When was the last time your house burned to the ground? Besides, there's an automatic sprinkler system. Take my word for it, John. You have enough money to buy this house, you have enough money to protect it."

"I'm not buying this house. I have a house," Cochran replied. "You do know I'm only here because my son begged me to take a look at this place, right? He figured your boss Kominsky could talk me into selling my property even though there is absolutely no way in hell that's going to happen. I only agreed to come after Shane promised to help me clear the phragmites from the marshes this weekend."

"Mr. Kominsky can be very persuasive."

"Yes, I'm sure he can sell refrigerators to the Inuits."

"Don't you mean the Eskimos?"

"Whatever."

They entered the expansive great room. Since there wasn't a stick of furniture in the entire house, Cochran felt like he had just walked into an empty airplane hangar instead of someone's living space. He craned his neck for a view of the chandelier hanging from the ceiling thirty feet above his head. Crystal prisms dangled in clumps like giant stalactites, a vain mockery of the stately crystal chandeliers he'd seen in European opera houses. This thing was downright ugly.

"Isn't that chandelier something?" Owens asked. "An original design, handmade by a highly regarded artist name of Cameron Jericho. Works out of Chapel Hill, though I believe he's originally from Ohio. He's the best in art glass. You won't find another chandelier like that anywhere."

"Thank God for that."

Ignoring this remark, Owens ushered his charge into the kitchen, which boasted the obligatory array of industrial-sized stainless steel appliances tossed in among an endless jumble of cabinetry and granite counters. A gourmet cook's dream, Owens told him.

Then it was through the breakfast nook to the formal dining room, a look into the music room and finally into the first-floor master bedroom. Cochran saw their reflections in the mirrored doors to the closet and noted how ludicrous they looked together. The salesman and the beach bum.

"Walk-in closet, plenty of room for the wife to keep all her clothes and doodads. Even has a timed lock so the maid won't steal anything while the lady of the house is out."

"Is that a problem, maids stealing clothes?"

"Well, let me put it this way — if your wife had a closet full of shoes at fifteen hundred dollars a pair, wouldn't you want a lock on the door?"

"Women pay that much for a pair of shoes?" Cochran asked.

"And more."

"That's criminal."

"Tell me about it. Seems like fast as I earn my commission, my wife's spent it all on a pair of designer shoes. And the handbag to match, of course."

Owens walked over to the back wall of the bedroom. It was entirely made of glass, a sliding door flanked by floor-to-ceiling windows. The door opened onto a wooden deck, and beyond that Cochran could see the waves coming up on the beach.

"Now, who wouldn't want to wake up to this view?"

"That view won't be there for long," Cochran answered. "You guys built the house too close to the ocean. The sand will erode away completely in a couple of years. Maybe sooner."

"Nonsense, John. Kominsky Builders consulted one of the best structural engineers in the business when we selected this site. He assured us there would be no erosion problem."

Owens reached over and pulled the sliding glass door open. Cochran followed him outside. He noticed that the deck followed the jagged outline of the house. So many angles, so much wood.

He thought he noticed a bit of movement. He felt there was something or someone just out of sight, hidden by the corners of the house.

Owens leaned against the railing and took a very audible deep breath.

"Just smell that air," he said robustly. "John, come on over here and take a look at the ocean."

Cochran did not particularly want to look at the ocean — he had a much better view from his own property up the coastline; but he could see no reason for ignoring the man, so he went over to the railing and stood next to him, fidgeting impatiently.

"Isn't that the most beautiful thing on God's green earth?" Owens asked.

Cochran never got a chance to comment, as the sound of the crashing waves was drowned out by heavy footsteps running toward them. He looked up to find they were surrounded by four men, all dressed in camouflage army fatigues, their faces hidden by thin olive-colored ski masks. Each one held a revolver.

One thug grabbed Cochran's left arm, jabbing the gun to his back, while another took his right arm and pointed the gun at his temple. He knew nothing about guns, but he thought the one in his face looked a lot like the one Clint Eastwood used in the Dirty Harry movies. It certainly was intimidating, and he offered no resistance.

The other two did the same with Owens.

"Do exactly as you're told, and no one will get hurt!" one of them yelled as they pushed Owens and Cochran back into the house.

Once inside, one of them grabbed the handle on the mirrored closet door and slid it open. The others shoved the two frightened men inside and shut the door, plunging them into total darkness.

Cochran stood very still, trying to hear what the men were doing. It was difficult to do, since Owens was making so much noise stumbling around in the dark; Cochran assumed he was looking for the light switch.

"Here it is," Owens said, sounding relieved as the lights went on. He gave the door a shove. It didn't budge.

"Damn, those guys must have hit the timer lock," he said. "Well, I guess they're just here to steal the stereo equipment then they'll be on their way. Mr. Kominsky and your son should be here any minute. They'll let us out."

"Don't you have a cell phone? We could call the police."

"Yes, but I left it in the car. Reception is so bad here, there isn't much point in having it. Besides, the police should be here soon. Those guys must have tripped the alarm when they came in."

"You idiot! They didn't trip any alarms. Don't you remember? We let them in through the back door!" Cochran shouted in frustration.

Outside, four pairs of feet pounded about the room. There was the glug-glugging sound of liquid spilling out of a big container and splashing against the walls.

"Oh, God, they're trashing the house — they're throwing paint all over the place!" Owens moaned.

"It's not paint," Cochran said quietly.

Someone outside shouted "Let's go!" and they heard the men run out of the room, followed by a grim silence.

Then the house exploded into a fireball.

Welcome Aboard!

Sept. 3 — Kate Dennison has joined the staff of the *Winslow Beach Beacon*. Originally from Cincinnati, Ohio, Ms. Dennison worked as a reporter for the Suburban Press newspapers in Dayton, Ohio. She also taught second grade in the Dayton public schools. She lives in the Sunset Park section of Wilmington with her daughter, Molly.

Winslow Beach Beacon

2. FIRST DAY ON THE JOB

IT WASN'T EXACTLY AS SHE'D PICTURED IT.

Kate Dennison stood outside the door of the office of the *Winslow Beach Beacon. Office* was too kind a word. The newspaper was housed in an old discount store in a seedy-looking strip mall on Market Street. There was a chiropractor's office on the left and an empty storefront to the right with "Jenny's Treasures, Adventures in Consignment" still painted on the window. The southern charm of Historic Wilmington was only two or three miles down the road, but there were no graceful rows of live oak trees or antebellum mansions here. This part of town was known for its used car lots and half-empty strip malls.

Kate was not the least bit concerned with appearances. She was earning her own money. And her ex-husband would finally get off her back about finding a job.

She opened the glass door to find a circular plywood receptionist's desk with a bleached-blond fortyish (possibly fiftyish?) woman sitting behind it. There wasn't much else in the reception area, just a couch with yellow vinyl cushions and a metal frame, an occasional table with some old magazines and a couple of metal racks in front of the desk offering copies of the *Beacon*.

"Hey, there," the woman said with a big, toothy smile. She waved Kate toward her, and the dozen or so gold bracelets she wore clanked together. The bracelets were complemented by four or five gold necklaces and chunky gold rings on every finger (even her thumbs, Kate noted). This veritable jewelry store was set off nicely by a very red, very tight blouse.

"Don't be shy, hon," she said. "Come on in. What can I do for you?"

"Hi, I'm Kate Dennison. Roger Hoffman told me to be here at nine o'clock. He just hired me to work on the paper."

"So you're the gal Roger's so excited about. Glad to have you on board. I'm Janie Glenn. I'm the *Beacon* office manager. I do everything that needs doing around here and then some. You need anything, you come to me."

"Thank you," Kate said.

"Hang on a second and I'll have Roger take you back to the editorial office."

Janie picked up the phone on an ancient console switchboard and pressed a button.

"Get your buns up here, Roger. Your new reporter's here. And I've got your e-mails printed out so you can pick those up too."

Roger wasn't kidding when he'd said the office was informal.

"He's on his way," Janie said, hanging up the phone. "I'd tell you to have a seat, but you don't want to sit on that couch. Roger bought it and everything else around here at a municipal auction in New Bern. So don't expect too much as far as the decor goes."

"Believe me, I'm just happy to be working someplace where I don't have to say 'Do you want fries with that?'" Kate said. "Decor is not an issue."

"Guess you'll fit in just fine," Janie said. "Roger tells me you're a divorcee with a girl in second grade. If you don't mind me saying so, you must've been a child bride. You don't look old enough to have a daughter that age."

"I'm old enough," Kate said. "Thirty-eight on my last birthday."

"Well, you certainly don't look it, hon. Someday you'll have to tell me your secret."

"Thank you," Kate said. She had grown used to comments about her youthful appearance, and she knew she should be appreciative, but deep down she wished she looked her age. She always felt that if she had curves – real hips and a bosom instead of a slight figure, people would take her seriously. Here she was, approaching forty, and she still looked like a seventh grader.

"Does your little girl have red hair and green eyes like you?" Janie asked.

"She has the red hair, but she's got blue eyes like her father."

"You'll have to bring her in sometime."

"I will."

"Oh, I almost forgot your tax forms." Janie held up a stack of papers held together with a large paper clip. "Just bring 'em back here when you're done. We can't pay you without 'em."

The door behind Janie's desk opened and there was her new boss, managing editor and publisher Roger Hoffman. A distinguished-looking man in his sixties, Roger was well over six feet tall and heavyset, a very imposing figure. Moreover, with his thick white hair and mustache he bore a vague resemblance to Mark Twain

"Hey, Kate. You're right on time," he said. "I see you've met Janie. Be sure to stay on her good side. She knows where all the bodies are buried. Are those my e-mails?"

"Yes, they are," Janie said, handing him a stack of papers two inches high. "You know it would make my job a whole lot easier if I didn't have to print out all those e-mails about church picnics and the next meeting of the Whatchadoodle Bird Watching club every morning."

"Yes, but it makes my job easier to read them on paper, the way things should be read. And, as I've mentioned before, Janie — it's your job is to make my job easier."

"Yes, sir, Mr. Hoffman, sir!" she snapped back, giving him a mock salute.

"One of these days, Janie...oh, never mind. Kate, come on back."

Roger escorted Kate through the door and down a long dark hallway. On the left was a wall covered with cheap tan colored wood paneling, on the right there was a door marked "Advertising" and a second marked "Publisher." At the end of the hall, she could see the "Editorial Office" sign.

"As you can see, this is where our advertising office is," Roger said. "They don't have much contact with the editorial side and vice versa. Except for Clarisse Hopper, our business reporter. She calls herself a reporter, but her stories are all advertisements masquerading as news. I figure there's a place for that, so I let her write whatever she pleases as long as she doesn't libel anyone. Here we are, Kate."

Roger opened the door into Kate's new world, the *Beacon* editorial offices.

"This place is a bit gloomy but it works for us," Roger said.

Gloomy was right. The editorial office was a windowless box. The walls were covered with the same fake wood paneling as the hallway. The floor consisted of linoleum squares the color of old coffee with light brown flecks. Shoved against the walls were several metal desks, the cast-offs of the City of New Bern. Two had computer terminals on them, the rest were empty. One bit of the wall was glass instead of paneling, which appeared to be the managing editor's office.

"Where do I sit?" Kate asked.

"This one right here. Yes, a lot of empty desks. I may fill them some day. Aside from the stringers and the occasional intern, we only have two full time reporters here – you and Barry Moore, who also doubles as our staff photographer. He should be here soon."

Kate sat down in the four-wheeled office chair behind her new (to her) desk and swiveled from side to side.

"It's perfect," she announced.

"I wouldn't go that far," Roger said. "Adequate is the best I can hope for. I know the office leaves a lot to be desired. Windows and a laminate floor would be nice."

"It's your newspaper. You can redecorate if you want. Didn't you make a fortune when you did public relations in New York?"

"Yes and no. You need to make a fortune just to live in New York. Somehow we got this crazy idea of retiring to North Carolina and buying a newspaper. I know I complain a lot about this place, but it wasn't easy to find something large enough to accommodate a newspaper right here on Market Street. We got a great deal when the old Dollar Saver went out of business. But we still have barely enough money to make ends meet, let alone put in new paneling and track lighting. Marlene does the books, and she says if it's not broken, we don't fix it. And if it is broken, we try to get along without it. That's why we're so glad to have you onboard. It's damned impossible to find reporters willing to work for what we pay them."

"Well, the free daycare is a definite plus."

"That's only for reporters who live next door to the publisher," Roger said. "Honestly, Kate, I can't believe our luck. I was going nuts trying to find someone to fill this spot and then Marlene called to say that our nice new neighbor just happened to have a degree in journalism, a year of experience and was looking for a job. All we needed to do was look after that sweet little girl of hers after school. I wish all my problems could be solved that easily."

"Are you sure Marlene doesn't mind looking after Molly? She can be a handful."

"Nonsense, Molly is a joy. Marlene adores her. And besides, you don't need to be in the office all the time. It's fine with me if you want to be home when Molly gets home from school. With the evening meetings you'll be covering, your hours will be erratic anyway; early one day, late the next. Today will be almost banker's hours, but don't get used it. I called Barry in today so you could meet him. We're having a staff meeting at nine. In the meantime, make yourself comfortable."

Kate pulled open the large file drawer. There were several empty manila file folders; the previous occupant had cleared them out before leaving. She slid them back and put her purse in the drawer.

"Would you like some coffee?" Roger asked. "We keep the pot out this way in the breakroom. It's free, too, by the way, and that's the only fringe benefit we provide besides the mileage stipend. I think we have some extra mugs out there. Remember to bring one in tomorrow; we don't have plastic cups. It saves money and cuts down on waste in the landfill. How do you take your coffee?"

"Black with sweetener, if you've got it."

"We do. Janie insists on it. Although a little bit of sugar in your coffee wouldn't hurt you, Kate. You don't need to lose weight."

"It's bad for your teeth."

A dark-haired young man walked in the room. He looked to be in his mid-twenties, dressed in blue jeans and a red plaid flannel shirt over a plain black T-shirt. His red canvas sneakers made squeaking noises as he walked across the linoleum floor. He carried a backpack with him and looked a bit miffed when he saw Kate sitting at her desk.

"David, thanks for coming in," Roger said. "This is Kate Dennison, our new reporter. Kate, this is David Hatcher. David is deserting us for the greener pastures and bigger paychecks of the Raleigh News-Observer."

Kate stood up to shake his hand. So this was the former occupant of her desk. Guess he wasn't quite ready to give it up. Oh, well, the News-Observer should provide him with a much nicer desk and chair. And possibly an office with a window and track lighting.

"Hello, Kate," he said politely. "You don't know how glad we all are to see you. We were sure it would be months before Roger found someone to take the job."

"What can I say? No one wants to be a reporter anymore, and if they do, they don't want to start at the bottom," Roger complained. "Kate, David was kind enough to come back to this hell hole to fill you in on his beat. You'll be covering the schools, the Winslow Town Council and that hotbed of controversy, the New Hanover County Planning and Zoning Board, at least whenever it relates to our readership, which is basically the top half of New Hanover County, from the Cape Fear River east to Winslow Beach and north to the Pender County line. David, I'll let you get started. Kate, pay attention. I'm off to get Kate some coffee. Would you like some, too, David?"

"Yes, thanks, Roger, double cream no sugar."

"Got it," Roger said and walked out the door.

"He gets you coffee on your first and last day. In between you get it yourself," David said.

David set his backpack down on the desk and unzipped it. He pulled out several file folders and set them on the desk. He slid a chair over from the next one and motioned for her to sit down.

"I put all this together for you last night. It should help you sort out the mess you're going to have to deal with in planning and zoning. Schools and Winslow Beach Town Council are pretty straightforward, but development here is spiraling out of control and the zoning board is just letting it happen."

He thumbed through his files, opened one up and spread its contents of newspaper clippings and typed papers across the desk. He pointed to a slick color brochure for something called Normandy Sands.

"Okay, this is a new development by Ed Kominsky. You wouldn't believe how fast this thing went through. The county ignored every single environmental regulation on the books. The house is way too close to the beach; somebody's going to have to pay for dredging up the sand when the beach erodes and you can bet it won't be Ed Kominsky. Then there're the water and sewer issues. And the emergency services problem. Fire and ambulance service is all volunteer in that area, and any calls to Normandy Sands would have at least a half-hour response time. It's all in this story I wrote last year when he submitted the plans for it."

He handed her one of the clippings with the headline "PLANNED DEVELOPMENT POSES CONCERNS."

"The name just kills me. Normandy Sands," David said. "It always makes me think of the invasion of Normandy and the opening scenes in *Saving Private Ryan*. Who'd want to wake up to D-Day every morning?"

"Yeah, it does have a kind of dour connotation, now that you mention

14

it. But I guess it's hard to come up with the names for these places. Maybe they were trying for something kind of quaint and European."

David nodded then continued.

"Let me tell you about Ed Kominsky. You're sure to end up hearing his inspirational speech at some community meeting. I've heard it at least a dozen times. I've got the whole thing memorized. 'I grew up poor and fatherless in the slums of Chicago. We were so poor we had to eat our cereal with a fork to save milk,'" he recited in a thick Chicago accent. "Well, you get the idea.

"His older brother Walter joined a gang and little Eddie was about to do the same. He was already doing small crimes. Then his brother was arrested for armed robbery and sent off to prison. His mom swore the streets wouldn't take her other son, and she made him promise he'd turn himself around. When he describes visiting his brother in Joliet, you can hear a pin drop. It's especially effective at DARE graduations.

"Anyway, Ed promises his mother he'll work hard and stay out of trouble. He gets a job in construction and works his way up to foreman. Then he starts his own building company. He always ends by saying he knows his mama is looking down from heaven on all the beautiful houses he's built, and the best reward is knowing he kept his promise and made her proud."

"How touching."

"Oh, it brings down the house every time," David said. "Seriously, though, you have to watch out for him. Kominsky is one smooth operator. He comes off as a really nice guy. He donates a lot of money to charity, sponsors a soccer team, and he holds a huge benefit every year for child abuse prevention. You can almost forget that he's destroying the Carolina coastline. When you interview him – and you will – be prepared to verify every word he says."

"Thanks for the heads-up," Kate said, a bit warily. She now wondered just what she'd gotten herself into with this job. Perhaps working at Target wasn't such a bad idea.

"Good. Now we get Kominsky's problems." He handed her the last clipping in his stack. The headline read "NEIGHBOR CHALLENGES BUILDING PLANS."

"This guy is Kominsky's worst nightmare. He's John Cochran – smart, rich and owns the best oceanfront property in the county. Made his fortune designing software then selling it to Microsoft back when they were buying up every innovation out there. You wouldn't know it to look at him, though. Most of the time he looks like an old hippie.

"Normandy Sands is going up right next to Cochran's property on Piney Point. More than anything, Kominsky wants that property, but Cochran will never sell it to him. Cochran tried like hell to keep him from building Normandy Sands. He managed to slow him down some but couldn't stop him. Kominsky kept ignoring the injunctions and no one around here bothered to enforce them."

"I heard about this – I remember seeing that on the news," Kate said, interested.

David gave her a look of disdain.

"You never get a clear picture of anything from TV news. As a reporter, you should already know that."

Kate said nothing, but felt her face growing hot with embarrassment, hoping that David didn't notice her blushing like an idiot.

She actually enjoyed reading newspapers but rarely bought them; she was irritated by the large amount of slick advertising inserts and felt like most of the newspaper ended up in the recycling bin unread.

"Never mind, you've been out of the business a while," David said, in a sort of apology.

She studied the photograph of John Cochran. He certainly was handsome, in a rugged, wind-battered sort of way. There was someone she'd enjoy interviewing. Especially if he was single.

"The man's got a ton of money and he looks like he belongs in a Tommy Hilfiger ad. Some men are just born lucky," David said.

"He's Wilmington's most eligible bachelor, you know. Divorced with a grown son. You'll get to meet him in the flesh this afternoon. He's president of Friends of the Carolina Coastline and you'll be covering their meeting at two o'clock. Oh, by the way, here's a list of the officers and their phone numbers. Frank Wells, the vice-president, is the best contact. Really helpful, but he'll talk your ear off if you let him. They're having the director of the North Carolina Chapter of the Nature Trust Corporation speak today."

"I used to volunteer for the Nature Trust back when I lived in Dayton. They do great work. Preserving diversity by working with the developers."

"Yes, they do. Cochran hopes they'll be able to make some headway with Kominsky."

Roger arrived with the coffee.

"Kate, Barry Moore is here," he said as he handed David and Kate their cups. "I'd like to meet with the two of you now."

"Don't think so, Roger!" a male voice shouted from the back of the room.

Kate had been so engrossed in her conversation with David, she hadn't noticed the young man sitting at the other reporter's desk. The voice belonged to an overweight, baby-faced man with a head full of brown curly hair. She noticed a police scanner, with lights flashing, sitting on his desk.

"Yes, Barry?" Roger replied calmly.

"There's a huge fire at Normandy Sands," he said in a thick North Carolina drawl. "That McMansion on the beach is burning out of control. If I leave right now we can have pictures for this issue."

"Okay, Barry, you take your camera and get what you can. Fill in the rest later."

"One more thing – they think someone might be inside the house. There are a couple of cars parked outside, but there's no word on the owners."

"What a shame," Roger said soberly. "Let's hope they're taking a walk on the beach. See if you can find out who they are, but for God's sake, Barry, if the worst happens, don't go graphic on me. I won't print it, and you can't sell it to anyone else."

"Sure thing, chief." Barry grabbed three cameras and a large camera case and lumbered out the door.

Kate sat at her desk in stunned silence, trying not to think about the horror of burning alive.

"Sorry, Kate, looks like it's just you and me for now."

Out and About

Fcc Meets Tuesday

Sept. 3 — The Friends of the Carolina Coastline will meet at 2 p.m., Tuesday, September 4, in the Oak Room of the Regional Public Library. Featured speaker will be Bryan Haas, director of the North Carolina Chapter of the Nature Trust. Mr. Haas will discuss ways in which residents can help slow down the development of the area's beaches. All are welcome.

Winslow Beach Beacon

3. LIKE RIDING A BICYCLE

NOW KATE WAS ON HER OWN; THE TRAINING WHEELS WERE OFF. IT was time to start covering her first news story in fifteen years.

She pulled her car into the lot of the New Hanover County Regional Library, gave herself a quick once-over in the rearview mirror, then collected her purse and notebooks. With as much confidence as she could muster, she strode across the lot to the sprawling brick building.

Kate paused in the library's large high-ceilinged anteroom, separated from the main library by two doors and a wall of glass. She could see mothers with young children standing in line at the circulation desk, waiting to check out the latest batch of picture books.

She knew this branch well. During the years that she and Keith lived in Carrington Downs three miles away, she'd brought Molly here many times.

Next to the glass doors into the main library was Dodo's Room, the children's library. This section of the building had been designed to resemble a boat, consisting of black bowed walls with metal trim and tiny windows for portholes. She and Molly had enjoyed many a spirited albeit squirmy story hour in that room.

For a second, she completely forgot about her meeting, recalling the days when Molly was an adorable pre-schooler. Back then, the sheer joy she and Keith felt at being Mommy and Daddy was enough to keep their marriage going.

Too bad that real life is not like the stories the cheery librarian read to Molly at story hour. Not everyone gets to live happily ever after, no matter how many counseling sessions they attend.

Enough wallowing in the past, she had a meeting to go to.

She walked through the door to the reference librarian's desk.

"Hi," she said. "Could you tell me where the Friends of the Carolina Coastline are meeting?"

"Sure," the woman said. "They'll be meeting in the Oak Room. That's straight back through fiction, first door on the right."

"Thank you," she said.

Walking through the library, Kate couldn't help thinking about the fire at Winslow Beach.

The first day on the job was not going as she expected. She had read the *Winslow Beach Beacon*. It was all features and dry accounts of council meetings. Nothing bad ever happened in Winslow Beach. Now there was this huge fire with people possibly trapped inside.

I'll bet Barry is hoping for a dramatic rescue, Kate thought. What a shot that would make. Firefighters in full gear carrying the victims out, barely conscious but alive, thanks to the selfless efforts of the brave Winslow Beach Volunteer Fire Department.

She sure hoped everyone lived. More than anything, she hated interviewing grieving relatives; forget the public's right to know. She was painfully aware of her role as intruder, asking them to share feelings that were, in truth, none of the public's business.

She found the conference room and took a seat near the front. The room was laid out like a college classroom, with long counters in front of the chairs so the attendees could take notes. There was a printed agenda at each place.

She read through the usual items the call to order, the reading of the minutes, old business. Then her eyes fell on the name of the featured speaker.

Bryan Haas? There couldn't possibly be two Bryan Haases working for the Nature Trust. Well, look at that, she thought. The man she always referred to as The Tall Skinny Guy Who Can't Commit had been transferred from Ohio to North Carolina. He was listed as the chapter's director, so he'd gotten a nice promotion. He was only the coordinator for the Dayton Prairie Grass Project when she knew him.

It's been ten years. A lot can happen. Hell, she'd gotten married, given birth, bought and sold two houses, moved out here and struggled through separation and divorce in all that time. Who knows what Bryan was doing those same nine years?

It was so long ago, a past life so far removed from the life she led now, it seemed as if had happened to someone else entirely.

She had been Miss Reid, a second grade teacher in one of the worst sections of Dayton. Even now, she could see the faces of her students, mostly black, with a few Appalachian whites and Asians thrown in. All of them dirt-poor and all of them needing more than she could possibly give. The other teachers told her it would get easier, but each day was more frustrating than before. Looking back, she wondered how she managed to stay with it for two years.

Her only escape was the volunteer work she did with the Nature Trust. She loved working on the stewardship projects. Nearly every Saturday she was out on the preserves, weeding out invasive species, harvesting the seeds for native prairie grasses or clearing out trash. Occasionally, she helped out during the week in the small office for the Prairie Grass Project, forming an easygoing friendship with coordinator Bryan Haas. Lanky and tall, with thick brown hair, Bryan had a quick smile and a ready joke.

"Go home, we saved the planet yesterday!" he always called out to her whenever he saw her.

Eventually, they found themselves in an on-again, off-again sexual relationship that never seemed to go anywhere but never seemed to really end, either. Finally, Kate gave up on Bryan, Dayton and teaching when she moved back to her hometown of Cincinnati. Friends introduced her to Keith Dennison, and before she knew it, she was married with a baby on the way.

She looked up at the podium and scanned the Friends officers seated at the head table. Yes, there was Bryan, no mistaking it. The man must have gotten himself into some kind of time warp. Ten years had passed since she'd last seen him, but he showed no signs of having aged a day. There was not a touch of gray in his brown hair and it looked to Kate that he hadn't lost any of it; it was just as thick as ever. No wrinkles, no middle aged paunch; he looked exactly the same as the last time she saw him in Dayton. He was still just as skinny and from the way he was talking with the other people, he still liked to joke around. Never one for suits, he was wearing a short-sleeved button-down shirt with no tie and a pair of blue jeans.

Now the day's really getting interesting. She never dreamed she'd run into an old boyfriend at the Friends of the Carolina Coastline meeting. But where was John Cochran? None of the people at the head table looked anything like the ruggedly handsome man she'd seen in the photograph. The man was the president of the organization. He wouldn't be late.

The members seemed to be uneasy about it as well. They glanced at their watches and whispered to each other. Then a middle-aged man, dressed in jeans and a blue denim shirt, entered the room. All the officers stood up and joined the man in a huddle by the door.

Kate couldn't hear what he was saying and wished she could. After a few minutes, they all returned to their seats.

One of the women was dabbing her eyes with a tissue. She appeared to be in her sixties, wearing jeans, hiking boots and an embroidered cotton tunic. Her salt-and-pepper hair hung in two thick braids nearly to her waist.

The middle-aged man approached the podium and spoke into the microphone.

"Good afternoon. For those of you who don't know me, my name is Frank Wells, and I'm the vice president of the Friends of the Carolina Coastline. I have some very bad news for all of us," he said in a firm voice, though it was obvious what he had to say was very difficult. "I just spoke to Shane Cochran. He has told me that this morning John was killed in that terrible fire at Normandy Sands. Shane says he'd gone there to meet with Ed Kominsky, but the fire broke out before he and Mr. Kominsky arrived. There was nothing anyone could do."

A rustling of gasps and shuffling rippled through the room.

"Now, the obvious thing to do would be to cancel the meeting, but I'm not going to do that. We're here, Bryan is here from Raleigh and when I say that John would want us to go on it's no cliche. It's imperative that we save the coastline from destruction, and as a tribute to John, I feel we should continue with the work he started."

"Frank?" the teary-eyed woman at the front asked timidly.

"Yes, Eleanor?"

"We should have a moment of silence for him."

"Of course, by all means," Frank replied. "Let's bow our heads and remember our dear friend John Cochran. We know his spirit lives on and will sustain us in the fight to save the beautiful beaches he loved so much."

Kate bowed her head along with the rest of the audience. Out of the corner of her eye she could see that Bryan's face was somber and serious. She'd never seen him look like that before.

And with a sinking heart she realized that, after the meeting was over, she'd have to ask grief questions.

Local Environmentalist Dies in Fire

Sept. 10 — "John Cochran was tireless in his fight to preserve the gorgeous beaches we have in southeastern North Carolina," said Frank Wells, vice-president of the Friends of the Carolina Coastline. "We will miss his passion and his drive, but we will carry on with the work he started."

A memorial service for Mr. Cochran will be held at St. Andrew's Episcopal Church on Market Street tomorrow at 7 p.m. Donations can be made to the Audubon Society and the Friends of the Carolina Coastline.

Winslow Beach Beacon

4. FOR THE RECORD

FOR THE NEXT TWO HOURS KATE TOOK COPIOUS NOTES, DUTIFULLY marking what she didn't understand for clarification later. Despite their grief, the members launched into the complex mechanics of land management with a passion. They cited statutes, rattled off lists of endangered species, encouraged attendance at upcoming government meetings and quoted John Muir.

She sat through it all, except for the five minutes when she ducked out to the hall to phone Marlene. On finding out that Molly was safe and sound under Marlene's watchful eye, she returned to what she now considered the longest earth science class she'd ever been to. Even Bryan was boring. He droned on forever about the effects of sand dredging on the sea birds.

She did find it amusing to think she was probably the only one in the room who'd seen the Nature Trust director naked. She was pretty sure about that. Unless his tastes had turned to dowdy matrons well into their sixties, none of the other women in attendance was remotely his type.

Things heated up a bit when Bryan asked for questions from the audience.

"Mr. Haas," a man in the back shouted defiantly. "When the Nature Trust compromises with developers, isn't that just giving in to them? So they build ten houses instead of fifty. That's still ten houses too many. And a year later, while you're sitting back in your nice office in Raleigh, those guys build more."

Kate turned to see who was speaking.

"Excuse me, Timmy," Frank Wells interrupted. "Please give your full name for the record."

"I'm not giving my name and I don't care about your stupid record."

"Let the record show that Timothy Kessler is addressing Mr. Haas."

29

Checking her list of officers, Kate noted that the group's secretary was Eleanor Kessler. So the aging flower child at the front table was related to the young radical. Mother? Grandmother? Aunt? Cousin? Kate would have to find out.

"So, Mr. Nature Trust, are you going to answer my question?"

"Timmy, please," his mother/aunt/grandmother pleaded. "Not today. Have a little respect for John's memory."

Frank said nothing, fidgeting in his seat uncomfortably. He also appeared to have an idea of what Timmy was about to say and that it wasn't going to be pleasant.

"You have a valid point," Bryan said calmly. "In a perfect world, there would be no developers and we'd have strong biodiversity in all our protected habitats. In fact, we wouldn't even have to protect them. But the developers are not going to go away, and in order to save what's left we need to work with them, not against them."

"You've heard of the Forces of Nature, Mr. Haas?"

"Yes, I have, unfortunately," Bryan said with a sigh. "And if you're a member, you'd better take cover. I understand the FBI has you at the top of their most wanted lists of subversives."

"You know as well as I do that the FBI, and every other governmental body, is owned by big business," the young man continued. "The only way to stop the developers is to hit them where it hurts the most, in the pocketbook. All this 'let's work together and compromise' crap is just the fat cats' way of making themselves look good to the rich yuppies who drive those huge SUVS to the recycling station."

"Burning buildings doesn't change anything. It only makes the rest of us look like radicals. And last I heard, arson was still a felony," Bryan said.

Kate furiously wrote down everything she heard. Forces of Nature, she noted in big letters to check on later.

"One man's felony is another man's civil disobedience." The young man was passionate in his response. "The Forces of Nature have never harmed a living thing, unlike the developers who bulldoze over baby birds and turtle eggs without a thought. Those developers you're so cozy with can afford lawyers to dance circles around your precious injunctions. But imagine what would happen if every trophy house, every ski lodge, every shopping mall burned to the ground before it opened? The money would dry up and the developers really would stop."

"Yeah, well, if you believe that, I've got a bridge in Brooklyn I think you might be interested in," Bryan answered. A small wave of nervous laughter rippled through the audience. "Look, I don't want to get into this argument here. If you like, we can talk afterwards."

"No, thanks, Mr. Haas. I've heard enough." The young man walked out the door.

Militant Environmentalist Timmy had left the building.

"Well, if there are no more questions, how about a motion to adjourn?" Frank announced in a shaky sort of voice, looking relieved the subversive was out of the room. His request was greeted with a "So moved!" and a "Second!" shouted from the audience.

"Meeting adjourned. Thank you all for coming, and we'll be letting you know about funeral arrangements for John."

Kate made her way through the crowd, waiting patiently as Frank spoke to the other members until she had a chance to get his attention.

"Hello, Mr. Wells. I'm Kate Dennison from the *Winslow Beacon*," she said, extending her hand in greeting.

"Yes, yes, good to meet you," he replied enthusiastically. "David told me he was going to the *Raleigh News-Observer*. He did a great job explaining the issues we're dealing with here. He helped us a lot in getting our message out."

"Yes, he's going to be a tough act to follow, but I'll do my best. And I have a lot of questions about today's meeting. Especially this Forces of Nature group."

"Oh, let me introduce you to Bryan," he said as the man walked by. Frank grabbed his arm and steered him over to Kate. She was a bit irritated at the attempt to avoid her question, but since she had been dying to speak to Bryan since she first saw him, she didn't mind all that much.

The Forces of Nature could wait.

Now that they were face to face, she could see a faint glow of recognition in his eyes, and she was sure he was telling himself this woman looked a lot like the one he knew back in Dayton.

"Bryan, this is the reporter for the *Winslow Beacon*, Kate...I'm sorry, I am so bad with names."

"Kate Dennison," she said, smiling. "Formerly Kate Reid."

"Oh, my God, I thought it was you," he said, his voice registering happy surprise. "You haven't changed a bit."

"You know each other?" Frank asked, surprised.

"Ten years ago, Kate was our number-one volunteer for the Prairie Grass Project in Dayton. We were sorry to see her go."

"That's because you had to file your maps yourself."

They all laughed.

"Yep, I'm still looking for maps I filed nine years ago." He gave her that goofy grin of his, and she felt like they were picking up where they'd left off.

Wait a second, she was at work here, she reminded herself. Report first, flirt later. She turned her attention back to Frank.

"Mr. Wells, I am so sorry about John Cochran," she began. "David told me about him, and I was looking forward to meeting him today. How do you think his death will affect the work of your organization?"

"John was an integral part of our group, and to be honest, I don't know how we'll get along without him," Frank said solemnly, as if launching into a carefully rehearsed speech.

Kate scribbled furiously in her notebook.

"We will do our best to maintain the course he set. As vice-president, I'll be taking over his duties temporarily, but I won't even begin to try to replace him. Fortunately, I'm working with a group of very dedicated individuals. We will not give up our fight to save the beaches from the developers."

"What about the protection of the sea turtles on Normandy Sands? It sounds like you really lost the battle there."

"Lost the battle but not the war," Frank said confidently. "I have a lot of information on that back at my office. I'll fax it over to you tomorrow morning. Here's my card, you can call me anytime." He handed her a business card then began stuffing his papers in his briefcase. "Bryan, if you'd like to stay here and talk old times with your friend, that's fine. I have to get back to the office. Thanks so much for coming down. I'm sorry about the fracas with Timmy Kessler. I'll be in touch."

"No problem, Frank. I'm willing to take those wackos on any time, any place. They give us all a black eye, as far as I'm concerned."

"Pay no attention to Timmy," Frank said. "He's Eleanor's grandson, and we've all known him since he was born. He changes causes like he changes his underwear. Last month he was passing out petitions to dissolve the World Bank. Before that he was trying to ban the internal combustion engine. For a while, he was a strict vegetarian, but I saw him at McDonald's the other day. He's harmless."

Then he spoke directly to Kate.

"I hope you won't sensationalize Timmy's little outburst here," he said earnestly. "He only wants attention and quoting his latest craze in the newspaper would only encourage him. David never mentioned him in his stories."

Now, wait a minute, buddy, Kate wanted to say. You can't tell me what I should write, and I don't care what David used to do.

Instead, she smiled politely and said, "I'll keep that in mind."

Frank waved goodbye as he walked out the door.

"So, Bryan, can you fill me in on this Forces of Nature group?" she asked.

"You got the gist of their mission from that guy Timmy. It's a group way out on the fringe, a conglomeration of radical environmentalists and animal rights activists. They think that if they burn up enough buildings, developers will stop building them. They're scattered across the country in secret cells with no organization to speak of. I've had to share the stage with them before. I've got some pamphlets and stuff I downloaded from their website."

"Thanks. I don't have business cards yet. I just started today. Let me give you my number at the paper." She tore off a piece of notebook paper and wrote her name and the paper's phone number, then paused and boldly wrote her home phone number.

"So, how's married life treating you?" he asked in an offhanded way.

"Not all that well. The divorce was final a year ago," she said brightly.

"Oh. I'm sorry." He had an embarrassed look.

Kate immediately tried to put him at ease.

"Don't be sorry. I'm not. It turned out to be the best thing for all of us."

"I heard you had a baby," he said quietly.

"I did, but she's not a baby anymore. She's in second grade now."

"It's been that long? Jeez, time flies. So, how'd you end up as a reporter?"

"My neighbor is the publisher of the *Winslow Beacon*, and when he found out I had a degree in journalism, he made me an offer I couldn't refuse. His wife watches Molly for free while I work."

"That's a good deal."

"You're telling me. I checked into daycare and it costs a fortune – of course, that's not something you have to worry about, is it?"

"No kids that I know of. No wife, either, for that matter." He shoved his hands in the pockets of his jeans and grinned. "Hey, maybe we could get together sometime. I've got to get back to Raleigh today, but I'll call you."

He's said that before. She probably should be careful. He was a source, after all. But as far as she could tell, Bryan's appearance was a one-time thing. After the story was written, he was fair game.

"Good luck getting through the Wilmington traffic. This is when rush hour begins, you know."

"Hey, you know me. I'm used to it. Back in Ohio, seemed like I lived in my car. It's the same in North Carolina, only I have a lot farther to drive. "Here, let me walk you to the parking lot."

With Bryan's six-foot, two-inch frame towering over her, she felt almost like a giddy high school girl walking through the library with her new beau.

Good God, I'm dating again, she thought.

Family Talk

BALANCING WORK AND FAMILY

Sept. 10 — For a homemaker, re-entering the work force can be a daunting prospect. Many women find the stress of a new job combined with the ongoing responsibilities of raising children and running the household overwhelming. However, with some advance planning and organization, the transition can run smoothly for all involved.

Here are a few tips the *Winslow Beach Beacon* recommends:

— Cook several meals ahead of time.

— Avoid working late hours

— Make sure you have reliable child care and a backup caregiver.

— Set aside family time

— Set aside time for yourself

5. HAVING IT ALL

KATE WAS EXHAUSTED WHEN SHE PULLED INTO THE DRIVEWAY OF HER small bungalow in Sunset Park.

She adored this neighborhood. It had been built in the 1920s, so the streets had sidewalks and trees. Kate had sorely missed those things during her exile to the suburban cul-de-sac. Thick old live oaks draped with Spanish moss lined the streets. The houses were all fairly small and built close together, but Kate never minded the fact that she could see into her neighbor's kitchen. That's what curtains were for.

It was already dark, the sun having set an hour ago. She knew she had to get out of the car, go next door, collect Molly, take her home and feed her, but it all seemed like so much.

That was the problem with children – you had to feed them every day. Plus bathe them and wash their clothes and help them with their homework.

"You can't stay here all night," she told herself. "Just do it." Somehow, she mustered the energy to get out of the car and walk over to Roger and Marlene's white two-story Charleston-style house.

"There's your mommy now," she heard Marlene say as she stepped onto the porch. Before she could knock the door opened.

"You see, Molly, I told you she wouldn't forget."

Marlene stood in the doorway wearing a purple velvet caftan and strings of brightly colored beads. Her long gray hair was pulled back in a ponytail, and her brown eyes sparkled through the lenses of her enormous glasses. It had been nearly a decade since she and Roger had moved to Wilmington, but she still maintained her image as a Greenwich Village bohemian artist.

"Mommy, I missed you so much," Molly announced, rushing out from behind a tangle of purple velvet. She flung her arms around her

37

mother. Kate bent over to return the embrace, drowning all her senses in the beauty of her red-haired, long-legged, scabby-kneed daughter.

"I missed you, too, pumpkin," she murmured.

"What are you doing standing outside, Kate? Come on in and warm up while Molly gets her things."

Kate stepped carefully across the hardwood floors, hoping she left no scuffmarks. As always, she admired the Mission-style furniture, the Native American wall hangings and original folk art paintings. Marlene had such great taste. Kate felt a twinge of jealousy, as her house was a hodge-podge of cast-offs and thrift shop finds, with no sense of style whatsoever.

"We had a wonderful time, didn't we, Molly?" Marlene said.

Molly beamed at her.

"We made cookies, and Miss Marlene helped me make this collage. See, Mommy?"

Molly pointed to a huge piece of poster board on the kitchen table. The poster board was covered with bits of construction paper, sequins, feathers, glitter, and glossy pictures cut from magazines.

"It's not finished yet," Molly continued. "Miss Marlene says it's our work in progress."

"It's lovely," Kate exclaimed with motherly pride. How does Marlene manage a project like this? There wasn't a speck of glue or glitter anywhere, and Molly was known for making huge messes when there was cutting and pasting involved.

"Molly did her homework as soon as she got home from school," Marlene told her reassuringly. "I'm proud to say she has not watched one second of television while she's been here. After we finished cleaning up, we read about Ramona and Beezus."

"I read a page and Miss Marlene read a page. She can read real good — better than my teacher."

"I don't doubt that," Kate said. "Listen, kiddo, we need to get home. It's dinnertime, and I am so hungry I could eat a horse."

"Okay, Mommy." Molly ran to the kitchen and retrieved her bookbag.

"Remember, you're inside, Molly," Kate called after her. "No running!"

"So, how was your first day on the job?" Marlene asked. "I hope Roger didn't work you too hard. I warned him to go easy on you."

"It was certainly interesting. I much prefer it to cleaning out the refrigerator and doing the laundry. But, Marlene, I am soooooooo tired."

"I'm sure you are. This is going to take some getting used to."

Molly ran over to her mother, pink Barbie doll backpack in hand.

"Let's go. I'm hungry, too," she said, grabbing Kate's hand and pulling her out the door. Seconds later, they were crossing the lawn, heading for their own house.

The porchlight was on, and another car had pulled into the driveway. Kate's heart sank as she recognized her ex-husband's well-maintained Nissan Altima. She just didn't have the strength for another confrontation with Keith. Not tonight.

"Daddy!" Molly squealed, dropping her bookbag on the grass and running to the tall figure standing on their small porch. Her father scooped her up in a giant bear hug.

Kate sighed heavily. She picked up the discarded bookbag and continued after her daughter.

Well, it's good for Molly to spend time with her dad, she thought. Even if he was the last person Kate wanted to see right now.

"Hello, Kate. Just came by to see my best girl," he said, planting a big kiss on Molly's forehead and setting her back down. "And to find out how you did on your first day at your new job. I am so proud of you, Kate, starting a career like this. You've really come out of your shell, and I know you'll be a fantastic reporter."

Keith was a handsome man, six feet tall and muscular, with a neatly trimmed brown beard; but Kate stopped noticing his looks years ago, when he started micromanaging her life. She especially hated that condescending tone in his voice. Last week he was furious about her job, telling her she could make more money waiting on tables.

"Thanks, Keith," she said curtly as she fumbled through her purse for the keys. She unlocked the door and turned the lights on inside the small house. The three of them moved into the living room.

"You're welcome," he said. He was looking at the floor now, not a good sign.

"You know you guys really shouldn't wear your shoes in the house. I can see at least three new nicks in the hardwood floor since I was last here. And I still think you should sell this place and get something larger. You need more than two bedrooms and one bathroom."

"No, Keith, two bedrooms and one bathroom really is all we need. There are only two of us living here."

Why did he always have to carp on the house? It was fine just the way it was. The front room had just enough space for Kate's Salvation Army couch and chairs and the round oak claw foot table she'd found at an estate sale. From the dark green-and-burgundy Oriental-style rugs on the floor to the family photographs and Japanese prints hanging on the celery-sage painted walls, everything was there by Kate's choice and hers alone. Keith had nothing to do with how she lived now.

She was just about to tell him so, but fortunately her daughter intervened.

"We're going to have dinner now, Daddy," Molly said, taking his hand. "Do you want to eat with us? We're going to have tuna casserole."

"Actually, I thought I'd treat you all to dinner at China Doll."

"Yay! We're going out to eat!" Molly sang, clapping her hands and hopping up and down.

"But, Keith, it's a school night, and she has to go to bed pretty soon."

"Oh, come on, Kate. By the time you get dinner ready we could be sitting down and enjoying our meal at the restaurant. And you won't have to clean up afterwards. It'll be fun. A nice family get-together."

She was just about to remind him they were not a family anymore and the last thing she wanted was to get together, but she stopped herself. Molly was so excited. Like all children of divorce, she missed her father terribly, and this was an unexpected treat for her.

"Oh, all right," she said, less than enthusiastically. She carefully placed her notebooks on the dining room table, reminding herself of the spot where she left them so she wouldn't have to go looking for them in a frenzy tomorrow.

Remembering Molly's bookbag, she held it out to her daughter.

"Go put this where it belongs."

"Yes, ma'am." She scampered off.

"When did you start making her call you ma'am?" Keith wanted to know.

"I don't make her. She started doing that about a year ago," Kate said testily. "I think she picked it up at school. It's a Southern thing. Anyway, if you'd been paying attention you would have noticed."

"Look, Kate, don't start," he demanded. "I'm just here to have some quality time with my little girl, and I've been generous enough to invite you both to dinner. The least you could do is be civil."

"Sorry," she muttered. "I've had a long day and I don't feel very sociable. But thank you for taking us to dinner. Molly will love it."

"And you?"

"I'll just be happy someone else is doing the cooking."

"Aren't you just a little bit glad to see me?"

"Only because I know you'll be leaving after dinner."

Molly came bouncing back, having hung her bookbag on the peg in the utility room.

"Let's go," she called out to her parents. "I'm starving!"

Kate followed her daughter, wondering if the free meal was worth an evening with her ex.

Fatal Fire Deemed Arson by NHCFD

Sept. 10. — Arson is the most likely cause for the fire at Normandy Sands last Tuesday, according to investigators from the New Hanover County Fire Department.

The fire, which took the lives of wealthy philanthropist John Cochran and real estate agent Warren Owens, apparently was ignited by several gallons of gasoline poured throughout the structure.

"Looks like they drenched the carpets and the walls, threw a match and then ran like hell," said Fire Chief Norman Pearson.

Winslow Beach Beacon

6. NO ONE CAN RESIST THE FORCES
OF NATURE

KATE WAS ALONE IN THE PRESSROOM. SHE TYPED AWAY FURIOUSLY ON her terminal, only stopping every few minutes to sift through reams of faxes on her desk. She was at her peak, taking her notes of the meeting along with what she'd received from Frank Wells and distilling all that information into a precise, coherent news story with lots of quotes and a snappy lead to boot.

"Good morning, Kate," Roger said, startling her out of her work-induced trance. "You know you don't have to be in this early."

She looked up to find him standing behind her. She felt a powerful urge to organize the haphazard piles of papers on her desk but resisted.

"Good morning, Roger," she said, as she turned away from the terminal. "I'm here now because this is the best time to get stuff done. And I know it sounds dumb, but I've always had to go to work to work. At home there are just too many distractions, even when Molly's at school."

"I'm the same way." He sat on corner of the desk opposite hers. "Last year Marlene tried to talk me into setting up a home office so I could cut down on the hours I spend here, but I told her not to bother. I like having that separation between work and home. There's a certain joy when you walk in the door, knowing that you've left work behind and you can do what you enjoy."

"You got that right," Kate agreed. "If you can work anywhere, anytime, pretty soon you're working everywhere all the time."

"I don't mean to look over your shoulder, but it looks like you've just about finished with the Friends of the Carolina Coastline story."

"Yes, and I got a few quotes about John Cochran from Frank Wells, the group's vice-president. It's the usual he-was-a-good-man-and-he-will-be-missed kind of thing but it should sound good in the obit."

"Ironically, John Cochran really was a good man and he will be missed," Roger said. "And that's something I want to discuss with you. I assume you saw the news last night?"

"Well, no," Kate said, a bit flustered. She really should pay more attention to local news events now. "Keith showed up as soon as Molly and I left your house, and he took us out to dinner. By the time we got home, it was all I could do to get Molly into bed before I collapsed. I was asleep by nine-thirty."

"Come in the office and I'll fill you in."

Kate hit the "save" button on the terminal, then followed Roger into the glass enclosed cubicle that served as his office.

He motioned her to take a seat in one of the two metal high-backed vinyl covered chairs crammed in the space between the wall and his desk. Roger's desk was from the city of New Bern, just like everyone else's, but his sumptuous leather chair was a relic of his days in public relations. Award plaques and framed certificates lined the walls, along with one of Marlene's paintings, a caricature of Roger in swirls of orange and blue.

The day's printouts of e-mails were on the corner of the desk in a neat little stack, ready to be edited for publication.

She sat in one of the chairs opposite his desk.

She hated private office meetings. Her original reporter's job had ended in an office very much like this one. She found herself flashing back to that horrible afternoon fourteen years ago when the newly hired editor, Mel Hornsby, had gleefully announced that her services were no longer required. She knew it was a ploy to shake up the staff so they'd quit and he could hire his own people. It worked, because that was exactly what happened. But it was a painful memory.

Mel the Malevolent, her co-workers called him. As well as Monstrous Mel, Smelly Mel and Mel from Hell.

"Don't be nervous, Kate," Roger said. He knew exactly why she'd left journalism. "Nothing bad is going to happen. No one ever gets fired from this paper. Look at our Clarisse Hopper — she submits every business-provided press release that crosses her desk word for word, doesn't even bother to correct the grammar, and she's been here for years. I need all the warm bodies I can get.

"Now, back to John Cochran. According to the news last night and the daily this morning, the cause of the Normandy Sands fire is considered suspicious. It's under investigation, but it's a safe bet that it was arson. No surprise there, of course. An empty house doesn't just burst into flames of its own accord. What is surprising is who may have set it. There is evidence pointing to a radical environmental group called the Forces of Nature."

Kate felt an ominous chill.

"That is so strange. There was a guy at the meeting yesterday who brought that up. He accused the Nature Trust of getting too cozy with the developers and said the Forces of Nature was saving the planet by setting fires. Sounded like he was an avid supporter."

"Really?" Roger leaned forward in his chair. "Did you get his name? Did you talk to him?"

"His name is Timothy Kessler, and he walked out before I had a chance to ask him any questions. Afterwards, Frank Wells really tried to play it down. He said that Timmy was the grandson of one of the members — that he's always got some radical cause, and the Forces of Nature is his flavor of the week. Wells also said he was harmless, and that's an exact quote. I did get a lot of background info from Bryan Haas on this outfit, though. Should be useful."

"Excellent," said Roger. "You see, the police found a flyer under the windshield of a car belonging to one of the victims. It said 'No one can escape the Forces of Nature.' The placement of the flyer on the car suggests the probability they knew people were in the house when they set it on fire."

"Wait a minute," Kate said, alarmed. "The Forces of Nature may be run by extremists, but they're extremists with principles. Every article I've got on them says they only destroy property, not lives. If they knew someone was in the house, they would never have started that fire."

Roger nodded, leaning back in his battered leather chair, causing it to squeak.

"Last night I went on the internet to check up on them and that's true. They make much of the fact that they've caused millions of dollars

47

of damage to property but have never harmed a living being." he said. "But they are very loosely organized. Small cells operating independently in secret all across the country, with no idea what any of the others are doing. It's entirely possible one of these groups decided to take that extra step from vandalism to first degree murder."

Kate remembered Timmy, so far the only face she had for the Forces of Nature. Could a passionate idealist like that young man intentionally take a life? Could somebody's beloved grandson burn two men alive and feel justified in doing it?

"If that's the case," she began carefully, not wanting to get into an argument with the boss, "were the victims chosen at random or were they targeted? I can see the rationale for killing Warren Owens – he represents the company that's destroying the beaches. But John Cochran was on their side. He was working as hard as he could to save the beaches."

"And he was doing it through mainstream groups like the Sierra Club, the Audubon Society and the Nature Trust." Roger replied. "They could have taken the attitude of you're either with us or against us, and those against us are fair game. Then again, they might have logically assumed that whoever was in the house with Owens was a prospective home buyer."

"What was Cochran doing in that house, anyway? It doesn't add up. I know he was supposed to be meeting his son and Ed Kominsky there, but why meet at a house out in the middle of nowhere? You'd think an office would be easier for everyone."

"And that's exactly what I want you to find out," Roger said.

There was a knock at his door. Before he could answer, Barry barged in with a handful of photographs he tossed on the desk.

"Here's the shots of the Normandy Sands fire, Rog."

"Good morning, Barry, nice to see you, too. Have a seat. I want to talk to both of you about the direction we'll be taking on the fire."

"Too bad David is gone. He'd have been all over this story like a bad suit," Barry said as he settled his bulk into the chair next to Kate. Wasn't that the same plaid shirt he was wearing yesterday? And those jeans looked like they could stand by themselves.

She smarted at the reference to her predecessor. It was only her

48

second day, and she was already fed up with hearing about what a great reporter David had been.

Roger said nothing. He was focused on the photographs.

"Great job, Barry. Here, Kate, take a look at these." He handed her the stack of photographs.

It was definitely a spectacular fire. Kate found it hard to believe that it happened locally. Although it was hard to tell the perspective from the photographs, the flames looked to be twenty feet high, engulfing the entire house, top to bottom. Clouds of thick, black smoke filled the sky. With a sickened feeling, she thought of John Cochran and Warren Owens trapped inside that inferno. Realizing she didn't want to look at them any more, she put them back on Roger's desk.

"That's unbelievable," Kate said.

"Yeah, it really got out of hand," Barry said, happy to play the role of expert. "It was already in full swing when Ed Kominsky reported it. The sprinkler system failed, likewise the smoke detectors. The house had this fancy security system that was supposed to call the fire department at the first sign of smoke. Turned out, it wasn't even hooked up yet. Kominsky Builders didn't plan to activate the system until the house was occupied and someone else was paying the bills."

"Listen, Barry, I want you and Kate to work together on this," Roger ordered. "I know the daily paper and the TV stations have the jump on us, but we have the time to go in depth. Barry, you get the police side. Follow the investigation and get the particulars. Kate, you do the human side. Interview Shane Cochran. It must have been devastating to come up on that house, knowing his father was inside.

"And poor Warren Owens is like the pilot flying Buddy Holly's plane. We don't know a thing about him. The man was thirty-nine years old. He must have done something in his life worth noting."

Kate squirmed in her seat and tried not to show her distaste for the assignment.

"Uh, Roger, it may be kind of difficult to reach Mrs. Owens and Shane Cochran right now," she said tentatively.

"Do what I do," Barry said before Roger could answer. "Just go to the visitation. They have to be there. Say you're working on the obituary and ask them if there's anything they'd like you to include. You won't be able to shut them up."

"That's just what I was going to tell her. Go up front and ask Janie for the times. She does our death page," Roger agreed. "And, Kate, see if you can talk to this kid from the Forces of Nature."

"You know a member of the Forces of Nature?" Barry asked, sounding incredulous.

"I'd say he was more of a Forces of Nature wannabe," she said. "It's Timmy Kessler. His grandmother is one of the little old ladies running that save-the-coastline group."

"That little crackpot?" Barry scoffed. "No one ever takes him seriously. I'd stick with the internet."

"Maybe it's time someone did take him seriously," Roger said. "I'm not saying he set that fire, but he could be part of a Forces of Nature cell. He sounds like someone they'd like to recruit, a young idealist who's not afraid to question authority."

"Timmy's a wimp, through and through. When it came time to light the match, he'd have run home crying to Grandma," Barry sneered.

"Be that as it may, Kate will still do the interview, right, Kate?"

"Yes, Roger," she replied, although she was inclined to agree with Barry. Timmy Kessler was no more a radical, fire-setting eco-terrorist than she was.

"And one more thing, Barry. I'd like you to go back out to the site. Take some more shots of the house so we can get the full scope of the damage. Kate, I'd like you to go along too. Get a feel for the destruction. Then go talk to the firefighters, get their take on it."

Barry stood up and retrieved his pictures.

"Anything else, boss?"

"No, that's it," Roger said.

"Well, let's hit the road, Kate."

Great, a road trip with Godzilla. And Normandy Sands was at least forty-five minute drive to the northern part of the county.

She followed Barry out of Roger's office, stopping at her desk to pick up her pens and notebooks.

"Wait a second, I want to check my voice mail," Barry said, pulling a small mobile phone out of the back pocket of his jeans. He punched in a few numbers and listened.

"Whoa, he must be shitting me!" he exclaimed and punched in some more numbers. "My contact in the sheriff's department says they've made an arrest. I'm just calling to confirm."

"Really? Are you sure? Hang on, let me get something to write with." He perched on the corner of his desk for about five minutes, scribbling in his notebook as he listened intently.

"Okay, thanks, buddy," he said, then closed the phone and popped it back into his pocket.

"Roger!" he yelled.

Roger came into the newsroom, looking a bit perturbed they hadn't left yet.

"What's up?"

"There's been an arrest in the Normandy Sands fire," he said with an air of self-importance. "It's our old pal Timmy Kessler."

Arrest Made in Cochran, Owens Murders

Sept. 10 — A Winslow Beach man was arrested for the murders of John Cochran and Warren Owens.

Timothy Kessler, 19, has been charged with aggravated arson, and two counts of first degree murder. Cochran and Owens lost their lives in a five alarm fire set in an empty house at the Normandy Sands development.

He is being held without bond in the New Hanover County Jail.

Winslow Beach Beacon

7. PRESUMPTION OF INNOCENCE

THAT POOR KID," KATE MURMURED.

"Aside from his opinions, and God help us if that was the only reason for his arrest, what evidence do they have?" Roger wanted to know.

"Plenty." Barry flipped through his notebook. "His fingerprints are on the handles of the empty gas cans left by the house, and on the flyer. He's got no alibi for the time of the fire – said he was at his apartment alone, sleeping late. And there's a witness who said Timmy told him the whole plan, including that he hoped he'd be able 'waste a couple of the corporate bastards' in the process. In fact, it was this witness who tipped them off to go after him in the first place."

"How convenient," Roger commented. "Does this witness have a name?"

"Not for publication," Barry answered. "Hey, Rog, I tried. My source tells me it's for the safety of the witness. They're worried about retaliation from the FON."

"The Forces of Nature are an environmental group," Kate countered. "They've taken a huge turn away from the mainstream, but they aren't the Mafia."

"The FBI considers them terrorists. You know, armed and dangerous," Barry said. "Anyway, it will be a while before I can talk to Kessler. They're keeping him isolated from the press for now, but they should let me see him tomorrow or Friday at the latest."

"Barry, I'd like Kate to interview him," Roger said.

"But, Rog, I've worked for a year to build up these contacts. It's not easy when everyone sees the *Beacon* as the piss-ant little shopping paper they sell at Food Lion. No offense, Kate, but this is only your second day on the job."

All the animosity she'd been sensing was bubbling to the surface. Barry was not about to let her take his big story away from him. The ironic thing was that she didn't even want it. She'd never done a jailhouse interview and had no desire to do one now.

"That's okay, Roger. He can do it. I don't mind."

"Now there's method in my madness," Roger said. "Barry, you've had dealings with him before, and I would wager that they weren't particularly pleasant for Timothy, were they?"

"It was just that one time," Barry protested. "I mean, he was such a goofball, chaining himself to the front gate of the Bellamy Mansion, saying they should use it as a homeless shelter."

"You threw a water balloon at him."

"Hey, it was hotter'n hell that day, it probably cooled him off."

"You were lucky he didn't charge you with assault and I didn't fire you," Roger said. "My point is that Mr. Kessler will be more open and forthcoming with Kate than he would ever be with you. Kate's an attractive woman with a kind face. And she's never smacked him with water balloons."

Barry, his shoulders slumped, stared at his feet and said nothing.

Great, thought Kate. She was going to have to work with this big bully and now he probably all-out hated her for stealing his big story. She might have to dodge a few water balloons herself.

"Still want us to go out to the Battle of Normandy?" Barry finally asked.

"Yes, I do."

"I'm driving," Barry said defiantly.

"Fine with me," Kate said with a sigh. She was not looking forward to doing this story at all.

They left the building in silence. Barry's car, a grungy maroon Chevy Lumina, was parked at the far end of the parking lot. There was a tattered bumper sticker proclaiming "If you like Wilmington, you should have seen it before you moved here." Unlocking the door on the driver's side, he eased behind the steering wheel then reached over to the passenger door and unlocked it from the inside.

Kate slid in, kicking the empty Port City Java Styrofoam cups under the seat. The smell reminded her of the time she chaperoned Molly's field trip to the local Krispy Kreme Doughnut Shop.

The vinyl dashboard was cracked and dirty, but boasted a shiny chrome stereo system with lots of blue buttons and a digital display. Barry reached over and gently dropped his camera case onto the backseat where it rested on top of a stack of photography magazines, a couple of camera tripods and more empty coffee cups. A tatty blue garter dangled from the rearview mirror. "Sorry, maid's day off," Barry mumbled

"No problem," she said. "Neatness is the sign of a sick mind."

"You'll get no argument from me on that." He shoved the keys into the ignition. The car sputtered to life, lurching across the parking lot toward Market Street.

For the first time ever, she saw him relax, dropping his guise of the hard-bitten reporter. He was even smiling.

"Look, I guess we kind of got off on the wrong foot," he said, clearing his throat. "David and I were friends, and I really hated to see him go. Course, we all knew the *Beacon* was just a stepping stone for him. He was too good not to get noticed. I wouldn't be surprised if he won a Pulitzer some day. And I bet you're sick of hearin' how good he was, aren't you?"

"That I am."

"Anyway, even though I haven't seen you in action, I know you work hard. Janie told me you get in before she does. You take the job seriously. That's good."

"I meant what I said to Roger," she said. "If you want to interview Timmy Kessler, that's okay with me. You're the one with the most experience right now."

"Much as I hate to say it, Roger's right. Little Timmy would take one look at me and ask the guard to take him back to his cell. I doubt if I'd get a word out of him. But you look like the all-American girl next door. I'll bet you were homecoming queen in your high school."

"Actually, the girl who was homecoming queen in my class has been married three times, has substance abuse problems and weighs two hundred pounds."

"Sounds like my kind of woman. Got her phone number?"

They both laughed. Kate decided her first impression of Barry was wrong. She always liked being around people who could make her laugh.

"You're from Dayton, aren't you?"

"Yup, same as the Wright Brothers."

"Probably the only folks from Ohio who went back home after seeing

57

the beach."

Kate laughed again.

"Seriously, though how did you end up here?"

"My ex-husband took a transfer five years ago. " Kate explained. "He's an engineer with GE Aircraft. When this job came up in Wilmington, he said it was a great opportunity, so we packed up and left Cincinnati."

"My dad worked at GE Aircraft for twenty-six years," Barry said. "He's retired now. Best thing that ever happened to him. Before the plant opened up, he was a fry cook downtown and doin' odd jobs on the side. Then a friend helped him get in at the plant, next thing you know he's working regular hours plus overtime and double time, and we can go to the doctor without worryin' about how we'd pay for it. When you got six kids, that's a pretty big deal. Course that all happened before I was born, but I heard enough stories about how hard it used to be before GE."

"So how come you're not working at GE?"

"Never wanted to," Barry answered. "When I went off to college, my dad was hopin' I'd be an engineer and get a job at GE or Corning. He liked to beat me within an inch of my life when I said I was majorin' in journalism. And again, when I took this job a couple years ago. I probably could've gone to work in Charlotte or Raleigh for more money. But this place is my home and even though it's full of carpetbaggers now, I decided to stay. I do all right, got my own business doing wedding photography."

"That must be interesting," Kate said.

"Yup, I'm there to record the happiest day of your life," he said, the sarcasm biting. "You know these folks have to be mortgaging the farm to pay for it all. There's the cake, the flowers, the dresses, the band, the sit-down dinner for three hundred friends and relatives. It's ridiculous. Everyone keeps tellin' the bride how beautiful she looks and she's always a mess, stressed out to the max. I remember one wedding I did where the ring bearer peed his pants, the flower girls smacked each other with their little baskets, and the bride was red as a beet, cursing like a sailor."

"That sounds like my wedding," Kate laughed.

"If any woman ever does consent to becoming Mrs. Barry Moore, there's no way I'm going through a big wedding like the ones I photograph. I say it's city hall or Vegas. Well, look, here we are at what's

58

left of Normandy Sands."

Barry turned off the highway down a side street. A twenty foot billboard welcomed them to the development, still peddling its beautiful beachfront lots.

Even with the windows up, the acrid smell of burnt wood and plastic found its way into the car. They followed the newly laid blacktop road to a high masonry fence with an arched stone entrance. Two large concrete lions scowled from either side of the archway. Beyond the impressive gate, a small guard house stood empty.

"Gotta keep the riff-raff out," Barry said, pointing to the guard house

They pulled up to where the house used to be. It was nothing more than a huge pile of rubble.

"That's what happens when there's no fire hydrant," Barry said. "It was pathetic. They had to hook their hoses up to a water tanker. They couldn't get to the water supply; it's underground and inaccessible."

The house was surrounded by yellow crime scene tape. A New Hanover County Sheriff's car was parked just outside the confines of the yellow tape. Its lone occupant, a young deputy, jumped out and walked directly into the path of Barry's car. He stood in the middle of the road with his arms outstretched.

Barry brought the car to a stop and turned off the engine. The deputy walked around to the driver's side and motioned him to roll the window down. He put one hand on the car roof and peered inside.

"Sorry, folks, this is a crime scene. No sightseers."

Kate did not like the way this was going. The deputy looked like he wanted to arrest somebody and seeing as how the two of them had driven past signs announcing they were on a private road – residents and guests only, criminal trespass seemed likely.

"We're with the *Winslow Beach Beacon*," Barry said, sounding respectful and cooperative, at least to Kate. "We're doing a story on the fire and we just want to look around, take a few photos. We won't stay long. We'll be gone before you know it."

"You got any ID?"

"Yes, of course," Barry said. He pulled his wallet out of his back pocket and took out a laminated identification card. The deputy took it and examined it carefully.

Kate sat quietly, wondering if they'd even get past Barney Fife here. He couldn't believe they'd print up fake IDs from the *Winslow Beacon* just to see a burned out building, could he? She was glad Barry was the one he was talking to, she was never good at pushing her way past anyone in authority, especially someone who carried a gun.

"Well, I guess it's okay," the deputy said, handing Barry's card back to him. "Just make sure you don't disturb the crime scene. Stay outside the tape."

"Not a problem, sir. Thanks. You guys are doing a great job here."

"Thank you. We caught the guy, that's all that matters, right?"

"That's for sure."

With that, Barry started the car and the deputy went back to his cruiser, still keeping a watchful eye on the reporters.

"You handled that very well," Kate said, once the deputy was out of earshot.

"I know my way around the local law enforcement," Barry said. "Most of them work pretty hard and feel like no one appreciates them. Take this guy, for instance. He's stuck with guarding the crime scene, which has to be the most boring duty he could be assigned. Everyone else is out chasing bad guys and he's got to sit on his keister all day, protecting a burned out hulk from vandals and rubber-neckers. I'll bet we're the most excitement he's had all day."

Barry stopped the car at the edge of the crime scene tape. The ruins of the house were still a good thirty to forty feet away.

"You're not going to cross that tape, are you, Barry?"

"Nope, don't need to. I can get as close as I need to, even closer. Take a look at this baby."

Barry rummaged through all the camera equipment he had in the backseat and pulled out a black leather case. He unzipped it to reveal a foot long telephoto lens.

"Bought it the last time they filmed one of those big Hollywood pictures here in town. I was hoping I'd get a nice shot of Ashley Judd nude sunbathing or something, but that never happened. Still, it's come in handy more times than I can count."

He attached the lens to his camera and went to work shooting the wreckage from every angle possible.

With Barry immersed in his photography duties, and the deputy reading a paperback on the county dime, Kate now had a chance to see the damage caused by the fire.

Standing at the end of the long driveway, Kate was dumbstruck by the destructive power of the fire. There was nothing left of the house. Even the garage had been destroyed, although one of the doors remained standing, the edges charred but still intact. The day before John Cochran had driven his car right where she was standing, unaware he only had an hour or two left to live.

But the smell was the worst of it. The acrid, smoky fumes hung in the air. After this, she could never complain about her neighbors burning leaves.

"Amazing what you can do with just a few five-gallon jugs of gasoline and a match," Barry said finally.

Kate decided to walk around the perimeter of the caution tape. She paused at the flagstone pathway to what used to be the front door. Only the concrete foundation of the front porch remained. However, the clear plastic box full of brochures had escaped the fire. Although streaked with soot, it was still possible to make out the words "TAKE ONE" emblazoned on the front.

She opened the top and pulled one out, inspecting the color photographs of the house in all its glory.

Six thousand square feet of luxury, she read. Five bedrooms, seven bathrooms, four wood-burning fireplaces, a great room, a home office, a gourmet kitchen, a wine cellar, a gameroom. She surveyed the ruin, trying to see if she could make out where the parquet floors had been. She caught the glimmer of sunlight reflected off a piece of glass. Perhaps that was the designer chandelier, its broken shards scattered among the mounds of burnt wood and mortar.

The spectacular views of the Carolina coastline remained.

Why had John Cochran come here? Had he relented on selling his property? Maybe he was thinking about buying this house and tearing it down. Would Kominsky Developers rebuild? And if they did, would anyone buy the house, knowing of the gruesome deaths that occurred on that very spot?

Kate took her notebook out of her purse, flipped it open and began to write. So far all she had was a lot of questions.

But she fully intended to get some answers.

She was startled by the sound of a camera shutter clicking away behind her. It was Barry; having circled the property, he was now photographing this side of the house. In dismay, she realized his camera was aimed at her.

"Don't take my picture!" she shouted.

He put the camera down.

"It's not for publication. But it would make a great shot. A nice artsy-fartsy kind of thing. I could title it 'Woman at the Ruins' and sell it for hundreds. Or I might just sneak it into the pictures of the next wedding gig and see if anyone notices."

"They'll notice. That's all the bride has to show for all the trouble she went to."

"True. And that's why I can charge them so much." He put his camera back into the bag slung across his shoulder and looked at his watch. "If you don't mind, I'd like to get back to the office, I've got appointments this afternoon, and I'd like to get these shots uploaded soon as I can."

"Fine with me, I've seen enough." She followed him back to his car.

Twenty minutes later, walking through the door to the *Beacon*, Kate knew she brought the fire and brimstone stench of Normandy Sands along with her. Maybe no one would notice.

"Whoa, where have you been?" Janie asked her pointedly from her perch behind the paneled reception desk. "I haven't smelled anything that bad since my ex-husband accidentally set the sofa on fire. I'd worry about setting off the smoke alarms if I were you."

Uh-oh, she really did smell as bad as she thought she did. Well, not much she could do about it now.

"Sorry, Janie, Roger asked Barry and me to go out to the site of the fire. It's pretty potent. I promise I'll go home and shower as soon as I finish what I'm working on. By the way, do you have the visitation times for John Cochran and Warren Owens?"

Janie reached over to a neat stack of papers adorned with the logos of local funeral homes.

"Let's see, Cochran; here it is. Memorial service Friday night at seven, St. Andrews Episcopal Church, with visitation four to six. And visitation for Warren Owens will be held the same afternoon at the Bethany Methodist Church on Chestnut, two to four with the funeral at five o'clock. You'll be cutting it pretty close."

"At least they're in the same neighborhood."

"Here, let me make a copy of these for you. It's always best to have the right information before you leave." Janie scampered back to the ancient copier behind her desk. It wheezed into action and produced a pair of smudged copies of the funeral announcements, which she handed across the counter.

"Thanks, Janie."

"No problem, happy to do it."

She headed the hallway to the pressroom. Smell be damned, she had to get her thoughts and feelings about the murder site down while they were still clear and sharp.

"A few five-gallon jugs of gasoline and a lit match," she typed.

Forty-five minutes and six hundred words later she hit the save button and turned off the terminal. It wasn't finished. She would fill in more later after she spoke to Shane Cochran and Mrs. Owens this afternoon. Still, she was proud of it. Writing opinion columns was the best thing about the reporter's job.

She was so pleased with her work she managed to put out of her mind the daunting prospect of interviewing a murder victim's widow — the worst thing about a reporter's job.

FIRE TAKES ITS TOLL

By Kate Dennison

Sept. 10 — A few five-gallon jugs of gasoline and a lit match. That's all it took to destroy six thousand square feet of luxury.

The beautiful home on Normandy Sands, with its huge bedrooms, its hand-crafted parquet floors and designer chandeliers, today is nothing more than a hulking mass of charred wood and brick.

Even worse, two lives were cut short. Two good men died in that fire, two men with families and friends who are left behind asking why this had to happen.

8. TERRIBLY SORRY FOR YOUR LOSS

THE DREADED MOMENT HAD ARRIVED.

Friday afternoon, Kate drove downtown, parking her car a few blocks north of the business district, where there were no meters. Nervously, she walked towards the limestone edifice that was Bethany Methodist Church. At least she was dressed appropriately, wearing her gray "interview suit" with the maroon blouse.

This was a serious event, and she wanted to look serious.

People were ascending the steps to the church, and they were not the people she had expected to see. She'd assumed all of Warren Owens's friends would be the country club type rich white men and their well-tended wives. Instead, she saw several nicely dressed black women and a Hispanic man with four school-age boys in tow.

Maybe she was at the wrong church.

She entered the hushed sanctuary and saw the closed casket at the altar.

Picking up a laminated funeral card, she found she was, indeed, at the right place. It had a photograph of the late Warren Owens and a short account of his life. Apparently, he did a lot more than sell McMansions. He was a soccer coach. He was the treasurer for his church and was responsible for raising money to restore the stained glass windows. He also did a lot of volunteer work for some organization called Abigail's Attic.

The cornerstone outside was dated 1920, which made Bethany Methodist one of the newer downtown churches, but it was built in a traditional style which made it feel much older. The ceilings were high and arched, lined with heavy crown molding all the way around. Looking over at the newly restored stained glass windows, Kate was surprised to see that they were done in the simple Craftsman-style design of green and yellow rectangles, with slivers of clear glass which let the sun shine in. The walls and the pews were painted white, with red cushions and carpet. It seemed so open and airy, as if the building itself was welcoming her inside.

Apparently, Warren Owens had a lot of friends and relatives. The place was packed. Kate had never been very good at crowd estimates, but she guessed there were a dozen people standing in line to speak to the widow and at least fifty more milling about, speaking to each other in hushed tones. She joined the mourners, going over her opening lines. Before she knew it, she was at the head of the line.

Beside the wooden casket, Mrs. Warren Owens was shaking hands with one of the mourners. She was dressed in an elegant cherry red suit with a red and gold scarf tied neatly around her neck. Next to her were three blond boys, like steps, their faces white and somber. They wore matching navy blue suits, so new the pants were creased and stiff. The boys did not look at all comfortable in their church clothes. They tugged at their collars and fiddled with their ties. The youngest one had removed his tie and was inspecting the clip-on mechanism.

That must have been one dreadful shopping trip. Imagine taking three young boys to buy suits to wear to Daddy's funeral.

"I'm so glad you could come, Arlene," Mrs. Owens said to the woman ahead of Kate, taking her hand and holding it in both of hers. "Warren was so proud of you. He always talked about what a great job you've done. Of course, he always knew you would."

"I don't know where I'd be now if it weren't for Warren," the woman replied, dabbing her eyes with a tissue. "He's with Jesus now, but I sure wish we still had him with us."

"Well, you just have to keep on making him proud, Arlene," Mrs. Owens said gently.

Then the Hispanic man stepped up, enveloping Mrs. Owens in a huge, teary embrace.

"Warren was a good man," he said when he released her. "He let Manuel go out and play on the team with his brothers when none of the other coaches would. He treated Manuel just like the other kids."

"That's because Manuel is just like the other kids, Carlos." She gave him a tearful smile. "Only sweeter, isn't that right, Manuel?"

Now that she had a closer view, Kate noticed that one of the boys had the distinctive features of Down Syndrome. That boy reached up to hug

Mrs. Owens as well. His brothers followed suit.

Oh, my God, I think I'm going to cry, Kate thought. She'd had the impression Warren Owens was just another money-grubbing real estate agent, only interested in selling big houses. But he had helped people. And she could see they all were going to miss him.

Taking a deep breath, she approached the widow.

"Mrs. Owens," she said, "I'm Kate Dennison, from the *Winslow Beacon*. I'm so sorry about your husband. I'm writing a piece about his life, and I wanted to get an idea of what kind of person he was. Can you talk to me for a few minutes?"

"Certainly, if you don't mind standing here with me and the hooligans." She indicated the boys, who were starting to poke each other. "And please, call me Caroline. What would you like to know?"

"How did you meet?" Kate began, taking her notebook and pen out of her purse, ready to write.

"Just a minute," she said and turned to her sons. "Kevin, put your tie back on. Boys, remember we're in God's house. No horseplay. Bobby, can you fix your brother's tie? That would be a big help."

The oldest boy smiled at his mother.

"Sure, Mom." He took his brother's tie and clipped it back into place.

"Come on, Kev. Stop playing around," he said.

"Thank you, Bobby," she said, then turned back to Kate. "Now where was I? Oh yes, how Warren and I met. We were high school sweethearts. We started going steady in tenth grade. I wasn't allowed to date until I was sixteen, but Warren didn't mind. He said he could wait. We knew even then we'd get married and spend the rest of our lives together." She paused, blew her nose in a tissue, then continued. "I've always been, you know, kind of heavy, but Warren would tell me I was the most beautiful woman in the world and when we were rich he'd fill the closet with expensive clothes. And he did. I never really cared all that much for designer clothes, but it made Warren so happy to buy them. That's how he got involved with Abigail's Attic."

"Yes, I was going to ask you that. What is Abigail's Attic?"

"It's an organization that provides quality clothes to low-income women so they can look good on job interviews. Warren was buying me so many designer outfits, I had to get rid of the old ones, and I read an article about Abigail's Attic in the paper. I just wanted to dump off the load and be done with it, but Warren really latched on to their mission.

"They do more than just give out clothes, though," she went on. "They work on the women's interview skills, help them with resumes, provide career counseling, and basically build up their self-esteem. Warren just loved the girls to pieces. He taught an interview class, and he always told the ladies they looked like a million bucks and they were worth it, too.

"And he'd check up on each one in his class to find out how they did. Most of them got jobs and went off public assistance. He was so proud of them. Arlene, the lady who was just here, she has three children and was on welfare all her life. Now she's got her realtor's license and she's the top agent in her office. Warren gave her a start in the business, helping her get a job as a receptionist at the agency where he used to work."

Just then another mourner approached, a large, burly man in his sixties. He had an air of importance about him, as if he expected everyone to defer to him. Judging from Caroline's reaction, everyone did.

He took her hand and, for a moment, just looked at her with a deep, sorrowful look in his eyes.

"Caroline," he said finally, his voice breaking, "I just don't know what to say. You know I tried to go in that building. I would have died to save Warren, I would have. But the heat of that fire was so intense. There was nothing we could do."

"Hush, now, Ed, it's not your fault. I know you did your best," Caroline soothed him.

"If only I'd gotten there sooner," he said, taking out a handkerchief and quickly wiping his eyes.

"There's nothing you can do about that now, Ed. Don't blame yourself. Warren wouldn't have wanted that." Caroline turned to Kate. "Ed, this is Kate Dennison from the *Winslow Beacon*. She's writing a story about Warren for the paper. Maybe you could help her. Kate this is Warren's boss, Ed Kominsky."

"A reporter from the *Beacon*?" Kominsky looked straight at her.

Remembering what David had told her, Kate studied the man's face. He had a large, bulbous nose, and his skin was ruddy and acne-scarred. His hair lay haphazardly in thin wisps across the top of his pink scalp. He smiled, displaying a row of crooked teeth. Apparently, he had never bothered to have them straightened when the money came in.

"Good to meet you, Kate," he said, gripping her hand in a firm shake. "Warren Owens was the finest man I've ever known. He worked hard for me and worked even harder for his kids on the soccer team and the ladies at Abigail's Attic. I don't know how we can get along without him."

"You saw the fire. That must have been horrifying."

"Worst moment of my life, and I've had some pretty bad ones," Kominsky agreed. "It was like looking into the back acres of hell. Shane Cochran was with me, he couldn't stop screaming. Me, I just felt helpless. All I could do was call nine-one-one." He turned back to Caroline and took her hand again, "Listen, Caroline, I just wanted you to know how sorry I am. If there's anything I can do for you and your family, just let me know. You take care." With a last sorrowful look, he walked away, taking his seat among the mourners.

As the next person stepped up to offer condolences, Kate noticed how long the line had become and decided she'd taken enough of the widow's time. She had more than enough to finish her column.

And she was feeling very sad for Manuel and Arlene and especially Caroline and her three boys.

She thanked Caroline for her help, said she was sorry once again, then left the church.

Sometimes a reporter's job could be downright miserable.

Fire Takes Its Toll (cont.)

By Kate Dennison

What would you do if you came upon a raging inferno, knowing your father was inside?

Last week, Shane Cochran was faced with that horrible situation.

All he could do was scream.

9. GRIEVING RELATIVES REVISITED

STEPPING OUT INTO THE LATE AUTUMN SUN ON CHESTNUT STREET, Kate took a deep breath and pointed herself in the direction of St. Andrew's Church. She wiped her eyes with a tissue, deciding that if Timmy Kessler was the one who set the fire he should have to come here and see all the pain he'd brought to a lot of very nice people.

Now she was on her way to interview a man who'd watched a building burn knowing his father was trapped inside. At this moment, she would sit through twenty of the dullest planning-and-zoning meetings just to avoid having to talk to Shane Cochran. From what Ed Kominsky had said, she expected Shane would be hysterical with grief. Hysterical people never gave very good interviews.

She could see the stone spires of the centuries-old Episcopal Church on the next block. Kate loved old churches, but this one was so big and imposing. It had an aura of wealth and privilege, the sort of haughty attitude that comes from generations of old money and even older connections. She had the sense that a man like John Cochran very seldom set foot in this church, and was certainly not an active member.

The sanctuary seemed to go on forever with row upon row of ornately carved pews all in dark wood. Marble statues of Jesus and eight saints adorned the altar, along with a marble baptismal font the size and shape of an oil drum.

Although there were dozens of people milling about, it was strangely quiet. No one dared speak above a whisper.

An odd assortment of mourners had gathered in the vestibule. Apparently, the society matrons and country club gentlemen she had expected to see at Warren Owens's funeral had come to this one instead. They clustered off to one side, keeping their distance from the scruffy folks decked out in their best khakis and Oxford shirts with only slightly frayed collars.

Frank Wells stepped out from this crowd and called out to her.

"Kate, good to see you again. Come to pay your respects, have you?" he said, shaking her hand.

"Well, yes, but I'm also writing a column about John Cochran and I needed to talk to his son."

Frank shook his head gravely. "Oh, I don't know about that. Shane is having a hard time with his father's death," he said in hushed tones. "They never were very close, you know, although Shane idolized him when he was growing up. John and his ex had a nasty divorce, lots of fighting over money, with the boy caught in the middle of it. Shane always felt abandoned, that his father cared more about the environment than for him. And to a certain extent, that was true. John was a lousy father. Very distant."

Kate was starting to be a bit uncomfortable with the direction this conversation was taking. What he was telling her was interesting and provided some insight into the Cochran family, but she had no desire to write a column about John Cochran's dysfunctional home life.

"I see," said Kate. "Well, sometimes it helps to talk."

"Of course, Shane's a rich man now." Frank was obviously in a talkative mood. "John left everything to him. It's a real blow to all of us, as John was always talking about leaving the land to the Nature Trust, but he never got around to putting it in writing. Shane can do anything he wants with that land, and it looks like he'll sell it to Kominsky. Oh, there he is, over there."

He pointed to a young man looking very lost among his aristocratic handlers. One in particular seemed to be assigned to him. A pale, thin woman in her fifties, dressed in a perfectly tailored gray silk suit, stood next to him with a gentle grip on his arm.

Kate knew the hold. She had used it on her own daughter a number of times, usually when she was bored and cranky and about to make a scene.

"He looks lucid enough," Frank commented. "He was in a terrible state this morning. Has been ever since the fire. That's John's sister Olivia Claymore. Upper crust all the way. You'd never think someone like that would be John's sister."

"He comes from a wealthy family then?"

"No, as a matter of fact. His parents were teachers, well educated but not a whole lot of money. He and his sister both ended up rich, though. John made his millions from his software business and his sister married hers. That's why we're here with all these snobs. Aside from Shane, Olivia is his only relative. And she made all the arrangements. If you knew John at all, you'd know this is not the sort of funeral he'd have wanted."

Frank looked anxiously around to make sure none of Olivia's friends had heard themselves referred to as snobs then continued.

"The Friends of the Carolina Coastline will be holding our own memorial service at John's Piney Point Preserve, though I expect we won't be able to call it that much longer. It's tomorrow night at six o'clock. You're welcome to come. We decided to have it at sunset. John often said watching a sunset on the beach was his favorite way to spend an evening."

"That's certainly true," Kate said, smiling, ignoring the invitation. She wasn't sure she was up for another memorial service, even if it was on the beach.

The receiving line had thinned out a bit, and it looked as if Aunt Olivia had been distracted by one of her cronies. Shane was left unattended, and now seemed as good a time as any to get that interview.

"Thanks for your help, Frank. I think I'll try to get a word with Shane Cochran now."

Maneuvering through the crowd, Kate joined the receiving line. Shane stood alone, his aunt completely engrossed in conversation with her friends.

He was a younger version of his father, having the same sharp features and thick hair, only sandy blond instead of gray. His eyes were an intense blue, though right now they were red-rimmed and bleary.

"Mr. Cochran?"

"What?" he said, as if waking from a deep sleep. "Oh, hello."

"Hello. I'm Kate Dennison from the *Beacon*. I'm so sorry about your father. I'm working on his obituary and I wondered if you could fill me in on some of the details."

"Okay, but I don't know how I can help you. My dad and me kind of lost touch over the years."

"But you were supposed to be meeting him at the Normandy Sands property. How did that happen?"

Shane's face contorted with grief, and he looked like he was fighting back tears. Kate felt like a class-A jerk.

"Yes, that's right. I was supposed to meet him there," Shane said, regaining his composure. "When my boss, Ed Kominsky, found out about the property my dad owned, he asked me if I could arrange a meeting with him. He said maybe if my dad saw the house at Normandy Sands he might change his mind about selling his land to him. I knew my dad and knew it would be a waste of time, but Ed kept saying all he wanted to do was have a dialog, find common ground. So I called my dad up and asked."

"What did your dad say?"

"Pretty much what I expected. That he'd talk to Ed Kominsky when pigs fly. But I told him if he came I'd help him clear the phragmites from the marshes on his property this weekend. That's miserable work, you know. You stand in muddy water up to your knees pulling out hundreds and hundreds of these tall reeds. He used to make me do that when I was a kid. I hated it. Funny, this time, I was kind of looking forward to it."

His intense blue eyes glistened with tears now. Blinking them back, he smiled meekly at her.

"I guess you want to hear what it was like to come up on the fire."

"Not if you don't want to talk about it," she told him softly.

"Everyone else wants to know. The police, the fire department, the guy from arson investigation, the newspapers, the television people, everyone wants to hear me say what it was like. How it felt. Why would anyone want to know what that feels like? You'd think they know it feels horrible."

Kate had no idea what to say to that, so she nodded and hoped Shane would keep talking. He did.

"Okay, here's what it was like. Ed and me are running late. I've done my level best to get to his office on time, but he's stuck on the phone or in a meeting that's running long or something. I don't remember. Anyway, we have a nice drive to Normandy Sands. We talk about the usual stuff, football, hockey, maybe going fishing some time.

"Then we turn down that road to the development and we see the smoke. Huge clouds of black smoke. I think maybe it's the pine trees on fire. Ed hits the gas, and we must be going a hundred miles an hour down that road to the house. Then we're skidding to a stop and there isn't even a house any more, just fire and smoke. I see my dad's car parked in the driveway, and I'm looking for him everywhere. I keep hoping he's on the beach or down the road. Somewhere, anywhere but inside that house. And then, I don't know, I just start screaming and screaming like I can't stop."

His voice cracking, he paused. "There, that's what it was like," he said in a flat tone.

"You're right, you know," Kate said gently. "Nobody should want to know what that was like. How about telling me what your father was like?"

Shane shifted his feet, deep in thought.

"We had our differences. Actually, that's about all we had. He was so serious all the time, you know? My aunt's the same way; it must run in the family. Anyway, he worked hard at whatever he did. Always working."

"Did you ever do things together, like fathers and sons?"

"Not a whole lot," Shane replied wearily. "Fishing. We both liked to fish. We'd go to this one special spot and spend all afternoon there. He'd point out the birds and tell me their names in Latin. That was a good time."

"Shane, dear, I'm so sorry to leave you by yourself. Are you all right?"

His aunt appeared at his side, once again taking hold of his arm, all the while giving Kate a look of disdain.

"Aunt Olivia, this is Kate Dennison. She works for the *Beacon*."

"I see." The look of disdain became utter loathing, and Kate figured she'd better be on her way.

"Listen, dear," Olivia said patronizingly. "My nephew has had a horrific experience, and he does not need to speak to anyone else in the media. You understand, don't you, dear?"

"Yes, of course," Kate said, feeling her face growing hot. "Terribly sorry for your loss, Mrs. Claymore."

"Thank you," Olivia replied coldly. "Now you'd best be on your way."

Kate turned and left the church. She had been ready to go anyway but couldn't believe the gall of Shane's aunt, throwing her out of a funeral, for God's sake.

Hey, it's over, she told herself. It was time to go home to Molly. That was all that mattered.

Family Talk

PARENTING TIPS

Don't burden your child with your worries. Children are not little adults, they can't help you with your problems at work, and telling them about how much you hate your job will only make them anxious and upset.

The *Beacon* recommends that you only tell your children what they need to know and only when it affects them. This means don't complain about your boss, your co-workers or your money woes around your children. And please do your best to avoid venting any anger and resentment you may be harboring toward an estranged parent around your children.

10. MOTHERHOOD AND MESSAGES

MOLLY WAS WAITING AT MARLENE'S DOOR WHEN KATE ARRIVED, HER forehead pressed against the glass panel on the left side of the door. As soon as she saw Kate, the door swung open, and she bounded onto the porch and hurled herself into her mother's arms.

"Hey, Mommy! Did you have a good time at work today?"

What a question to be hit with after a day like today, Kate thought. She wasn't sure what to say.

"I worked hard, and I did a good job," she said, pleased with herself for coming up with a truthful response without having to go into the gloomy nature of her afternoon.

"I did, too. Come inside and I can show you my spelling test. I got all the words right, even the bonus words, and they were hard!"

Molly scampered across Marlene's hardwood floor to the utility room in the back of the house where her bookbag hung.

Marlene was in the kitchen, in the midst of preparing what was no doubt a marvelous meal. The delicious smell of spices and roasting lamb filled the room.

"You look like you've been through the wringer. What's Roger got you doing now?"

"Grieving relative stories."

"Ooh, that's the worst. It's a good thing he's the publisher because he could never do that kind of story. It's too intrusive. This was about that fire, wasn't it? Those poor men. It must have been horrible."

"Yes, especially the real estate agent. Did you know he helped welfare mothers get good paying jobs? And he was a soccer coach?"

"I read something about that in the Star, but they really didn't go into it. Said he was active in several volunteer organizations."

"He was a really nice guy. And I'm writing a column that says so."

Molly arrived, her bookbag in one hand and a grubby piece of ruled notebook paper in the other. She held it up for Kate to see.

"Well, look at that," Kate said, taking the paper and reading it. "One hundred percent. And you can spell 'independence.' That's hard for grown-ups. I'm impressed."

Molly grinned proudly and stuffed her paper back into the chaos of her bookbag. "Let's go home, Mommy." She hoisted the straps around her shoulders and headed for the door. "I want to have pizza."

"Ordering pizza tonight? That sounds like fun," Marlene said.

"No, it's a frozen deep-dish. They're pretty good, and we always add extra stuff. Molly likes olives, and I put on some of that imitation crabmeat."

"Mommy used to make us pizza every Friday, but now she doesn't have time because she has to work," Molly announced from the door. "We have to buy it from the store."

"Ouch!" Kate clutched her chest. "I've just been hit with a ton of Mommy guilt. Of course, she doesn't remember the times it came out with a soggy crust and burnt cheese."

"A meal shared with someone you love is always special no matter where it comes from," Marlene said. "Go on home and enjoy it."

"Thanks, Marlene," Kate said, as she hurried out of the house. Molly had the door wide open and all the heat was escaping, even though Marlene was too polite to say anything about it.

Her daughter stood outside, hopping from foot to foot impatiently.

"It's been a hard week for you. Take it easy over the weekend," Marlene called as they crossed the yard to their house.

"I'll try," Kate called back from her own front porch.

Molly ran inside, dropping her bookbag on the floor by the door.

"Don't run in the house!" Kate yelled after her. "And you know your bookbag doesn't belong on the floor."

"Sorreeee!" she wailed.

Molly managed to slow down to a kind of trot, retrieving her bookbag and dutifully taking it into the kitchen, where she hung it on the special hook Kate had put up for her.

"Oh, Mommy, we got three phone messages!" she called "Can I check them?"

"No, let me. Last time you erased them," she said, grabbing Molly's hand away from the machine.

"It was an accident. I didn't mean to, Mommy." She was close to tears.

Dammit, this was supposed to be quality time and here she was jumping all over the poor kid. Reminding herself that her daughter was "the best kid in the whole world," she vowed to stop the recriminations right now.

"I know it wasn't your fault, sweetie. It's just that someone from work might have called, and I want to make sure I hear it. You're not in trouble. Just settle down a bit, okay?"

"Okay, Mom."

Kate gave her daughter an affectionate squeeze to let her know all was forgiven then pressed the play button on the answering machine attached to the wall of their kitchen.

"Message One," came the mechanical voice of the machine.

"Katie, this is your mother. Just wanted to know how your new job is working out. I'm so glad you've gone back to journalism. I don't know why you ever left. Anyway, give us a call this weekend. Love you."

"Message Two," the machine announced.

"Hey, it's me." Keith always identified himself that way. "Can you have Molly ready by seven-thirty tomorrow morning? I know it's early, but I'm going out for breakfast with Jennifer and the boys and I want Molly to come with us. See you tomorrow."

At the mention of Jennifer, Kate felt an annoying twinge of jealousy. The divorcee with two sons had been their next-door neighbor when they'd been married. Although Kate had wanted to end her marriage to Keith, she was still shocked at how quickly Jen had moved in on him. Now she suspected the woman had had her eyes on him all along.

Keith was free to date whomever he pleased, Kate reminded herself, even if it was a woman she found overbearing, rude, and totally inept at parenting. Jennifer let her sons get away with murder.

Kate could only hope Molly had the good sense not to imitate them.

"Message Three."

"Uh, hi, Kate. This is Bryan. I'm going to be out your way tomorrow night for John Cochran's memorial service. Are you going? If you are I can give you a ride. If not maybe we could meet up afterwards. I'll be home this evening, too bushed to party on a Friday night. Anyway, give me a call."

In a frenzy, Kate rushed to find a pen and paper so she could write down the number. It was supposed to be right here by the phone. Why couldn't she be more organized?

"Who's that guy?" Molly asked.

"Just a second, sweetie, I need to get this phone number." Having found a pen, she pushed the replay button and carefully wrote down the number, all the while feeling a tingle of excitement at the sound of Bryan's voice.

He called, he called!

"Mommy, who is he?" Molly asked again.

"An old friend," she replied. "What do you say we get that pizza started? Olives on your side, crabmeat on mine, right?"

"Right," Molly said, now very subdued. She leaned against the counter while Kate searched through the cluttered refrigerator for their dinner.

She found the olives and crabmeat then pulled the pizza out of the freezer.

"Do you want a lot of olives?" she asked as she took a handful out of the jar and began slicing them.

"Yes."

"You're awful quiet. What's going on with you?"

"Are you going to marry that guy who just called?"

Stunned, Kate didn't know what to say. Her daughter looked so distraught, she stopped chopping olives, wiped her hands and leaned down and gave her a hug.

"Of course not, Molly. He's just a man I knew before I met your daddy."

"Was he your boyfriend?"

"We used to do things together, but I don't think you could call him my boyfriend. And it was a long time ago. We just want to get together and talk."

Good lord, she thought, even I can't swallow that one. But considering her habit of falling asleep at nine-thirty, talking is probably all she'd be able to manage.

"Jennifer is Daddy's girlfriend," Molly said woefully.

Kate returned to her olive chopping.

"How do you feel about that?"

"Jennifer is nice, but Austin is mean to me sometimes."

"That's nothing new. Austin used to tease you when he lived next

86

door to us."

"I know," Molly said sadly. "It's just weird. It's like, you know, I'm supposed to be happy and I'm supposed to like Jennifer and Austin and Matthew and all because Daddy wants me to but sometimes I don't like them. I don't want them for my family. I want you and Daddy."

Kate stopped the pizza preparations and led her daughter over to the couch.

"Sweetie, they aren't your family, and you don't have to like them if you don't want to. Your daddy and I expect you to be polite and respectful to Jennifer, as you would for any adult. And to try to get along with the boys. But that's it. How you feel is your own business. No one has the right to try to make you feel something you don't feel in your heart. You understand that, don't you?"

"Yes, Mommy," a very relieved-sounding Molly replied.

"Good, I'm glad we've got that cleared up. Now, let's get this baby in the oven."

"It's a pizza, Mom, not a baby. You don't put babies in the oven. That's scary."

"Sorry, kid, that's just a figure of speech. I know it's a pizza."

Kate returned to the kitchen and slid the pizza into the oven, all the while making sure Molly was nowhere near the heating elements. Then she slammed the door shut and set the timer.

"Would you like to sit on the couch and read some more of Ramona while we wait?"

"Okay." Molly quietly went down the hallway to get the book from her room.

"Hey, I like the way you remembered to walk in the house," Kate called after her.

Catch them being good, the books always said.

Molly returned with the dog-eared copy of *Beezus and Ramona* and presented it to Kate.

"So, is Bryan nice?"

"Yes, he is. He's kind of tall and he smiles a lot and he tells funny jokes."

They sat together on the couch, and Kate paged through the book for where they had left off reading the day before.

"Mom?"

"Yes, Molly?"

"It's okay with me if you have a boyfriend."

"That's good to know, pumpkin."

Later that night, after the pizza had been finished off, Kate tucked Molly safely into bed, kissed her on the forehead, and standing at the door, she said "Goodnight, sleep tight, I love you. You're the best kid in the whole world."

And Molly replied, as she did every night, "You're the best mommy in the whole world. I love you."

Then Kate shut the door and headed to her own bedroom across the hall.

Once the door was closed, she took out Bryan's number and dialed, surprised at her own nervousness. Come on, it's just Bryan.

"Hullo?" came the voice at the other end.

"Hey, Bryan, this is Kate."

"What's up?"

"Oh, not much. I just put Molly to bed. I tell you, I don't know if I'm ever going to get the hang of this working mom juggling act."

"You'll get used to it. You just went back to work this week, right?"

"Yes, the Friends of the Coastline meeting was my first day on the job."

"So, it's only been a few days."

"Yes, and they're running me ragged. Still it's a lot of fun to be working again. I really like what I do. Just wish I had more energy. And more time."

"Speaking of time, you got any to spare tomorrow night? I know it's a memorial service, but it's on the beach so it shouldn't be that much of a downer."

"I don't know. I got thrown out of his last funeral."

"You're kidding. What did you do, show up drunk?"

"No, I was perfectly sober, thank you. I was just interviewing his son Shane Cochran for the paper and Mrs. Olivia Claymore, sister of the deceased, asked me to leave. Have you ever met her?"

"No, never had the pleasure, though I've heard about her. I only met with John a couple of times on Nature Trust business. He didn't talk much about his family or personal stuff. Never knew anyone so focused. He must have slept, eaten and lived that preserve. Anyway, when Frank asked me to the memorial service, my boss said it would be good for us to have a presence, especially since the conservative politicians are making out that all environmentalists are militant extremists."

"Frank asked me, too, so I suppose it would be okay for me to go. Molly will be at her dad's tomorrow night so I won't have to get a babysitter."

"Great. It'll be nice to have someone to talk to afterwards. Would you like me to pick you up?"

"I don't know, you'd have to go pretty far out of your way to get to my house. Maybe I could meet you there. Oh, wait a second, I don't know where it is."

"Piney Point Coastal Preserve. I've been there. It's out of everyone's way. And it's hard to find. You have to go up a dirt road to get to it and there's no sign on the road. I drove around in circles looking for it the first time I went there."

"Maybe you should pick me up then."

"Tell me how to get to your house and I'll be there around five. That should give us plenty of time to look for that dirt road." Kate explained how to get to her house from the highway, giving him the simplest route even though it wasn't the shortest.

"That sounds good. If I get lost, I'll call you on the cell phone."

"You have a cell phone? I thought you hated those things."

"I do, but the office insisted I get one so now they can track me down wherever I am. They do come in handy sometimes. Like when you get lost."

"Just make sure you pull off the road before you call."

"Always do. Well, I gotta go, see you tomorrow."

Hanging up the phone, she felt excited about her first date in ages then remembered where she was going.

At least this funeral would be on the beach.

Defense Lambastes Star Witness

Sept. 10 — Adam Steiner, lawyer for accused murderer Timothy Kessler, is insisting the state's star witness is lying and that Kessler is innocent in the deaths of Warren Owens and environmentalist John Cochran. Both men perished in a fire which has been determined to be arson.

"They aren't even giving out his name," Steiner told reporters at a press conference Friday. "We've been threatened with contempt charges if we so much as mention it. And they won't let us near this man, a clear violation of our client's right to confront his accuser."

Winslow Beach Beacon

11. YET ANOTHER MEMORIAL SERVICE

PINEY POINT WAS CERTAINLY A BEAUTIFUL PLACE FOR ANYTHING, EVEN a memorial service. Members of the Friends of the Carolina Coastline had gathered in a semi-circle along the beach, facing west toward the Intracoastal Waterway. The setting sun shone through wispy clouds, turning the sky purple and scarlet. Seagulls dipped and hovered above as the water from the inlet lapped at the sandy beach. Scuttling about on their tiny stilt legs, sandpipers searched along the beach for their supper.

This service was far more relaxed and, if it could be said about a death ritual, more enjoyable than the one Kate had almost attended the day before. There were about thirty or so people in attendance, counting herself and Bryan. She stood next to him as they listened to Frank give the first of what would be many tributes.

"Take only pictures, leave only footprints. We've heard it a million times. And I know we've all tried to live by it," he began. "But John has left us a lot more than just footprints. He left us his vision and his challenge..."

About five minutes into Frank's speech, the John Muir quotes and bumper sticker buzz phrases seemed to merge, and Kate found her mind wandering. No matter, she was on her own time now and didn't have to take notes.

She looked across the Intracoastal Waterway, marveling at the lack of development. She had never seen an area like it without at least some houses along its shores, most often built one on top of the other. All she could see on the opposite shore here were long-leaf pines, which Frank was now explaining were an endangered species, nearly wiped out in this area.

She could understand Cochran's desire to protect this spot, and she hoped his friends could manage to keep it exactly like this forever.

Frank was followed by a woman who introduced herself as Sara, and with shaking hands and a trembling voice, she read a very long abstract poem she had written for the occasion. Her monotonous delivery sent Kate into a bored stupor, so in an attempt to keep from falling asleep on her feet, she turned her attention to the ocean side of the beach. About two miles away, she could see a large black pile of jagged beams. With a shock, she realized it was the ruins of the house where Cochran died.

"I didn't know Normandy Sands was this close to Piney Point," she whispered to Bryan, pointing up the coastline to the burned house.

"Yup," he whispered back. "Now you see why Kominsky was so hot to buy this property. Nothing but prime beachfront as far as the eye can see. Location, location, location."

The woman standing to her right turned sharply and gave them both a look that Kate had not seen since she was a fidgeting little girl during Sunday mass at St. Monica's. It had the same effect. She stopped talking immediately.

The next speaker stepped up, a blue-jeaned child of the sixties now well into a potbellied middle age. He wore his thinning gray hair in a ponytail and carried a battered guitar. The man moved slowly, almost in a daze, and Kate thought he may have gotten too much of the bad brown acid at Woodstock.

"We all know John was a man of few words. He let his actions speak for him," Guitar Man said. "So I won't waste your time with any of my own words. I'm here to sing one of John's favorites 'Whose Garden Was This?' by the great folksinger Tom Paxton. Feel free to join in if you know the words. Or even if you don't."

Kate was not surprised that nearly everyone in attendance knew the words to this 1960s anthem to ecology.

The sun had disappeared behind the horizon, and it was now very dark along the beach. No houses also meant no lights. A woman moved through the crowd, handing out small white candles with cardboard circles from a box. Once she got close enough to them, Kate recognized Timmy Kessler's grandmother, Eleanor.

"Bryan, how nice of you to come," she said as she handed them both a candle. "And you're the girl from the *Beacon*. I'm so sorry, I've forgotten your name."

"Kate – Kate Dennison."

"Oh, yes. If you don't mind, I'd like to talk to you about my grandson after we're done here. That is, if it's not a problem," she added, glancing at Bryan.

"Oh, no, of course, it's not a problem. I'd be glad to," Kate replied.

Frank was back, holding a large lit candle.

"It is better to light one candle than curse the darkness," he proclaimed loudly. "Let's all pass that light along and think of John as we do it." Then he leaned over and lit the candle of the person standing in front of him, who in turn lit another person's candle. Sara began singing "Amazing Grace" while the guitar man accompanied her.

Once again, Kate felt her eyes tearing up. The beach, the candlelight, the old hymn; you would have to have ice water in your veins to remain unmoved by it all, she told herself.

"Go in peace," Frank said solemnly when they finished. He blew out his candle, and everyone else followed suit. In silence, the crowd headed toward their cars, parked a good half-mile away.

Most of the attendees, including Bryan, had remembered to bring flashlights, and the line of beams bobbed up the coastline. Kate scrambled up the path through the dunes, remembering how hard it was to keep up with Bryan's long strides.

They approached the clearing that had served as a parking lot for the dozen or so member vehicles, most of them beat-up fuel-efficient compact cars with a few high-dollar Volvos thrown in. Kate was impressed that no one had driven a gas-guzzling sport utility vehicle and that several had carpooled.

She had a lot of respect for people who practiced what they preached.

Eleanor stood at the entrance to the clearing, collecting the used candles as everyone passed her.

"Do you mind waiting while I talk to Eleanor? I don't think this will take long. If it does, I'll just tell her to call me at the office."

"No, I'll wait in the car," he said, heading toward his old red Geo.

Kate dropped their candles in the box and Eleanor waited as the last of the mourners filed past.

"I'm so glad I can talk to you," she said, perching the box on her hip and carrying it to a car where Frank was standing, with his hands in his pockets. He stared up at the night sky, then turned to Kate and Eleanor.

"Beautiful night, isn't it?"

Kate looked up to see the stars and had to agree. Away from the city lights, even the faintest stars were visible.

"Here, let me take care of that for you, Eleanor." He took the box, opening a door and sliding it into the backseat

"Frank, I'm going to have a word with Miss Dennison, here."

"Take your time, Eleanor," he said. "I'm watching the cosmos."

"You know what's happened to Timmy, don't you?"

"Yes, I know. We're doing a story on it now."

"He didn't set that fire. He told me. That boy can't tell a lie to save his life. Whenever he was in trouble and tried to make up a story, he always gave himself away. Eyes on the floor, face beet-red. He's telling the truth when he says he didn't do it. It's that so-called witness they've got who's telling the lies here," she said, her anger and frustration evident in her voice.

"But what about his fingerprints on the gas can? They aren't making that up."

"I went to visit him today and he told me everything that happened, and I think I know the name of the person the police are so all fired up about protecting from the Forces of Nature who, by the way, haven't got a damn thing to do with this."

Eleanor's kindly demeanor had disappeared. By the glow of the flashlight, Kate could see she was quite angry and, if she'd been able, would have torn down the county jail to free her grandson.

"So what really happened?"

"He was at that Normandy Sands house Monday night. He went there with this young man named Brandon Fawkes he'd just met at the library. Brandon said he had some marijuana and knew a great place to get high. So Timmy went with him to Normandy Sands. He said they went down to the boat slip and he had to pull some gas cans out of the way to get to the dock. The cans were empty, and he wasn't anywhere near that house when it burned.

"They were there a couple of hours then they left around midnight. Brandon dropped him back at his apartment. Timmy had a few beers and fell asleep. He didn't wake up until about ten-thirty the next morning. The first he heard about the fire was at the meeting."

"So you're saying this Brandon Fawkes set him up."

"Yes, that's exactly what I'm saying. And if you'd like to get it from his lawyer, I've got his phone number," Eleanor said. She pulled a business card from her pocket and gave it to Kate.

"His name is Adam Steiner," she continued. "And I wrote my name and phone number on the back, in case you have any more questions. Really, I'm not supposed to talk to anyone in the press. But I know I can trust you. Roger Hoffman is a good man, and I know he wouldn't have hired you if you weren't fair and honest. Talk to Adam, he'll set everything straight."

Kate could hear the desperation in the woman's voice.

"I'll try to call him this weekend," she said, putting the business card into the inside pocket of her jacket.

"Thank you," Eleanor said with an exhausted smile. Then she went back to Frank's car.

Kate stood alone for a second, trying to decide if what she'd heard was the truth or the only plausible story a young murderer could come up with to explain away the evidence against him. A grandmother could not be seen as impartial by any stretch of the imagination.

She'd have to talk to Roger about this.

"Hey, Kate!" Bryan called. "How about dinner?"

This was not how she envisioned her first date.

The Beacon Family Advisor

Q: I'm newly divorced, with a young daughter and I need some advice. How should I handle dating?

A: Very carefully.

12. CHINESE TAKE-OUT

THAT'S IT, RIGHT THERE ON THE RIGHT. THE WHITE ONE WITH THE porchlight on."

"Kate, they all have their porchlights on."

Bryan swung the car around the corner, creeping along through the narrow streets of Sunset Park. At this time of night, all the houses did seem to look alike, even to Kate, who knew the neighborhood well.

Still, Kate was feeling a bit annoyed with Bryan. She wanted to get home and eat. The car was filled with the aroma of Szechuan shrimp with garlic sauce and all she could think of was how great it would taste.

"Okay, it's the one with the big live oak in the front yard and the garden gnome at the foot of the driveway."

"Oh, that one."

Bryan pulled the car into the driveway.

The night was warm with a gentle breeze, the oppressive heat of the Carolina summer now a distant memory. A faint scent from the flowers blooming on the crape myrtle bushes hung in the air. Everything was so still; the traffic on the main road, the dogs barking on the next block, the mournful tones of her wind chimes, all seemed muted and far away.

Kate got out of the car, keenly aware that she was with a man, and this man was not her ex-husband. Walking with Bryan up the walk to her door, she could feel her knees wobble a bit and her heart pounding.

She hoped she didn't look as nervous (or as eager) as she felt.

In the dim light of the porch lamp, Kate dug through her purse for her keys.

"You still carrying all that junk around with you?"

"Even more now. My ex-husband got me into carrying a flashlight and a cell phone on top of everything else." She pushed the key into the temperamental lock, jiggled it and opened the door, switched on the overhead light in the living room.

He handed her the soggy brown paper bag that held their dinner.

"Looks like the garlic sauce leaked a bit," he said.

"Yeah, those little cardboard containers tend to do that, especially when you take the turns a bit too fast on the way home from the restaurant."

"Hey, I wanted to make sure it was still hot by the time we ate it."

"Ever heard of a microwave oven?"

"Oh, yeah," he said, grinning.

"Make yourself comfortable. I'll just be a minute while I get some plates. How about a beer?"

"Thanks, I'd love one."

Kate took the bag into the kitchen and set it down on the white tile counter while she got the beers out of the refrigerator. It was so nice to hang out with a guy who drank beer that came with twist-off bottle caps. Keith had always been such a snob about having imported beer.

Kate opened the cupboard and went into shock.

Oh, my God, there are no clean plates! This was her big romantic evening, and she certainly didn't want to be washing dishes while Bryan waited to eat. Panic gripped her until she remembered she'd run the dishwasher that morning. Thank God for the All-Electric Kitchen.

Okay, Kate, get a grip, she told herself. Everything's under control. All you have to do is get the food from the carton to the plates to Bryan. Not a big deal.

She opened the dishwasher door and reached in, grabbed a couple plates, and the serving spoon, then began dishing out Szechuan Ginger Beef and Shrimp. She kept a watchful eye on her gentleman caller pacing across the living room floor.

He'd made his way walked across the front room to the built-in bookcase where she kept her stereo. Her CD collection filled two shelves, end to end, in no particular order.

"Hey, Kate, is it okay if I put on some music?" he asked.

"Sure, go right ahead. Play whatever you want."

"Do you have any Led Zeppelin?" Bryan said, thumbing through the disks.

"I've got 'Houses of the Holy' on vinyl somewhere, but I never got around to connecting the turntable to the stereo. Anyway, I don't have the patience to deal with records. I know for a fact that I have exactly two hundred-seventy-two CDs, so there must be something there you want to hear."

"Okay."

She heard the CD player opening and closing, followed by the sounds of Miles Davis's trumpet.

"Good choice," Kate said. "Your tastes have changed."

"A lot of things have changed." He walked back over to the kitchen and took one of the beers. "Listening to classic rock stations gets old. Makes you think that people are really afraid to age, and think maybe if they keep hearing the same songs they can convince themselves they're still in high school. Besides, I've always liked jazz."

Kate brought the plates in along with an assortment of eating utensils and everything down on the coffee table.

"Okay if we eat sitting on the couch? I didn't have a chance to clear all the junk off the dining room table."

"Fine with me."

He flopped down on the couch, putting his feet up on the coffee table, just like he used to do years ago when they shared pizza at her shabby little apartment in Dayton.

"Thanks, Kate, this looks great," he said, picking up his plate. "Take-out was a great idea. You ever been to this place before?"

"Yeah, it's pretty good. When you ask for extra-spicy, it really is extra-spicy. Chopsticks or fork?" she asked, holding the chopsticks in her left hand and a fork in her right.

"Chopsticks, of course," he said, taking them from her. "Forks are for wimps who can't take extra-spicy." Expertly, he dipped them into the mound of sauce-covered shrimp and took a bite.

"Whoa, you weren't kidding! This is great stuff!" Tiny beads of sweat popped up on his forehead.

"Glad you like it," she replied. "I had to go without hot and spicy food for my entire marriage. My ex couldn't take it. Looking back on it, I should have seen it as a warning. Stay away from compulsively neat guys who only eat bland food."

Bryan took another mouthful of shrimp. They both said nothing for a long moment, reveling in the shear joy of spicy food while Miles Davis played on.

"Hey, is this your daughter?" Bryan asked, pointing to a black-and-white photo hanging on the wall.

"Yes, when she was two years old. She's a lot bigger now."

"That's a really nice picture. How did you get all those pigeons to fly away like that?"

"A real professional photographer managed that, not me. It was just before we moved out here. Molly was toddling around the park benches and this woman all dressed in black appeared out of nowhere and took her picture. When the woman had me sign a release, she told me her name was Lisa Watson. A couple years ago, I heard her interviewed on National Public Radio. She'd just published a book of art photos. And guess what? That picture of Molly was on the cover. We had a copy of the book, but Keith got it."

"She looks like a great kid."

"I think she is. Even though the marriage didn't work out, it was worth it just to have her."

"So what went wrong, if you don't mind my asking?"

"Lots of things," she said. "In the beginning, I was sure it would work out. He was a nice guy with a good job, ready to settle down and have kids. It wasn't until after we were married and Molly was on the way that I realized how..." she stopped, searching for words. "How controlling he could be. He had a system for everything – how to fold towels, how to fill the dishwasher, how to vacuum the carpet, how the bed should be made. It took me years to figure them all out. I managed pretty well, until we moved out here, and then it all fell apart."

"How?"

"It was the house that did it."

"This place? What was wrong with it? Too small? He didn't like the neighborhood?"

"No, this is my house. I bought it with my half of the equity when we sold our other house after the divorce. You wouldn't believe that place – hardwood floors, twenty-foot ceilings in the great room, stainless steel appliances in the kitchen. It was impossible for one person to keep clean. Okay, impossible for me to keep clean. I hated it from the second I saw it."

"Then why did you buy it? Didn't you tell your husband you didn't want to live there?"

"I did, several times. But Keith loved it. It was his dream house and, as far as he was concerned, it was my dream house, too. He said the only reason I didn't want to buy it was because I just didn't feel worthy of it."

"Not worthy?"

"Yes, it was all a problem of self-esteem. I have plenty of self-esteem, and I've got dreams, too, but they don't involve waxing parquet floors on a regular basis. Not only that, I thought the house had too much bad karma."

"You could tell?"

"Well, the realtor gave us the history and it wasn't good. Some rich entrepreneur commissioned it, but his business tanked halfway through construction and he couldn't afford to finish it. Another builder took over after that, but he went bankrupt after the last major hurricane. When we came around it was in pretty rough shape, and the bank had foreclosed on it. We got a hell of a deal, though. We only paid a third of the original asking price, and we got more than that back when we sold it last year."

"Well, at least you made a profit."

"There are easier ways to make money," Kate replied. "Don't get me wrong, I am so glad I had enough to buy this house plus have some left over to live on until I found a job. But I wouldn't want to go through that again."

"I'm sorry things didn't work out for you. You deserve to be happy."

"I am happy. Happy enough for now, anyway. Not many people can say that. How about you, Bryan? Are you happy?"

"I used to think so," he said. "But I'm starting to wish I'd settled down and had a family. Like you did."

"Trust me, Bryan, settling down and having a family is a lot harder than it looks."

"Even so, I'd like to come home to something more than an empty apartment. You know, I really missed you when you left. I meant to call you, but then I heard you were engaged. I was a fool to let you go, Kate. I guess I just always thought there was plenty of time and you'd always be there."

She set her plate down on the coffee table and edged over towards his side of the couch.

"I'm here now. And there's still plenty of time."

"Plenty of time for what?" he said, draping his arm around her shoulders.

"Whatever we want. Whatever happens. Whatever."

Kessler to Plead Not Guilty

Sept. 10 — Timothy Kessler, represented by noted trial lawyer Adam Steiner, is expected to enter a plea of not guilty before Superior Court Judge J. Allen Hulick. Sources at the New Hanover County Court House say his trial is set to begin sometime in October and will probably last at least three months.

Winslow Beach Beacon

13. POP QUIZ ON THE BILL OF RIGHTS

WELL, I GUESS I'D BETTER GO," BRYAN SAID.
They stood next to the garden gnome, surrounded by early-morning sunshine. Bryan's arms were draped around her; they'd just ended a goodbye kiss that seemed as if it would last well into the afternoon.

"Yes, I suppose it's time you hit the road."

He made no move to get into his car, instead leaned down for one more kiss.

"You know we can't stand out here all day," she said. "You have to go back to Raleigh, and my daughter will be home soon."

"Oh, I don't know, this is kinda fun. You think we could do it again sometime?"

Kate smiled dreamily, remembering the evening's sexual acrobatics. Dating sex sure was a lot more fun than married sex. Of course, now that she thought about it, even the dating sex she'd had with her ex-husband had never been much to write home about.

"Sure, Bryan. Give me a call, and we can work out the details."

"Can I call you at work?"

"At home, at work, on my cell phone. You can even e-mail me if you like."

He finally let go so he could pull a pen and pad of paper out of his pocket. He handed it to her.

"Write 'em all down."

She did, making sure they were legible. Now all she could do was hope he didn't lose them.

He put the pad back in his pocket, and actually opened the driver's door, slid in behind the wheel and put the keys in the ignition.

"Well, I'll be damned, you really are leaving," Kate said, leaning over the car window.

"Yeah, but I'll be back." He started the engine. She stepped away as he backed out of the driveway. She waved, and watched him drive away.

The sweet euphoria evaporated, replaced with that long-forgotten anxiety of waiting for The Phone Call that never seemed to come. And he hadn't even gotten to Carolina Beach Road yet.

"Morning, Kate!"

Roger was on his porch waving to her. She felt her face redden with embarrassment. Now that he was her boss, it was a bit tricky having him living next door where he could see the comings and goings of her gentlemen callers. Of course, up until now, she'd had no gentleman callers to speak of. Keith didn't count.

"Good morning," she said, crossing the yard.

"Nice young man you got there. It's about time you started dating again."

"Well, Bryan's an old friend from Ohio who just turned up."

"Even better to start off with someone you know. They've already heard all your important stories so you can skip ahead to the good stuff."

She climbed the steps. He held the door open for her.

"Come on in. Coffee's on, and I need to talk to you about the Kessler case."

The smell of freshly ground coffee brewing wafted from the kitchen. Marlene stood by the sink, rinsing off breakfast dishes.

"Looks like somebody had a good time last night," she said, her eyes twinkling. She poured a cup of coffee for Kate. "I told Roger we might have to hose you two down."

Kate blushed scarlet but smiled anyway. She knew Marlene was just teasing. And she and Roger would be the last people to judge. They were from New York City, after all.

"Have a seat, Kate." Roger pulled a chair out for her at the dining room table then sat down across from her, holding a reporter's notebook and pen in his hand. "I've got some ideas on how to cover Timothy Kessler's trial and I wanted to talk to you about them now."

"Roger!" Marlene scolded. "It's Saturday. Give the girl a chance to enjoy the afterglow, for God's sake."

"You know how the newspaper business is, we're always on deadline. Right, Kate?"

"Um, that's what they told me in journalism school."

"You see, Marlene? She understands perfectly. Now here's my plan. I want you to cover the human side of Timothy Kessler. Talk to his family, his friends, his teachers, anyone who knew him. We need to find out what could make him do something like this. As you know, Barry can't do that, he's pretty biased against Kessler, if you haven't already noticed. And you've got that wonderful, kind face. I read your piece about Warren Owens, and I could tell his widow must have really opened up to you."

"Speaking of people opening up," Kate said. "Timmy Kessler's grandmother talked to me last night about the case. She told me Timmy's side of the story, how his fingerprints got on the gas cans and even the name of the secret witness. It's some college kid named Brandon Fawkes."

"Guess it's not a secret anymore," Roger replied, sipping his coffee. "I don't expect we'll be able to get by with printing it, though. Judge Hulick just issued a gag order as far as writing anything about the main witness until the trial. They keep saying they fear retaliation from the Forces of Nature."

"Can they do that? Isn't there something in the Bill of Rights about confronting your own accuser? I know the First Amendment backwards and forwards, but I'm a bit fuzzy on the other ones."

"It's the sixth amendment, Kate. It guarantees the right to confront your accuser, along with other good things like a speedy trial and an impartial jury. Of course, we're talking some major First Amendment issues here as well. I've spoken to my colleagues at the big papers, and they've got their lawyers working on it. Unfortunately, that takes time.

"I would love to be the one who lifts the veil of secrecy, but I just don't have the resources to back up that decision. I know it's wrong and you know it's wrong, but it's Judge Hulick's courtroom and he can pretty much do what he wants. I will ask Barry to do a little digging into our friend Brandon Fawkes. Let me make a note of that."

Kate watched him write "Barry to check on Brandon Fawkes, UNCW."

"And that brings me to my next story idea. Barry will be covering the arraignment on Monday, but I'd like you to go along as well. For one thing, it will be a chance for you to talk to his family. They'll be out in full force for his court appearance. Plus I want you to be in the courtroom so you can get a sense of what's going on with Timothy. How does he act?

Scared, arrogant, submissive, remorseful – that sort of thing."

"How about guilty or innocent?"

"That's up to the jury. We certainly don't want to try him on the front page of the *Beacon*. Just write the truth as you see it."

"I don't know about this, Roger. The last trial I covered was eighteen years ago in Ravenna, Ohio, and that was for my Reporting Public Affairs class. It was just some guy charged with siphoning gas from his landlord. This is way out of my league."

"Welcome to the majors, Kate," Roger replied. "You'll do just fine. Don't worry about it. Just keep in mind that whatever you write ends up at the bottom of a birdcage sooner or later."

She smiled but felt butterflies in her stomach. Despite Roger's cryptic words of encouragement, she still felt very uneasy about the prospect of covering a murder trial.

This job was certainly turning out to be more than she'd bargained for.

Defendant "Just a Regular Kid"

Sept. 17 — "I'll be the first to admit it, my grandson Timmy's is a bit of a hothead. Always acting first, then thinking about it later." Eleanor Kessler spoke tearfully of the young man she helped raise, now on trial for murder.

"But I can't for one second believe he'd kill another human being."

Winslow Beach Beacon

14. COURTROOM CONFUSION

WE'RE PRESS, *WINSLOW BEACON*," BARRY ANNOUNCED LOUDLY TO the bailiff, waving his county-issued press credentials in the old man's face. Whether it was out of a deep and abiding respect for the power of the First Amendment, which Kate doubted, or just that Barry was so intimidating, they were waved through and managed to squeeze into the last remaining seats.

The courtroom had rows of long benches like pews in a church. They were made of some kind of hardwood, probably oak, and through the years spectators had polished them to a fine sheen.

Barry pulled a maroon throw pillow out of his backpack and placed it on the seat.

"I swiped this from my Aunt Joan's sofa. You should get one for yourself. These benches will kill you, believe me," he said, lowering himself onto it. Kate watched him enviously and made a note to bring her own pillow the next time she had to cover a trial.

"This is just the arraignment," he continued. "Not much will be going on. All he's doing is entering a plea. It'll be over in a couple minutes."

The elderly bailiff shuffled over to the front of the court.

"All rise!" he bellowed. "Court is now in session, the honorable Keenan P. Hulick presiding."

Judge Hulick emerged from chambers. Kate was surprised at how small he was. The judge was no more than five feet tall, and his robes barely concealed a substantial potbelly. He stepped up onto the raised platform and took his seat behind the enormous bench. She expected him to nearly disappear in the massive chair, but he seemed to grow before her eyes. He had a commanding presence and looked about as friendly as a pit bull.

She hoped she never had to appear before him. The phrase "hanging judge" could have originated with him.

The crowd fell silent as he slammed his gavel down.

"First case, please," he said with a definite Wilmington drawl.

"The People versus Timothy Kessler," the bailiff answered.

Kate recognized the young man from the Friends of the Carolina Coastline meeting, now clad in an orange jumpsuit, his wrists in shackles. She saw his face briefly when he turned around, probably looking for his grandmother, who was sitting right behind the defendant's table. No longer the swaggering militant disrupting her meeting, he looked like very young and very terrified.

A tall man with dark curly hair and a beard to match touched his arm.

That must be his lawyer, Adam Steiner.

"How do you plead, Mr. Kessler?"

"Not guilty, your honor," Steiner said.

"So noted. Trial set for October second."

"What about bail, your honor?"

"No bail."

"But, your honor, this is his first offense. He has strong ties in the community."

"Mr. Steiner, I said no bail. Your client is charged with killing two men by burning them alive. He stays where he is. Next case."

Two uniformed jail guards led Kessler to the side door. Even though he was headed away from her, he kept twisting around, keeping his eyes fixed on his grandmother. He said nothing, but Kate could almost hear him pleading with her to take him home.

"Told you there wouldn't be much to it," Barry said, getting up and stuffing his pillow back in his back pack. "I'm going to try to see if I can get anything from the prosecutor. If I don't see you before then, I'll wait for you at the entrance. Don't worry. It won't take long."

"I see the Kessler group over there. I'll grab them while I can."

"Later," Barry said and huffed his way over to the assistant district attorney handling the case.

Eleanor Kessler was a few feet away; Kate nearly walked into her.

"Hello, Kate, didn't know you'd be here," Eleanor said. "Barry usually covers the trials."

"Actually, I'm here to talk to you. We're doing a story on Timothy. We want to give people an idea of what kind of person he's like, his background. I can use any comments from people who know him, specially family members. Are his parents here?"

Eleanor frowned. "Let's go have a seat at the coffee shop and I'll tell you all about Timothy's life. Starting with why his parents aren't here."

They pushed through the crowds and stopped at the cubbyhole that housed the courthouse cafe.

"How do you take your coffee?" Eleanor asked as they stood in line at the counter.

"Thanks for offering, but I can get this myself. Roger says we can't take anything from a source, and that includes coffee."

"Oh, I see. Well, far be it from me to compromise your ethics. Although I hardly think one cup of coffee will lead you down the road to corruption."

They took their cups to a Formica table off in a corner. Through a dingy window, Kate could just make out the outline of Thalian Hall across the street. She reached into her purse and pulled out her notebook and pen.

"So, tell me in your own words about Timothy's life."

Eleanor took a sip of coffee. "I'm not sure where to begin. We've made a lot of mistakes with him. His mother – my daughter Melissa had him when she was sixteen. I was all for putting him up for adoption. We didn't have much money. My husband had died and I was teaching school – earth science at Noble Middle School. There was barely enough for Melissa and me.

"Used to be getting pregnant was something you hid, but in Melissa's crowd it was the cool thing to do. Keep your baby and show it off. She had no idea of what being a mom meant. Oh, she tried hard at first, but I knew what was happening. I was the one taking care of him, not her. But I didn't mind. I wanted her to finish school, and I really loved the little guy.

"Melissa went off to college when Timmy was two, and I became his legal guardian. She married a nice guy and lives in Phoenix now. We hardly ever see her."

"What about Timothy's father?"

"Missing in action from the beginning." Eleanor sighed. "Melissa thought that boy hung the moon. He was captain of the football team, best-looking guy in school. Then when he got her pregnant he told her he wanted nothing to do with the baby, even called her a slut and said it probably wasn't even his. I think she had this ridiculous idea that he'd marry her and they'd live happily ever after. We lost track of him when his family moved away after Timmy was born. We didn't even bother to look for him. He never sent child support and pursuing it didn't seem worth the aggravation."

She reached into her handbag for a white linen handkerchief. She dabbed at her eyes then put it back in her purse.

"Did Timothy ever show any violent tendencies? Ever hurt anyone intentionally?" Kate asked.

"He's got a temper, always been a hothead with a tendency to act first and think later. But I can't for one second believe he'd kill another human being. He was raised to believe in nonviolence. From the time he could talk, I always told him to use your words, not your fists. There's always a better way than fighting. And he took it to heart. When he was in third grade, he stepped into the middle of a fight between two boys twice his size. I think those boys were so stunned that they forgot why they were beating each other up. And even though it was a foolish thing to do, I was really proud of him for that."

"What sort of interests does Timothy have? Did he belong to clubs and things in high school or was he a loner?"

"He's always been a bit of an odd duck, being raised by his grandmother, who's a bit of an odd duck herself. But he has friends. Very nice kids in high school, I thought. As far as activities, he wasn't much of a joiner, but he did start a group to patrol the beaches during nesting season, keeping the tourists from bothering the mother turtles when they laid their eggs. Now that he's in college and living on his own, I don't know who he's hanging out with these days. He's always been a bit too open-minded sometimes."

"Do you think he might have gotten in with the Forces of Nature?"

Eleanor's eyes flashed.

"All he ever did was go to their website and download one of their flyers. And he talked about their ideas at that Friends of the Coast meeting you went to. He was mainly showing off that day. I am absolutely positive he's not a member. In fact, I doubt if he's even e-mailed them. Kate, I know he'd never harm another human being. It's just not his nature. Good lord! What in heaven's name is going on in the hallway?"

Kate turned to see a crowd gathered outside the entrance to the coffee shop. The two women stood up to see what all the commotion was about. Kate recognized Ed Kominsky in the middle of the group, surrounded by reporters, photographers and a television camera man.

"That weasel sure knows how to grab the spotlight," Eleanor said.

"My friends and neighbors." Kominsky's voice boomed out over the crowd. "I'm just a concerned citizen, hoping to see justice done here. Yes, it was my property that was viciously burned to the ground, but that's not important. Lives were taken. I lost a good friend in Warren Owens and an adversary I both admired and respected in John Cochran. I'm hoping that the good folks of New Hanover County will see these environmentalists for the destructive, evil cowards that they are. We need to stop them here and now. Our entire way of life is at stake."

Eleanor turned away and hurried toward the nearest exit. Kate followed her.

"I'm sorry, Kate, I just can't take that. Not right now."

"I don't blame you. That's enough to turn anyone's stomach."

Outside, the rest of Wilmington went about its business. Traffic was backed up on Chestnut Street, and a woman stomped past them, yelling obscenities into her cell phone.

"This is better," Eleanor said. "Ed Kominsky's a sly old bastard, but this is a new low even for him. I can see what he's doing. He's trying to tar all of us who care about the environment with the same brush. We're all militants out to burn down everybody's house if they don't agree with us."

"Hopefully, people will see what he's trying to do. We did, didn't we?"

"There are a lot of people around here who think like Kominsky does."

"Hey, Kate!" Barry called to her from the bottom of the steps. "I thought we agreed to meet at the main entrance!"

"Be with you in a minute, Barry!" she called back to him. "Thanks so much for all your help, Eleanor. Is there anyone else I can talk to? Friends? Teachers?"

"Sure. He went to Laney High School, just graduated last year. Plenty of his old teachers are still there. And he spent a lot of time volunteering at the Fort Fisher Aquarium. Those folks will be glad to talk to you."

"Thanks, Eleanor."

She turned to go down the steps, but Eleanor grasped her arm

"I know I can't ask you this, but please, tell everyone my baby didn't do this, couldn't do this. He's all I've got."

Kate smiled ruefully.

"I'll do my best, Eleanor."

Winslow Beach Beacon

September 24

What kind of loco weed is that Dennison woman smoking? Tim Kessler burned down a house and killed two people. He deserves the death penalty. I can't understand why this paper is so supportive of a murderer. Kate Dennison should go back up north where she belongs.

15. ADVERSE REACTIONS

"YOU HAVE THIRTY-TWO MESSAGES," THE DISEMBODIED TINNY VOICE announced when Kate punched in her voicemail code.

The Timothy Kessler story had just hit the stands that morning or, more precisely, the subscribers' mailboxes. She had known there would be a reaction, but she hadn't expected it to be so swift. Or so voluminous. She hit the play button.

What she heard made her cringe. She took a deep breath and told herself they were just recordings and there was no point in trying to argue with them. Everyone had a right to their opinion.

Except these weren't opinions. These were vicious assaults on her character.

Message One:

"I've had just about enough of you godless, pot-smoking Yankees coming down here and trying to lay all your bleeding heart liberal crap on decent people. You deserve to go to jail with your murdering boyfriend."

Beep. Message Two:

"Didn't your mama teach you right from wrong? How dare you stick up for that evil hoodlum? You should be ashamed of yourself."

Beep. Message Three:

"I'm calling about that idiotic article you wrote in the paper. That's the worst piece of journalism I've ever seen. I can't believe this type of propaganda would be published in the paper I've subscribed to for thirty-seven years."

And on it went.

After the seventeenth message, it was all Kate could do to keep from deleting the rest, as she couldn't take much more verbal abuse. The only thing that kept her going was the knowledge that buried among the mean-spirited rants would likely be something important, a message she needed to hear.

Eventually, she found two of those messages, a reminder from her dentist about her appointment the following day and a call from the principal at Holly Tree Elementary School confirming the time for an interview and photographs of their kindergarten Green Thumb program.

"End of messages," Mr. Tinny Voice said.

"Finally." She pressed the delete button.

Despite the work she had to do, Kate was unnerved by the malevolence the *Beacon* readers had just thrown her way, so she decided to take a walk up to the front desk and talk to Janie. It was only nine-thirty and her voice mail was already starting to fill up again.

At least she didn't have to talk to these people. The phone's ringer was turned off.

She found Janie hunched over her terminal, typing what looked to be an office memo.

"Hey, Janie," she said. "How's it going?"

"Oh, Kate, you about made me jump out of my skin," Janie said. "Guess I was off in my own little world. What can I do for you?"

"Um, Janie, is it possible to turn off my voice mail?"

"Sure, hon. That's no problem at all. Just hit the menu and keep pressing the option button until you hear the guy say 'Disable voice mail' and you're set. But I thought you reporters needed your messages."

"Not the ones I'm getting. This morning I had to listen to thirty separate messages and all of them absolutely horrible. I can't believe people would say things like that to someone they've never met. Or even to someone they have met."

"Boggles the mind how rude people can be, doesn't it?" Janie said. "It was that Timmy Kessler story, right? I knew that would cause a stir as soon as I read it. Folks around here talk a lot about freedom and justice, but a good many of them believe that if the police arrest a man then he must be guilty of something and anyone who says otherwise must be guilty of something, too. It don't mean they're right."

"I know that, but it still hurts."

"Don't take it to heart, hon," Janie said with a kind smile. "I'll just take messages for you when you get calls, and if it's anyone you want to talk to I'll buzz you on the intercom. All right?"

"Is that going to be too much work for you?"

"Not a problem. I know how to deal with these jokers. Oh, I almost forgot." She reached over to her inbox and picked up a large inter-office communications envelope. "Someone left this for you. It's from Holly Tree Elementary School."

Kate took the envelope, which had an odd bumpy shape to it and was fairly heavy.

"Good lord, they really stuffed this one, didn't they?" she said.

"We're always getting things like that from the schools," Janie said. "They like to send us letters and little projects. 'Specially after Roger does one of his little talks at the schools about newspapers."

Kate turned to leave.

"Thanks for your help, Janie."

"That's what I'm here for."

Feeling much better, Kate returned to the dim bunker of the *Beacon* office. Barry was now at his desk, pulling his notebooks out of his backpack, a large cup from Port City Java balanced precariously on the corner of his desk.

"Hey, there, Kate. What's up?"

"My blood pressure, for one thing. Had to listen to thirty people ranting and raving about that Timmy Kessler story. I'm sure there's more piling up in my inbox, if you care to listen."

"Comes with the territory, my friend. Just get used to it. I don't even notice them anymore."

"Even when they say things about your mother?"

"Well, that does sting a bit, but I try not to take it personally." He smiled and took a swig of coffee. "What's that you got there? Fan mail from some flounder?"

"No, it's from the kids at Holly Tree Elementary School. Guess they sent me some handmade notes or something. Let's see what I've got."

She undid the string that held the envelope shut and dumped the contents onto her desk.

Suddenly, the room was filled with her screams.

"Jesus, Kate, what the — " Barry rushed over to her desk and stopped in mid-sentence when he saw the source of fright.

Lying on her desk in a bed of shredded newspaper was the biggest rat Kate had ever seen, dead or alive. Its neck was bent at an excruciating angle and a trickle of blood had dried around its mouth.

"Get it out of here!" she screamed.

"Well, damn, that sure as hell ain't from no elementary school," Barry said. "Looks like someone just took that bad boy out of the trap."

"Barry! Do something! Get it off my desk! It's still bleeding, for God's sake!"

"Now, calm down, Kate. It's just a dead rat and it stopped bleeding a long time ago. It can't hurt you." He came in for a closer look. "Hey, there's a note in here."

He reached over for it.

"Don't touch that!" Kate said, still very upset.

"Right," he agreed. "Don't want to mess up any fingerprints."

"I was thinking more about germs, but I guess the police will need it."

"Do you think we should move the rat? It's a crime scene now."

"Barry, I don't really believe the New Hanover County Sheriff's Department will need to see the rat in the exact position it fell on my desk. And who knows how long it will take them to get here? I just want it off my desk and out of the office."

"I got an idea." He rushed over to his desk, pulled out one of his cameras and began clicking. "Now we can show them exactly how it happened and still have the rat out of here."

"Guess we should find out what the note says," Kate said. She pulled out a tissue from the box on her desk and carefully picked up one of the corners of the note. It was a folded piece of copy paper. Printed in what Kate recognized as 72 point Arial type face were the words "YOU'RE NEXT TREE HUGGER!"

The two reporters stared at the paper, speechless.

"Wow, Kate," Barry said finally. "You sure did piss somebody off."

THE BEACON ANSWER MAN

Q: What is the best way to dispose of dead rodents?

A: First, wear gloves. Whatever you do, don't touch the animals. Like your mother said, they are teeming with bacteria and disease. Place them in a thick plastic bag. It's up to you what you want to do after that. At our house we throw them in the trash.

We expect there are already plenty of dead rats in the local landfill.

Another option is burying them in the backyard, but I prefer the landfill.

16. I SMELL A RAT

IT WAS MORE THAN AN HOUR BEFORE THE NEW HANOVER COUNTY sheriff's deputies arrived. Using plastic gloves from the janitor's closet in the pressroom, Barry picked the rat off of Kate's desk and placed it in a trash bag, which he shoved behind his chair.

"Are you sure you want to do that?" she asked him. "It's just so creepy. We could just throw him in the trash and show the pictures."

The recently printed photos lay scattered across his desk.

"I think it's a better idea to have him handy when the cops get here," Barry said. "I don't mind stashin' him, Kate. I used to go squirrel huntin' with my dad and carry five or six of 'em home in a burlap sack. Not much difference between a dead squirrel and a dead rat. Just that the squirrel's got a nicer tail. Come to think of it, there's not much difference in any of us, once we're dead."

"Well, that's true, but it's still depressing." She sprayed her desk for the twentieth time with the bottle of disinfectant she'd found in the women's restroom, then went at it with what was left of the roll of paper towels she'd also taken.

"Uh, Kate, I think it's clean now."

"Not clean enough."

"How 'bout we switch out your desk with one of these extras? Roger won't mind if it keeps you from going all obsessive-compulsive on us."

A tall deputy strode confidently into the room.

"Are you Kate Dennison?" he asked.

"Yes, that's me. Are you here about the dead rat?"

"Yes, I am," he said. "Deputy Kyle Moss, ma'am." He looked down at her desk, which was now much cleaner than it had been in years.

"I take it you disposed of the body," he said.

"No, it's right here," Barry said, picking up the trash bag with the rat in it. "And we've got pictures of what it looked like just after Kate opened up the envelope. Whoever did this wrapped the rat in newspaper and stuffed it into this."

Barry handed him the envelope and the pictures and held the bag open for Moss to take a look.

"That's a dead rat, all right," Moss said.

"Janie up front saw the person who delivered the envelope," Kate said. "Maybe you can get a description."

"I did, and she says she can barely remember what the person looked like. A man in a white jacket. Average height, average build. That's about it. We'll ask her to go through some mug shots, though. Maybe she'll recognize him."

"Oh, we almost forgot," Kate said. "Here's the note. It's a death threat."

She offered the note sent along with the dead rat. He read and stuffed it into the envelope.

"Well, there's not much we can do right now," he said. "I'll take the envelope and the note back to headquarters and we'll run it for fingerprints, see if we pull up anyone who's got a record for this kind of thing."

"Does Wilmington have a lot of people sending dead rats?" Barry asked.

"Actually, no," Moss admitted. "But once in a while we get a guy who wants to send a message with a dead cat on the doorstep or something like that. Might be one of those."

"What about the note?" Kate asked. "Isn't that a death threat?"

"I wouldn't take it that seriously, ma'am," the deputy said. "In these cases, the perpetrators are cowards with no intention of doing any real harm. Just wantin' to scare you."

"Well, he certainly succeeded in that regard. I don't believe I've screamed so loud in my life."

"I'll second that," Barry said. "She damn near broke my eardrums."

"Gotta go now," Moss said, shaking Kate's hand. "We'll keep you posted on any new developments. And call us if you get any more suspicious packages. But don't worry yourself. I'm sure it's just a one-time thing."

"Thanks for your help," Kate said, watching him walk out the door.

"There goes New Hanover County's finest," Barry said. "Don't you feel better now?"

"Not really." She sat down at her desk. "More worried than ever. But I suppose if I go home now, Creepy Guy wins. You can throw the rat out now, though."

"I'll put him in the trash on the way out."

"Can you do that with a dead animal?"

"The garbage guys aren't going to check your trash. They just dump it in the truck. And do you think there aren't any dead rats in the landfall already? Don't worry about it."

"Believe me, Barry, what happens to that dead rat is the least of my worries."

Obituaries

MOORE, WILFRED PLEASANCE. Age 74 years. Beloved husband of 54 years to Delores. Devoted father of Wilfred Moore, Jr, David Moore, Hobart Moore, Eileen Moore Graves, June Moore Wynn, and Barry Moore. Also leaves fourteen grandchildren and five great-grandchildren. Mr. Moore served honorably in the Korean War and retired from General Electric after 26 years of faithful service. Funeral service will be held at the Christian Holiness Church of the Living God in Hampstead. Donations to American Cancer Society.

Winslow Beach Beacon
October 15

17. CONDOLENCES AND A
COVERED DISH

KATE STARED AT HER BLANK TERMINAL, WILLING HERSELF TO COME UP with a passable lead for the planning commission meeting she'd just attended. She was having a hard time finding anything to write about, as all the items on the agenda had been approved without even a whimper of protest, eliminating the conflict angle she usually worked. Not only that, the changes were all fairly minor and so technical she was sure no one would want to bother reading through her laborious layman's-terms explanation to get to what happened.

She looked over at Barry's empty desk, knowing he was covering Timothy Kessler's murder trial. At this time of the morning, it was probably in full swing, though as Barry was fond of saying it was all a lot of talk about doodly-squat.

Six weeks after the fire, Barry handled everything having to do with it, leaving Kate to cover the school programs and zoning changes. She thanked her lucky stars her part in the Normandy Sands fire story was over and done with. She had managed to put the dead rat out of her mind, but it was still unnerving whenever she thought of it.

"Kate, do you have a minute?" Janie held an ornate greeting card in one hand and a pen in the other.

"For you, anything," she said, reaching for the card, which on closer inspection turned out to be a sympathy card.

"Who's it for?"

"Barry. His dad died early this morning. Wilfred Senior's been sick for a long time. They've been expecting it."

Kate was shocked. After more than a month working here, and all the conversations they'd had, she would have thought Barry would have mentioned something about his father's illness. He did talk about him a

135

lot.

She studied the card, noting all the signatures and expressions of condolence. It was one of those kinds with a Bible verse on one side and a long poem on the other. Not at all what she would have picked out for Barry, but the choice hadn't been up to her.

She carefully wrote her name and added "My thoughts are with you."

"The funeral is next Tuesday."

"That's a ways off, isn't it? That's a week from now."

"Delores – that's Barry's mom – she wanted to make sure the whole family could be there. And she means the whole family. The six kids, the fourteen grandkids and the five great-grandkids. That's going to take some time for them to get here. Barry's brother David is a lawyer in San Diego, and his sister Eileen lives in Boston. Those Moores are scattered all over the country. Except for Barry, of course. It's always the baby that stays behind to take care of the folks, you know. Anyway, thanks for signing. It will mean a lot."

Kate was quite sure her signature on a card probably would not mean much at all to Barry, but she smiled anyway and gave it back to Jane.

"See you 'round, Janie," she said.

"Yeah, see you." Janie turned, then stopped. "I almost forgot. Your boyfriend Bryan called. He says you've got the number. And if you don't mind me saying so, Kate, it's time you reactivated your voice mail. No one cares about that Timmy Kessler story anymore."

"I suppose you're right. But those messages were just so ugly. Not to mention the dead rat."

"And to think that thing sat at my desk for a good twenty minutes before I gave it to you. Did the police ever find out who did it?"

"The deputy who came to investigate said he'd keep me posted, but I haven't heard from him since he walked out that door last month. I guess making an arrest in the case of a dead rat sender is a pretty low priority. Barry's still keeping the photos for evidence if there's a trial, but no one seems interested."

"Well, I'd say it was a one-time thing," Janie said. "All your calls lately have been the usual stuff from the schools wanting you to cover science fairs and kindergarten pageants. The sickos have moved on."

"Okay, Jane, I'll switch it back on today."

"Thanks." Jane headed away toward the classified ad offices.

Even though she would have loved to drop everything and call Bryan, she turned back to her story. Just as she finally wrestled the last item on the planning commission agenda into something comprehensible, Barry walked in.

"Hey, Dollface. What's up?"

"Not much," she answered. "Janie told me about your father. I'm sorry."

Barry heaved his bulk into his chair, switching on his terminal.

"Thanks. We all knew it was coming. The man worked too hard, smoked like a chimney and wouldn't eat anything unless it was deep fried in lard and washed down with a cold beer. I'm surprised he lasted to seventy-four."

"Is there anything I can do?"

"No, the ladies of the C.H.C.L.G. are taking care of everything. We've got enough banana nut bread and ham casseroles to feed an army."

"The C.H.C.L.G.? What's that?"

"The Christian Holiness Church of the Living God. We used to go to a run-of-the-mill Baptist Church, but about twenty years ago, my mom decided the minister was diluting the message to appeal to liberal Yankees. 'They've lost the fire,'" he drawled, raising the pitch of his voice to mimic his mother. 'They've lost the SANCT-ti-fi-CA-tion. They're denying the Lord, lettin' these folks believe they can get to heaven without the sufferin' and the heartache.'

"Myself, I'm not too keen on this church. They won't shut up about this pain and suffering thing. But they're wonderful people and they'd do anything for you. Plus they throw the best damn pig pickin's you'll ever go to. I never miss a church pig pickin', even though most of the congregation feel I'm in league with the devil."

"That sounds a bit like St. Monica's, the Catholic Church I went to back in Ohio. Lots of talk about pain and suffering and guilt, followed by a huge potluck supper with fourteen different kinds of pie for dessert. You had to eat a little bit of everything, otherwise you'd hurt someone's feelings."

Barry sorted through his backpack and pulled out his notebook.

"How's the trial going?"

"Slow and boring. Judge Hulick declared a recess for the rest of the afternoon, which suits me just fine. Of course, starting tomorrow, you'll get to experience it all firsthand."

"What do you mean?"

"Roger will get around to telling you eventually, but I'll tell you now. With all my sisters and brothers coming in for my dad's funeral, I asked Roger for some time off and he gave it to me. He told me he'd have you take over for me covering the trial. He figures since you know the background, you can step right in."

Kate's heart sank. An entire week of sitting through the trial. More angry letters and voice-mail messages. At least it was temporary.

"Don't look so down. It's really not that bad. New Hanover County Superior Court is no 'Law and Order,' but I promise you'll get hooked on it like I did. It's at a pretty interesting point now – they're coming on with the heavy-duty witnesses, including the infamous mystery man a.k.a. Brandon Fawkes. He testifies tomorrow. And so does Shane Cochran."

"Eleanor Kessler already gave me Timmy's side of the story. Wish there was some way to fit it in."

"Oh, they'll get around to his side. Word is, he'll be taking the stand pretty soon. Anyway, I've got to get this story done right now so I can get home and start helping Mama clean the house."

"Can't the CH-whatever ladies help?"

"They'd love to, but Mama says she don't want those busybodies pokin' around her house. They're lovely women, but they sure do love to gossip, God bless 'em."

Kate smiled, recalling that in the South you can say just about anything about anyone as long the phrase "God bless 'em" followed it.

Just then her phone rang. Barry took the opportunity to tear into his last story.

"Kate Dennison."

"It's about time you answered your phone."

"Hey, Bryan, what's up?"

"Like to spend a weekend in Asheville? Hike through the mountains and maybe see the Biltmore Estate? One of our volunteers up here won the trip in a raffle but can't make it so she gave it to me. Says I've been working too hard and deserve a break. Two nights' stay at a luxury hotel. Meals included."

"Sounds great. Let's go right now."

"Sorry, the reservations aren't for three weeks; the sixteenth and seventeenth, to be exact. So, you'll go?"

"I'll have to talk to Keith about taking Molly for an extra day but I don't think he'll mind. He's been saying he wants to spend more time with her. I'll let you know."

"Great. See you then."

"Can't wait."

"Talk to you later, take care."

"Bye."

Kate hung up, savoring the anticipation of her weekend getaway.

"Kate's got a boyfriend!" Barry sang from across the office.

"You're just jealous."

"You bet I am. Don't forget I do wedding photos. I can give you and Mr. Wonderful a discount rate."

"Forget it. Been there, done that, fought over the plates."

"You'd be surprised how many second weddings I photograph. And third ones. It's the triumph of hope over experience."

"Get back to work, Barry."

He punched a button on his terminal and clicked it off.

"My work here is done," he said, getting up from his chair and gathering up his stuff. "Kate, have a good week in court. Any questions, feel free to call me. I'm off to douse everything in Pine-Sol. See you round."

Witness: Kessler Planned Fire

Oct. 15 — Stonefaced and emotionless, star witness Brandon Fawkes calmly recounted his conversation with defendant Timothy Kessler, charged with murdering John Cochran and Warren Owens.

"He looked me straight in the eye and said 'I'm going to burn that house to the ground. And I want to take a couple of them rich pigs down with it.'"

Winslow Beach Beacon

18. HANGING WITH THE HANGING JUDGE

BARRY WAS RIGHT. KATE WAS HOOKED ON THE KESSLER TRIAL, especially now that Brandon Fawkes was testifying.

Fawkes sat in the witness chair, stiff and attentive, looking very much like a prep school boy eager to impress the adults. She had expected him to be around nineteen or twenty, but he looked to be a few years older. Well tanned, well built and well dressed, he seemed at ease despite the commotion, as if testifying in a murder trial was something he did every day.

Martin Soames, the district attorney, stood next to the witness box. Kate figured he hadn't seen the light of day in years, he was so thin and pale. He must have spent his entire adult life indoors surrounded by law books. With an air of natural authority, he posed his questions.

"Mr. Fawkes, I've read up on the Forces of Nature. They have a policy of respect for life. They insist they never harm any living beings. When he spoke of his association with this group, did Mr. Kessler mention that policy to you?"

"Tim didn't say anything about the Forces of Nature having a policy of not killing living beings," Fawkes answered, speaking with the tiniest hint of condescension in his voice. "All he said was that it was time to take action and declare war on the developers. Then he said 'You can't have a war without some killing. The pigs are going down.' Those were his exact words."

"Why didn't you tell anyone of his plan?"

"Well, sir, at the time, I thought it was all talk. Tim is just a kid. He's only nineteen. I figured it was just an immature plea for attention, an attempt to sound big and important. I didn't want to get him into trouble, although now I am truly sorry I didn't go to the police then and there."

"Thank you, Mr. Fawkes. No more questions."

Judge Hulick turned to Kessler's defense lawyer.

"Any questions for the witness, Mr. Steiner?"

"Yes, Your Honor."

Timmy Kessler sat at the defendant's table, having traded in his orange jumpsuit for a suit and tie. The look of fury on his face was unmistakable.

Curly-haired, dressed in a rumpled beige suit, Steiner ambled up to the witness chair.

"Mr. Fawkes, do you know the victim's son, Shane Cochran?"

"Yes." Fawkes looked a bit surprised. "We went to school together."

"Would you say you're friends?"

"More like acquaintances. We attend a lot of the same social functions. I knew him enough to say hello and have a bit of small talk, but that's the extent of it."

"A bit of small talk. All right, in any of those chats, did he mention his financial situation?"

"Once or twice."

"Can you recall what he said?"

"That he needed money. Shane was always short on money."

"But his father, the victim John Cochran, was wealthy. As the son of a rich man, Shane Cochran should have had more money than he knew what to do with. Did he ever say why he couldn't get money from his dad?"

"Objection!" Soames called out. "Relevance, Your Honor."

"Showing reasonable doubt, Your Honor," Steiner replied.

"I'll allow it," Hulick replied. "Go on, Mr. Steiner?"

"Shane's dad wouldn't give it to him. Shane had expensive tastes and racked up a lot of debts."

"By the way, where do you work, Mr. Fawkes?"

"I don't work for anyone. I run my own consulting business."

"And Kominsky Builders is one of your clients?"

"Among others, yes."

"Don't you find it a strange coincidence that, as a friend of the victim's son and an employee of the builder of the burned house, you are the one person who can connect the defendant with this crime?"

"Objection!" Soames shouted.

"Withdrawn. No further questions."

"Thank you, Mr. Fawkes, you may step down," Judge Hulick said.

Fawkes descended from the witness stand and took his seat among the spectators.

"The People call Edward Kominsky."

There was a rustling among the spectators as Kominsky strode to the witness stand. With his big frame, he towered over the bailiff who administered the oath, to which he answered "So help me, God" in a booming voice that filled the courtroom.

The district attorney approached.

"Mr. Kominsky, can you describe the events of the morning of September fourth?"

"Yes, of course. That was the day I was going to meet John Cochran at the house my company built at Normandy Sands. I was supposed to be there at nine o'clock, but just as I was about to go out the door, there was a phone call from a client I'd been trying to get a hold of for weeks. Let me tell you, I will go to my grave wishing I'd told the guy to call back later. I might have gotten there in time to pull Warren and John out of that house."

"Did you go alone?"

"No, my assistant Shane Cochran went with me. We drove in my car."

"For the record, Shane Cochran is the son of John Cochran, who died in the fire."

"Yes, that's right. Shane had arranged this meeting at my request. John owned the property adjacent to Normandy Sands, and I was very interested in purchasing it. I knew it was a long shot, but I thought maybe if I let him see what we'd do with the property he might change his mind about selling it."

"Tell us what happened when you arrived at Normandy Sands."

Kominsky paused, a pained look on his face. He made a choking sound then took a handkerchief out of his pocket and wiped his eyes.

"I'm sorry. Talking about it brings it all back. Give me a second, please."

"Take your time, Mr. Kominsky," Soames said in what probably passed for a soothing tone.

The entire courtroom fell silent, waiting to hear Kominsky describe the horrific scene everyone had seen on the evening news. He took a deep breath and continued.

"We pulled into Normandy Sands about nine-forty-five. The house was a mile away, but we could see a huge cloud of black smoke. And smell the smoke, too, even with the windows closed.

"I hit the gas and drove as fast as I could to the house, probably made it in under a minute. Shane and I both tore out of the car, but the heat was so intense I couldn't get within ten feet of the front door. The whole house was engulfed in flames, and they must have been twenty feet high. There were two cars parked in the driveway: Warren's Mercedes and an old Volvo that belonged to John. Shane took one look at that car and started screaming."

"What did you do next, Mr. Kominsky?"

"I did the only thing I could do. I called nine-one-one on my cell phone. Then I grabbed Shane and put him back in my car. The state he was in, I was worried he'd try to go inside looking for his dad, even though it was hopeless. No one could survive that kind of fire."

"Your honor, we'd like to play a tape of the nine-one-one call," Soames said to Judge Hulick.

"Go ahead, Mr. Soames."

Soames walked over to a tape recorder and pressed a button.

"Nine-one-one, what is the nature of your emergency?" came the calm voice of the anonymous operator through the courtroom speakers. In the background was the sound of a man screaming. Kate could not quite make out the words, except for "Dad!"

"The house! It's on fire," Kominsky answered. "We're at Normandy Sands off Highway Seventeen. The whole house is burning. We think there are people in there."

"Sir, please stay out of the building. The fire department is on its way. Is anyone hurt? I hear someone screaming."

"My assistant, Shane; he's not hurt, but his father may be in the house."

"Get him away from the house, sir. The fire department will be there shortly."

"I'll wait for them at the front gate. That's on Normandy Drive."

The tape ended.

"For the record, Mr. Kominsky, that is your voice on that tape?" Soames asked.

"Yes, sir, it is."

"And what did you do after you made the call?"

146

"Well, sir, as I said, I managed to get Shane into the car, and I drove back to the gate. We waited for the fire department there."

"How long did you wait?"

"It was a while, maybe half an hour, forty-five minutes? All I know is it seemed like forever. I kept telling Shane his dad and Warren must have left the house when it started to burn and that they were safe on the beach somewhere. I had no idea that monster Kessler had locked them in the closet."

"Objection!" Steiner shouted.

"Sustained," said the judge. "Mr. Kominsky, please limit your answers to that of which you have firsthand knowledge."

Kominsky said nothing but nodded.

"Thank you very much, Mr. Kominsky. No further questions."

"Any questions for the witness, Mr. Steiner?" Judge Hulick asked.

"Yes, Your Honor," Steiner said. He got up from the defense table and ambled to the stand. "Mr. Kominsky, I'm curious. What sort of consulting does Brandon Fawkes do for your company?"

"I've never dealt with him directly. He works with the accounting department, advising them on what kind of software to buy and how to use it. To tell you the truth, I've never met him."

"Another question about your employees, now. How did you come to hire Shane Cochran as your assistant?"

"I met him a couple years ago at a charity golf tournament organized by Olivia Claymore; that's Shane's aunt. He was helping out with the logistics of the whole thing, and I was very impressed with him. He has great people skills, something we can use in our business. His aunt told me he was looking for a job. I invited him to lunch that day. Liked what I saw in the young man, and I hired him as my personal assistant that very week."

"He's your assistant. What does he do for you, exactly?"

"Whatever needs doing. He meets with clients when I can't. He makes sure I have the papers I need when I go to a closing. He deals with the contractors when there's a problem. He takes calls when I'm busy and people insist on talking to someone important."

"But not you."

"That's right, someone important, but not me."

"And for all his hard work, how much is Mr. Cochran paid?"

"I'm not sure if I can tell you that. Our salaries are confidential, and besides that's something the human resources department handles."

"Mr. Kominsky, let me remind you you're under oath and this is a murder trial. Please answer the question."

Kominsky's pink skin flushed to beet red.

"I'm sorry. I really don't know."

Steiner returned to the defense table, pulled a paper from a file folder and handed it to Judge Hulick.

"Let me refresh your memory, Mr. Kominsky," he said. "The defense offers exhibit seventy-two, a copy of Shane Cochran's tax return for last year. According to the IRS, Mr. Cochran's salary comes to a grand total of thirty-five thousand dollars. Does that sound about right?"

"Yes, that sounds right."

"And Mr. Kominsky, can you tell us how much you were willing to pay for that piece of property belonging to Mr. Cochran's father?"

"Thirty million dollars."

"And were you aware that Shane Cochran was his father's sole heir? That with his father's death, he inherits everything the man owned, including the property adjacent to your Normandy Sands development?"

Kominsky's calm demeanor changed. His jaw clenched as if he was trying to keep himself from losing his temper.

"No, of course not," he said. "Shane never talked about his father's financial affairs with me. Obviously, it was none of my business."

"Thank you, Mr. Kominsky. No further questions."

Family Talk

DEALING WITH STEPCHILDREN

The nuclear family of mother, father and two-point-five children, once the norm, is rapidly disappearing. Now it's just mother and children. Or just father and children. Or, that trickiest of relationship models: mother-stepmother, father-stepfather, children and stepchildren.

Trying to keep this type of family together can be a monumentally difficult task. But, as blended families attest, it can be done.

19. HOPE OVER EXPERIENCE

WITH THE SMACK OF HIS GAVEL, JUDGE HULICK DECLARED THE TRIAL adjourned for the day. Shoving her notebook into her purse, Kate grabbed her pillow and headed out the door. An increase of courtroom spectators created a bottleneck in the aisle. She found this extremely irritating, as she was in a hurry to get home and see Molly. It was after four, and she knew the traffic would be heavy on the way.

Forty-five minutes later, she trudged up Roger and Marlene's gravel driveway. The front door opened, and Molly burst out. She ran up and flung her arms around her. Kate knelt down and returned the embrace.

"Mom, you said you'd be home early. What took you so long?"

"Sorry, sweetie. The judge gets to decide when to end court and today he let it go longer than usual."

"That's not fair. You should have told him you had to leave."

"I suppose I could have, but I'm pretty sure he would have said no."

Hand in hand, they walked up the steps to the porch and opened the door.

"Marlene, I'm here to take Molly off your hands!" she called.

"She's in the art room, Mom."

The art room was at the back of the house, an old sun porch covered with glass panes. Marlene had turned it into her studio, and it was wall-to-wall canvases.

Wearing a paint-flecked smock, Marlene stared intently at the painting on her easel. Kate couldn't tell what it was, but she liked the blues and greens all swooshed around in it.

"Marlene?" she said quietly, not wanting to break her friend's concentration.

"Do you think there's too much of the cobalt blue here?" Marlene asked, pointing to the painting.

"No, I think it looks great."

"You always say that."

"Because they always look great."

Molly appeared at the door with her school bag.

"Come on, Mom."

"How about saying goodbye to Miss Marlene?"

Molly obliged, dropping her school bag in the doorway and going to give Marlene a big hug.

"I had fun today, Miss Marlene. I'll see you tomorrow."

"I'll be here. We can work some more on that collage."

"Haven't you got that thing finished?" Kate asked.

"Oh, no," Molly said. "Art takes time, you know. 'Specially great art like our collage."

"Let's go, pumpkin. Thanks again, Marlene."

"My pleasure," Marlene said, putting down her brushes. "I'll walk you to the door."

"No, don't stop painting on our account," Kate objected. "We can see ourselves out."

"No, it's time I started Roger's dinner anyway. And this baby doesn't seem to be going anywhere I want it to go, so it's a good time to stop."

They trooped down the hall to the front door.

"How's the trial going, Kate?"

"It was pretty slow at first, all those dull forensic reports, but it's picking up now. The mystery man Brandon Fawkes testified today."

"That was no mystery. Everyone in town knew it was him. Got any idea which side is winning?"

"That's hard to say. The defense is putting up a pretty good fight. They're suggesting Shane did it for the money."

"Well, it's been known to happen. Is the jury buying it?"

"I have no idea. They're a group of real stone-faces. Can't tell what they're thinking."

They arrived at the front door, and Marlene opened it.

"See you later, alligator," Marlene said to Molly.

"After while, crocodile," Molly responded, giggling.

They hurried across the lawn. Kate turned on the lights as she entered the dark house.

"Can I check to see if we have any messages?" Molly asked.

"Go ahead."

She ran over to the kitchen counter and inspected the display on the answering machine.

"It says we have one. Can I play it?"

Kate gave her approval, and Molly punched the play button.

"It's me," Keith's voice crackled. "Please call as soon as you get in. It's important."

Kate said nothing and went to the hall closet to hang up her coat.

"Aren't you going to call Daddy?" Molly asked. "He said you had to call him back as soon as you got in. That's now."

"Daddy can wait a few minutes."

"But he said it was important."

"All right. I'll call him."

She dialed Keith's number, wondering what minor crisis he was obsessing about now.

"Hello?"

"Hi, Keith. It's Kate."

"Oh, thanks for getting back to me. I didn't expect you to call this soon."

"Molly insisted."

"That's my girl. Anyway, I do have some news, but I don't want to tell you over the phone. Can you go to lunch tomorrow?"

"Can it be somewhere downtown? I'm covering the Kessler trial. There's a recess for lunch every day at noon. It's supposed to be an hour, but it usually comes to around an hour and fifteen minutes. I can meet you outside the courthouse at twelve o'clock."

"That'll work for me. How 'bout we go to that sandwich place we like so much on Front Street?"

"That's fine with me. What's so important you can't tell me over the phone?"

"You'll find out tomorrow. See you then. Bye."

"What's Daddy's news?" Molly asked, barely able to contain her excitement.

"Don't know. I won't find out till tomorrow."

"I hate having to wait."

"So do I, but tomorrow will be here soon enough. Let's start dinner."

Keith was waiting for her at the bottom of the courthouse steps.

"Over here, Kate!" he called. He smiled broadly and waved.

She made her way carefully down the stairs; she had her fancy heels on and didn't want to trip When she reached him, he gave her an affectionate hug, something he hadn't done in a very long time.

"Well, you're in a good mood. Does that have something to do with your good news?"

"Yes, it does."

"Can you tell me now?"

"No, not here on the street. Just wait."

They walked down to Front Street to the Morgan Cafe, where a crowd had already formed.

"Keith, I don't know if we can get in. That's an awfully long line."

"There's a new place down the street. Let's try that."

A block away, they found a cozy storefront restaurant with an open table inside just waiting for them. A friendly waiter seated them right away. As they ordered coffee and scanned the menus, Kate felt like she was ready to explode. The suspense was killing her.

"Okay, tell me now. I can't stand it. Especially you being so damn nice."

Keith took her hands across the table and looked at her soulfully. The same look he had used when he proposed to her.

Oh, my God, he wants to reconcile, she thought.

"Kate, I've asked Jennifer to marry me and she said yes. I'm asking your blessing."

Her jaw dropped. She didn't know what to say.

"You're speechless."

"Uhh, I wasn't expecting that. When did this happen?"

"Last weekend. We went to a beach house out on the island. It was beautiful. You could almost – "

"Keith, I'm really not interested in the details."

"Oh, yeah. Well, anyway, we're getting married in a couple of months. I'm putting the condo up for sale, and this weekend I'm moving in with her and the boys. We'll be a real family."

"Keith, are you sure this is such a good idea?"

"Sure it is. I love her and she loves me."

"Yes, but what about her boys? It's a safe bet they don't love you. Don't you remember back when we were married and they lived next door? You were always complaining about how horribly they behaved."

"That's because they had no strong father figure. I'm going to change

154

that."

"Have you talked to Jennifer about that? It's a pretty tricky business dealing with someone else's children."

"Once they see how happy I make their mother, they'll come around."

Kate took a sip of her coffee.

He's not your husband anymore, she reminded herself as she felt anger rising. It's his life. He can marry whoever he wants, even if it is a Class-A witch like Jennifer Tremont.

But she just couldn't let go. She had to say something.

"This will be your third time down the aisle."

"Third time's the charm." He smiled then noticed she didn't think the remark at all humorous. "Seriously, it's different this time. Jennifer and I are adults. We've learned from our mistakes."

Even though they'd been divorced for well over a year and hadn't lived together for more than two years, once again Keith had managed to push all her buttons and she couldn't hold back.

"Keith, you just hate being alone," she said loudly.

"Kate, keep your voice down," he whispered. "People are looking at us."

"I don't care," she whispered back. "I want you to hear this. You married your first wife right out of college, and when she left you four years later to, quote, 'find herself', you latched on to another wife, namely me, as soon as you could. And Jennifer pounced on you the second Molly and I left the house. You've always had a wife. Or a girlfriend soon to be your wife. You aren't learning from your mistakes. You just keep repeating them."

He gave her that condescending look she'd grown to hate during the course of their marriage.

"This is not a mistake," he said in his usual slow, measured tones, as if she were a child. "We complement each other. Jennifer's not needy and dependent like you. She's a strong woman. She has her own career and her own ideas. And I don't believe there's anything wrong with seeking lifetime companionship."

Needy and dependent? Kate wanted to scream. She had been doing just fine when she met him and was doing just fine now. She was itching to start screaming at him like a shrew, and she didn't care who heard her.

Fortunately, the waiter arrived. While Keith gave him his sandwich order, she used the time to calm down.

Relax, she ordered herself. It's not your problem, it's his. And Molly's problem on alternate weekends. Oh, God, how was Molly going to handle this?

As she contemplated her daughter's future stepfamily, Kate gave her lunch order to the waiter. He took it cheerfully then turned and hustled toward the kitchen.

"This place has great service, wouldn't you say?" Keith asked.

"That's because it's new and hardly anyone's here."

"But they're putting in the effort. That counts for something."

"Yes, it does."

They stopped to drink their coffee.

"Have you talked to Jennifer about how Molly will fit into your new family?" Kate asked, in what she hoped was a rational, not at all confrontational, tone.

"As a matter of fact, we've talked about it at length," Keith said. "Don't worry, Kate. Jennifer understands that you're Molly's mother, and she won't try to replace you. She thinks the world of Molly and just wants to be her friend."

"What about when Molly misbehaves? Have you talked about how we discipline her? We all need to be consistent, you know. I'm just worried that with Jennifer in the picture, we won't be able to keep up the united front we've always had with Molly. You know, what she can't do at Mom's house she can't do at Dad's house?"

"That's not going to change."

"I hope you're right."

He reached over and took her hands again.

"Kate, this makes me happy. Please try to see it as a good thing. For all of us."

He looked so disappointed. Knowing him the way she did, she was sure he had expected a wave of congratulations and good wishes from her. He never did think things through.

"I do hope it works out for you," she said grudgingly. "You know, it might be a good idea to get some family counseling. Or at least go to one of those step-parenting classes they have at The Parenting Place. You have to know this isn't going to be easy."

"Yes, you're right. I'll talk to Jennifer about that tonight. Oh, by the way, Molly tells me you have a boyfriend yourself. What's he like?"

Kate's felt her cheeks flush.

"He's nice. He's the guy I was going out with when I lived in Dayton. I told you about him, remember?"

"The tall, skinny guy who couldn't commit?"

"That's the one."

"Don't you think that might be a problem now that you've got a child to think of?"

"Right now, I'm not ready to commit to anyone, either; except Molly, of course. So, no, it's not a problem. But while we're talking about it, Bryan asked me to go to Asheville next Friday. I know it's not your weekend with Molly, but could you do me a favor and take her anyway?"

"Of course, Kate. I'd be glad to."

"Um, would you like me to tell her she'll be staying at Jennifer's house, not your condo?"

"No, I'll pick her up after school tomorrow and take her out for hot chocolate at Port City Java."

"You may need to buy a couple of those giant cookies as well. You know how she feels about Matt and Austin."

"Don't worry, Kate. I can handle Matt and Austin."

"For Molly's sake, I sure hope you can."

The food arrived, and lunch concluded uneventfully. Keith walked her back to the courthouse, with plenty of time before court went back into session.

"Thanks for lunch, Keith."

"My pleasure. We should do this more often."

"I don't think Jennifer will approve." She smiled, glad they'd managed to declare a truce even if she wasn't exactly thrilled at her ex-husband's news.

"Tell Molly I'll pick her up after school tomorrow. Make sure the school knows, too. I don't want them getting all bent out of shape when I get there. And don't you tell her about me and Jennifer, either. I want to do that myself."

"Don't worry. I won't spoil your surprise."

He gave her a hug.

"This is a good thing, Kate. I know it is."

"If you say so."

She stood by the courthouse door watching him go down the steps.

That man doesn't have a prayer, she thought.

Tips on Fire Safety

Fire safety is everyone's business. The *Beacon* encourages all its readers to conduct regular fire drills. At work, go around your office or work area and make sure that all doors can be opened from the inside. Quiz your fellow workers on where the closest exit is. Have a fire extinguisher handy. These precautions could save your life.

20. PYROMANIA

THE *BEACON* OFFICES WERE EMPTY SATURDAY MORNING, JUST AS KATE had hoped. Walking into the silent newsroom, she finally felt focused, able to put aside her worries about Keith's upcoming marriage. She immersed herself in her copious notes about the trial and went to work.

"Okay, let's see what we got here," she said out loud, as there was no one around to chide her for talking to herself. "Looks like we got enough for two or three stories. Shane Cochran; that's the big thing here. Defense suggests Shane Cochran set the fire. No, wait, they showed the connection with Brandon Fawkes and established a motive, but they didn't say he did it. Oh, this is so confusing. Give me a planning and zoning hearing any day."

After another fifteen minutes of ruminating, she fired up the terminal and began writing.

"Just get it all in there. You can edit it on Monday," she told herself.

Three hours later she was ready for a break and decided to get up and make some coffee. She hit the save button and headed out toward the break room where the coffee station was. She'd just set the pot to brew when she heard the front door open, accompanied by the sound of children laughing.

Who could be bringing their kids to work today?

"Hey, guys, settle down. This place is dangerous."

She recognized Barry's voice. Kate took her coffee back to the newsroom and found him at his desk. Standing next to him was a boy of about ten or eleven and a little girl who looked to be five or six.

"Kate, what are you doing here? It's Saturday."

"Just getting a little work done. I could ask you the same question. I thought you were spending time with your family. Who are your friends?"

"This here's my nephew, Cody Wynn. He's my sister June's boy. And this little lady is Caitlin Moore. She's my brother Wilfred's granddaughter. Kids, this is Kate Dennison. She's a reporter at the *Beacon* just like me."

"Barry's my great-uncle," Caitlin chirped, squeezing his hand.

"Makes you feel old, doesn't it?" Kate said to Barry.

"Not really. Bein' the youngest of six, seems like I was born an uncle. Which ain't exactly true, as Wilfred didn't become a daddy until I was four, when Caitlin's daddy was born. Then after that my sisters and brothers went forth and multiplied. I'm an uncle fourteen times over."

"Which is why we're here. The Moores have multiplied so much my mama's house is fit to burst at the seams. So me and my compadres here decided to take a look at where Uncle Barry works."

"Barry, is it my imagination, or has your accent gotten thicker?"

"That's a hazard of family reunions. I been around all the folks who ain't set foot outside Burgaw their whole lives an' it's rubbed off on me. You should hear my brother David. He lost his accent completely after twenty years in San Diego, but this morning he sounded like the Carolina good ol' boy he used to be."

"Where's the newspaper presses?" Cody asked. "Can we turn 'em on?"

"Sorry, buddy, we don't have 'em here anymore. Roger pays someone else to print the paper cuz it was costin' him too much to run it himself."

"That's no fun," Cody complained. "There's nothing to do here."

"Want to go back and hear Grandma tell embarrassing stories about you?"

"No way, Uncle Barry."

Barry took out one of his cameras from his bag.

"How about this, Cody? You take pictures of Miss Kate here and then we'll edit them on the computer."

The boy grabbed the camera with both hands, excited to hold one of his uncle's prized digital cameras.

"You okay bein' a super-model, Miss Kate?" Barry asked.

"I'm definitely okay with being a super model, Mr. Barry. Just let me make sure I saved my story. I'm pretty sure I did, but it's better to be safe than sorry. It's a good five or six pages, and I sure don't want to rewrite it from scratch."

She hurried over to her desk while the children watched her impatiently.

"Can I be a super model too?" Caitlin asked.

"Of course you can, honey. You can even go first. That is if it's okay with Ms. Kate. You know what they say – age before beauty."

"And you certainly are a beauty, swee – "

She was cut off by the sound of glass shattering. They all stopped and listened intently, frozen in their spots. There was the earsplitting sound of an explosion that shook the desks and plunged the room into darkness. The squealing of the smoke alarm mingled with Caitlin's hysterical screams.

"Kate, we've got to get out. This whole place could burn to the ground!" Barry yelled.

"It's too dark, we'll never find the way out," she cried. "Wait, I've got a flashlight!"

Though crazed with panic, she had remembered the flashlight in her purse. She felt along the desk, grabbing the handle of the right-hand drawer, reached in and felt her purse. She took a deep breath, thankful there was no smoke in the room yet, then pulled it out and unzipped it. She felt around inside. There was her comb, there was her wallet, there was the cell phone; they should call 911 when they got outside.

Oh, that's it, the flashlight.

With a tight grasp, she whipped it out of her purse, clicked it on and shone its tiny beam around the room. Barry and the children were by his desk, both kids clutching him for dear life.

"The exit is at the back of the room here. Out this door, through the storage room and we turn right to the rear of the building."

Kate shined her light on the door, and they opened it.

"Everybody crouch down. There's better air close to the ground," Barry instructed. "Kate, grab on to us. That way no one gets lost."

They all hunched down, forming an odd sort of conga line, and duckwalked as quickly as they could toward the exit. There were windows there, and the EXIT sign was illuminated. Thirty feet away. Twenty feet away. Ten feet away. Almost there.

Finally, after what felt like an eternity, Barry grabbed the handle and opened the door. They stumbled out into the sunlight and found themselves facing a ball of fire and sparks.

"Holy smokes! The transformer exploded!" Barry shouted.

Thick black smoke poured out of the mass of twisted metal that once served as the *Beacon*'s transformer box.

Kate took the children by the hand and led them away from the fire, with the intention of taking them around the building to the parking lot facing the street. Barry lagged behind, dialing his cell phone.

"There's a fire at the *Beacon* newspaper office. The street address? I can't remember: it's two thousand something. Just tell the guys to look for the building on fire. And you better call Progress Energy. Our transformer exploded."

"Never mind, Barry, they're here," Kate called back to him.

With siren blasting, a fire engine barreled into the parking lot at full speed. It screeched to a stop and several firefighters alighted, swarming out in all directions.

"Wow, that was quick," Barry said to the 911 operator. "What? Okay, thanks."

He snapped his phone shut and ran to catch up with Kate and the children.

"It was in the neighborhood, and someone already called."

"I wanna go see the firemen!" Caitlin said when Barry reached them. Now that they were safe, the children wanted to watch the action and they weren't the only ones. The traffic on Market Street slowed down as motorists in both directions paused to take a look at the fire, and a crowd gathered at O'Reilly's Used Car Lot next door.

"Sorry, kids, we're going home. Now. Your grandma is gonna kill me."

Coming around the corner of the chiropractor's office, they could see the reception room for the *Beacon* was burning, too.

"Barry, I think we both need to stay here. The police are going to want to talk to us."

He sighed, then reached into his pocket and pulled out his cell phone.

"You're right. I'll call for someone to take them home."

While he worked out getting a ride for his niece and nephew, Kate walked over to get a better look at what was going on. The front window was completely gone, only jagged shards left in its frame. The fire must have started at Janie's desk, burning through the plywood paneling to the particleboard frame. The newspaper rack was still there, though its contents were reduced to ash. The sprinklers in the ceiling had doused most of the flames, leaving a burnt soggy mess.

Smelled awful. She remembered hearing that plywood paneling was full of formaldehyde, so kept her distance.

A firefighter approached her.

"Ma'am? You need to get away from the building, right now."

"Yes, of course. Um, can I go to my car? It's parked over there."

"Yeah, that'll be okay."

Kate had parked in front of the empty unit in the strip mall, leaving room for customers, even though none were expected. Her Ford Focus appeared to be untouched by the fire.

Then she noticed hers had a page of newspaper stuck under the windshield. Who could have put that there?

She went over and detached it from the wipers. It was the insert commissioned by Kominsky Builders, showcasing one of their new developments, Whispering Pines. Scrawled across the page in black marker were the words NO ONE CAN RESIST THE FORCES OF NATURE, and below that "in league with the corporate monsters."

Kate stared, wishing she'd never seen it. She put it back under the windshield wiper, hoping she wouldn't get in trouble for tampering with evidence. She waved to Barry, leaned against her car and realized she was in for a long afternoon.

At least she'd saved her story.

Beacon Opens Temporary Office

Oct. 22 — The *Beacon*'s editorial staff has opened a temporary office downtown, at the corner of Front and Chestnut Streets.

"The damage to our building was fairly minimal, but it will take some time for repairs to be made," publisher Roger Hoffman said. "But we are still in business and we intend to keep right on putting out a newspaper."

21. DISPLACED AND DISGRACED

THE *BEACON'S* STAFF WAS ABOUT TO HOLD ITS TUESDAY MORNING editorial meeting, this time at Port City Java on Front Street. Kate was settled into one of the marvelously comfortable easy chairs when Barry arrived.

They had claimed a corner at the back of the shop, setting up their own cluster of easy chairs around a small coffee table.

"Hey, Kate, how's it going? This sure beats playing sardines in Roger's office," he said as he took the chair next to her.

"Coffee's better, too," she agreed, taking a sip of her special morning blend.

"Let's get on with this. Some of us have work to do," Clarisse Hopper snapped.

She glared at all of them across the table through her thick glasses, reminding Kate of a large white bulldog wrapped in a pink polyester pantsuit. She wondered how the local business people could stand dealing with the woman. Clarisse never smiled and was always complaining.

"Don't get your undies in a bunch, Clarisse," Barry said. "We can't do anything until Roger gets here, so relax. Have a nice cup of tea and some brioche or something. Roger's running a tab for us. Part of the expenses of being displaced from our premises."

"Waste of time and money, if you ask me." Still, Clarisse managed to lift her bulk off the couch and waddle over to the counter to order a double chocolate latte, charging it to the *Beacon*.

In the old office, Barry and Kate rarely saw Clarisse. With her desk in the advertising department, she only joined them at editorial meetings, and most of the time she never made those.

Now, however, everyone, from the classified ad girls to the reporters, was stuck in a small, three-room office suite in the old Hanover Bank Building on Front Street. Kate hoped they got their old office fixed soon. Clarisse was driving her nuts.

"Sure wish that old cow would retire," Barry whispered. "Not that she ever will. She's been here forty years. Outlasted eight publishers and God knows how many reporters like us. Janie told me she's got a shitload of money stashed away so she doesn't need to work, but she comes in every morning just the same."

Kate was about to say retirement would be a good thing for Clarisse and the *Beacon* staff as well when she saw Roger coming through the door. He hurried over and sat down on the couch next to Barry.

"'Hello, troops. Glad to see you're all here." He opened his briefcase and took out a yellow legal pad. Kate could see a list of items for this week's meeting. She was pleased to see it was short. She'd like to get home before the traffic got too bad; working downtown was awful.

"Good to see you, too, Rog," Barry said. "Any news on when we get back into the office?"

"I talked to the contractor, and he says three weeks at the earliest. Which in contractor time means a couple of months or more. According to the police, we were hit with two incendiary devices – a pipe bomb to the transformer, and a Molotov cocktail to the reception area. Low tech but lethal. The transformer has to be replaced, the wiring needs to be overhauled since what we had before wasn't up to code, and the reception area has to be completely redone. Whatever didn't burn was soaked by the sprinklers. The good news is that the insurance settlement turned out to be a bit more generous than I expected, so I decided to get a few things fixed up. Besides a new reception area, all the offices will be getting new flooring, new lighting, new everything."

"It's about time you got that reception area fixed up," huffed Clarisse, returning to her couch clutching her latte and a plate of cookies. "It was an embarrassment when our clients dropped off ad copy. That dingy linoleum and all those stains in the ceiling. That's why I always meet my sources at the Bistro in Lumina Station."

"By the way, Clarisse, you do pay for your own lunch at the Bistro, don't you?" Roger asked. "I'd hate to think you were selling the paper's influence for the price of shrimp scampi with garlic sauce."

"Why, of course I pay for my own lunch!" she bristled. "The very idea!"

"Just checking," Roger replied. "Can't be too careful about the appearance of impropriety. All right, let's get started. First off, I want to thank Kate and Barry for their quick thinking during the fire Saturday. You got yourselves and the kids out and you got the fire department there in time to save the building."

"Don't understand why those children were there in the first place," Clarisse barked. "It's a newspaper office, not a playground."

"Children are never too young to find out about a newspaper career," Roger said with a smile. "Future reporters, right, Barry? Anyway, I'm glad you were there to call the fire department and thankful no one was hurt."

"I wouldn't say that," Barry told him. "My mama was inches away from taking a strap to my backside for putting her precious grandchild and great-grandchild in mortal danger. Course, Cody and Caitlin thought it was the most exciting thing they'd ever seen. Cody's talking about being a fireman now. Sorry, Roger. No future reporters."

"Oh, well, give them time," Roger said. "The police are still looking for the perpetrator or perpetrators, as there had to be two of them. They've been talking to witnesses but aren't getting much. A couple of guys bomb a building in broad daylight on Market Street and no one sees a blessed thing.

"Next, I want to thank Kate for taking over for Barry on the Kessler trial. You did an excellent job, very insightful coverage."

Kate smiled, savoring the compliment. Wow, insightful.

"So, Barry, how's the trial going?" Roger asked.

"Looks to be a while before it goes to the jury. The prosecution is still going on, but they're supposed to rest their case tomorrow. My sources in Judge Hulick's office tell me the defense has quite a few expert witnesses lined up to refute the evidence."

"Well, all they had is Timmy's fingerprints on the gas cans," Kate pointed out. "Circumstantial, at best."

"Fingerprints on the murder weapon is enough to convict, if you ask me," Clarisse pronounced. "And that hoodlum has no alibi. An open-and-shut case."

"People, we're not hear to discuss the Kessler case," Roger

171

interrupted sharply. "You can do that on your own time. Right now, I've got to figure out what we're putting in this week's issue. Since Kate and Barry were both participants, I'll be writing a story on the fire, but I'd like one of you to write a sidebar about the experience."

"I'll do that, chief," Barry offered.

"Great." Roger checked off one of the items on his list. "Kate, what have you got for this week?"

She opened up her notebook for the stories she was working on.

"There's a planning-and-zoning meeting this week. They'll be handing down their decision on the addition to the Food Lion in Porter's Neck. Also, I'll be interviewing the third-grade teacher who received a volunteer award from Habitat for Humanity. This lady is amazing. Teaching is one of the hardest jobs there is, and still she managed to put in a thousand hours building houses.

"The school board meets Wednesday morning. Looks like there'll be another big flap about displaying the Ten Commandments in the schools along with all the other stuff on the agenda. There's the new after-school swimming program for the special ed kids at the YMCA. I've got an interview and pictures lined up. That's about it."

"Sounds good," Roger said.

"Oh, Roger, is it okay if I leave a bit early on Friday?"

"If everything's done, that's fine with me. After what you've been through, you certainly deserve a little time off."

"Thanks."

"Clarisse, what are you working on?"

Clarisse put down her cookie and picked up her notebook.

"I've got a lot on my plate this week, Roger," she said, not noticing the stifled giggles of Barry and Kate. "I've got an interview with Henry Reiker, who was just named Wilmington Business Person of the Year. They'll be having a lovely dinner for him at the White Swan in Wrightsville Beach. There's a new independent real estate agency just opening up. These gals have a lot of gumption. They're going up against Coastal Realty, and they think they can win. And there's a new boutique opening up in Independence Mall."

"That sounds good." He scribbled notes on his pad.

"Oh, and there's an event next week that should be a business story, but I can't do it. I've got an engagement I just can't get out of. Perhaps

172

Kate could cover it?"

"What sort of event, Clarisse?"

"It's the Young Entrepreneurs Expo sponsored by Cape Fear Community College. It should be quite interesting. All those young kids with their great ideas on display. There will be an awards ceremony with Ed Kominsky as the keynote speaker."

Kate looked pleadingly at Roger. It sounded just awful; another "grip-and-grab" photo of Ed Kominsky and some college kid.

"I don't know, Clarisse. I don't think we can spare Kate for that. Can't you just cobble something together on press releases? Have CFCC send you some photos?"

"Janie's nephew is getting an award, and I promised her we'd cover it in person."

Kate's heart sank. Now there was no way she could get out of doing that story. She owed Janie ten times over, and she would hate for the editorial department to let the receptionist down.

"For Janie, I'll do it," she said. "When is it?"

"Next Thursday at the Schwartz Center on campus. The expo goes on all day, but the awards ceremony is at two o'clock."

"Thanks, Kate," Roger said. "I appreciate your doing this. I certainly don't want to get on Janie's bad side. Okay, that covers this week's issue. Now, as far as our temporary office goes, I want to make sure we all understand we leave it the way we found it."

He looked over at Barry when he said this, but Barry just grinned.

"The building's owner is an old friend of mine and he was kind enough to let us use it. That's why there's no coffeemaker. No coffee, no coffee stains. Also, I've checked the finances, and the paper will not be able to cover the cost of parking downtown. So, for the time we're down here, I'd advise all of you to park your cars on Fifth Street where there are no meters and walk. Otherwise, you pay your own way."

"Do you know how far that is, chief?" Barry complained.

"Yes, it's four blocks. A pleasant stroll and we can all use the exercise." Roger looked around. "Well, that's all I've got. You folks have anything to say?" He looked around, but no one said a word. He checked his watch. "That's great, because if we all leave right now, I think we can avoid rush hour traffic. See you round."

PREPARE CHILDREN FOR REMARRIAGE

A parent's remarriage can be very stressful for a child, especially when the new spouse brings his or her own children into the household. Remember, most children of divorced parents cling to the hope their parents will reconcile. A remarriage means giving up this dream.

To make the transition easier, the *Beacon* recommends both parents make every effort to insure the child feels loved and secure.

22. QUALITY TIME

MOLLY WAS NOT HERSELF. HER USUAL EXUBERANCE AND BOUNDLESS energy had been replaced by a listless blue funk. Since Keith had brought her home Sunday night, there had been no running in the house, no excited squeals and no peals of laughter.

Kate had expected Molly to take her father's upcoming marriage pretty hard. Still, she hadn't expected this kind of reaction. Molly had lost interest in just about everything. It was as if she were sleepwalking through her day.

Kate had made a point of getting home early, hoping that some extra time with Mom might cheer her daughter up. But when she arrived at Marlene's house, Molly was sitting quietly at the table drawing pictures in blue crayon. She looked up at her, but said nothing.

"Has she been like this all day?" Kate whispered to Marlene.

"Yes, and the day before as well. I'm sure it's the news of her dad's upcoming marriage."

"Yes, I know that's it, but damn him, I didn't think it would turn Molly into a zombie. How can we snap her out of this?"

Marlene shrugged.

"I don't know what to tell you. I've been trying to get her away from that table all day, and she won't budge. She won't talk about what's bothering her, either. I've never seen her like this. I offered her favorite gingerbread cookies and she just said 'No, thank you.'"

"Molly! Let's go home, pumpkin."

Molly got up from the table and walked quietly over to retrieve her bookbag.

"How was school today, sweetie?" Kate asked.

"All right. Goodbye, Miss Marlene. I'll see you tomorrow."

"Good-bye, Molly. You think you can bring your smile with you then?"

Molly looked as if she were about to cry.

"I'll try," she said gravely.

Kate took her by the hand, and they headed out the door.

Molly barely made a sound as she walked into the house, putting her coat and bookbag away, just like she was supposed to but never did. Kate wished she felt happier about that.

"Would you like supper now?"

"Okay." Molly sat down on the couch, quietly reading a book she'd brought from school. Ordinarily, she'd be begging to watch cartoons or videos.

Kate opened up the freezer door and pulled out a large casserole. She quietly commended herself for finally following the advice in the paper's Household Hints column about making meals ahead of time and freezing them. All she had to do was warm up the oven and slide the dish inside. If ever she needed thirty minutes of extra time it was now.

A few minutes later she was sitting on the couch with Molly.

"Would you like me to read the new book we got from the library?"

"We've read it twice already, Mom," Molly answered. "It's not new anymore."

"Well, what would you like to do?"

Molly shrugged.

"I don't know."

"How about telling me why you're acting like this?"

"Like what?"

"Molly, you're scaring me. You've stopped being you. You don't run in the house, you don't yell and scream, you don't want to do anything fun. What's happened to you?"

She could see tears welling up in her daughter's eyes.

"I'm trying to be good."

Kate felt a terrible aching in her heart. What had she and Keith done to their beautiful little girl that she felt she had to try to be good? She reached over and took her now sobbing child into her arms.

"You're always good, sweetie. You don't have to try. Did Daddy tell you that you had to be good?"

"No, it was the fire in your office," Molly said, sniffing and wiping her eyes. "Jennifer said that if anything happened to you, I would have to come and live with them. I don't want to live with them so I promised God that if you could be safe, I'd be good all the time."

"I hope you didn't learn that in Sunday school," Kate said, dismayed at her daughter's skewed theology. She had searched long and hard for a church with a philosophy of love and forgiveness, light on the guilt. Market Street Presbyterian had seemed to be exactly what she was looking for. Now her daughter felt she had to live up to some impossibly high standard or God would smite down her mother.

Maybe this guilt thing was genetic.

"Well, they told us that God answers prayers and he can do anything. I figured if I promised to be good all the time, nothing bad would happen to you."

"Listen, Molly," Kate said, holding her daughter close. "The fire was a scary thing, but I'm all right. It wasn't very big, and we had plenty of time to get out of the building. Now, I can't promise you that nothing bad will ever happen to me, but I'm pretty sure I'll be fine. I always wear a seatbelt when I drive. I look both ways when I cross the street. I don't jump out of windows or eat uncooked meat. And I wash my hands a lot.

"Besides, your behavior has nothing to do with what happens to me. God's not going to hold you to that promise, and neither will I. So, how about you go back to being my old Molly, and we have a nice supper together. Okay?"

Molly smiled, a load lifted from her small shoulders.

"Mommy, I really don't want to live with Daddy and Jennifer. She yells all the time. And Matt and Austin are really mean now."

"How are they mean to you?"

"Saturday night before I went to bed, they came in my room and stole Elephant. They were throwing him back and forth and wouldn't let me have him. I went and got Daddy, and he made them give him back, but they called me a crybaby and a tattletale."

"Oh, Molly, I'm so sorry they did that to you. And I bet Daddy was, too."

"He said he would talk to Jennifer about it, but nothing happened to them. The next day Matt and Austin still got to play their video games and ride their bikes and get chocolate cake for dessert. Like they hadn't done anything. It's not fair."

"No, it isn't, sweetie. Do you want me to talk to your daddy about them?"

"I think he's afraid Jennifer will yell at him some more. She's not very nice sometimes."

"I agree with you on that one," Kate said. "But since Daddy has decided he wants to marry Jennifer, we're all going to have to learn to get along."

"I don't want to go back so soon. Can you stay home this weekend? Please?"

Molly's pleading eyes were almost more than she could bear. What to do? The child was going through some tough times. It had to be hard dealing with both of her parents finding other people. She might very well be thinking we're both going to leave her behind, Kate thought.

On the other hand, Kate had been looking forward to the weekend with Bryan for quite some time, and it wasn't something that could be re-scheduled. Besides, canceling would set a precedent she certainly did not want, that of letting her daughter dictate her social life.

No, Molly was a big girl. Like it or not, she would have to learn how to deal with her stepbrothers, and sooner rather than later.

"No, Molly. I promised Bryan I'd go with him. It wouldn't be fair to tell him no."

"You could tell him I was sick," Molly offered.

"That would be telling a lie, and you know that would be wrong. That's a real surprise coming from someone who was trying so hard to be good five minutes ago."

"Sorry, Mom."

"How about this? You spend the weekend with your dad and you can take that necklace of mine you like so much. Every time Matt and Austin are mean to you, just touch the locket and you can remember how much I love you and that I'll be home soon. And if things get really bad, you can call me on the cell phone. But ask Daddy first, okay?"

"Okay," Molly said, her eyes downcast.

"And when I pick you up on Sunday, we'll go to Port City Java for a smoothie."

"Promise?"

"Yes, I promise. Now, how about setting the table for dinner and maybe we can play a game after supper. You choose."

Molly flung her arms around her mother.
"You're the best mommy in the whole world."
No, I'm not. But I try.

Travel North Carolina

Destination: Asheville

North Carolina has a number of excellent resorts for weekend trips. Although it is a bit of a drive from Wilmington, The *Beacon* highly recommends a visit to Asheville, on the western edge of the state. Chimney Rock Park, the Biltmore Estate and the beautiful scenery of the Great Smokey Mountains are just a few of the attractions in this area.

Winslow Beach Beacon
October 29

23. WEEKEND GETAWAY

THE WEEKEND TRAFFIC IN RALEIGH WAS SPILLING TO THE RING ROAD, even though it was not yet two o'clock on Friday afternoon. Kate gripped the steering wheel, scanning the exit signs, looking for Poole Road. She was a bit anxious, as Bryan had a tendency to leave out key information in his driving directions. Once, she had driven around for an hour on a bumpy old country road in Montgomery County, Ohio, because he had forgotten to tell her there was no sign on the dirt road she was looking for.

With a great deal of relief she spied the Poole Road exit sign ahead on the right, only two miles away. Easing her car into the exit lane, she was startled by her cell phone ringing. Oh, it must be Molly. Kate had a hard time resisting the urge to pull the phone out of her purse and talk to her daughter, but she managed to let the phone ring.

Drive now, talk later.

As far as she could tell, she wasn't that far from Bryan's office. She would call Molly from there; she could wait ten or fifteen minutes.

She checked the street numbers and discovered the address she was looking for was on this block. Yes, there it was, a cluster of brick-and-glass office buildings. In the circular lawn at the entrance to the complex, she saw a stack of stone blocks about ten feet high, surrounded by a low brick wall. Driving by it, Kate discovered it was a fountain, now turned off for the winter.

"Building B, Building B. Where is Building B?" She followed the maze of directional signs in the parking lot. A few minutes later she had found Building B and took the stairs up to the second floor where the North Carolina Chapter of the Nature Trust had its offices. It seemed impolite to take the elevator as it was a waste of natural resources.

Reduce, re-use, recycle.

Walking up the stairs, she checked her cell phone to see who had called her. As she had expected, it was Molly, as she recognized Jennifer's phone number.

A cheery receptionist sat at the front desk, dressed in faded jeans and a Nature Trust T-shirt. She typed away at her terminal, filling in cells on a spreadsheet titled "Gains in Wetland Reclamation, 2004 To Present."

"May I help you?" she said, smiling at Kate. There was no trace of a Carolina accent.

Kate figured she was an environmental studies major from the north hoping to work her way up in the organization by starting in a lowly clerical job; jobs for environmentalists were few and far between. Bryan told her once he could paper his office walls with the resumes he received on a daily basis.

"Uh, yes. I'm here to see Bryan Haas."

"Oh, you must be Kate Dennison. He told me you'd be here. His office is down that hall and to the right. Go on in. He's expecting you."

"Thank you."

"No problem," she said, returning to tallying up wetland reclamation statistics.

Kate passed the framed colored photographs of all the preserves managed by the Nature Trust in North Carolina. It was a different chapter, a different state, but this office was exactly like the one in Ohio. It had the same slogans on the wall, the same type of nature photographs, the same cheery optimism from the director right down to the receptionist.

She found Bryan's office. He was on the phone but motioned for her to have a seat. He was leaning back in the chair, his long legs resting on his desk.

"Yup...Okay...Yeah, I'll do that." He covered the receiver and whispered, "Be with you in a minute."

Kate responded "Okay" in the same tone and sat in one of the chairs across his desk. She was eager to get started on their trip and didn't want to spend any more time in the office than they absolutely had to. She thought about calling Molly back on her cell phone but figured their conversations would clash. Maybe there was an empty conference room she could go to.

"Yeah, thanks, Al. You, too. I'll be expecting it in the mail. Bye." Looking exasperated, he hung up.

"That man is our biggest contributor and the biggest pain in the ass as well. Thinks he has the right to tell us exactly what we can and can't do with the money."

"Well, can he?"

"Unfortunately, yes. At least up to a point. Anyway, that's part of my job, telling him no without actually saying it so he'll keep on giving us money. Seems that's all I do these days. I haven't been out in the field in weeks. I spend all my time talking on the phone to people with lots of money and no idea what our mission is. And let me tell you, it sucks."

"No one said saving the planet would be easy. Or even saving parts of it."

"I never even get to see the planet anymore, let alone help save it."

He got up from his chair, grinning, and walked around the desk to take her by the hand. Kate stood up. With his arms about her, her face buried in his soft flannel shirt that smelled of Tide and aftershave, Kate felt all her trials and tribulations melt away.

Forget the trip, she thought as their lips met in a long, soulful kiss. I could stay here like this all day. And all night, too.

"It's good to see you," he said, still holding her in a tight embrace. "You ready to hit the road?"

"Yes." She pulled back from him. "I just need to call my daughter. She called me while I was on I-440 and I couldn't answer it."

She reached into her purse for her cell phone.

"Here, use the land line, save some minutes."

"No, it's okay. I've got one of those unlimited calling plans for work and it's easier to press the button on received calls. But thanks anyway."

She called and listened to the phone ring. She sure hoped someone picked up. If Molly was having trouble again, a message from her on the answering machine wasn't going to be of much help.

"Hello?" Jennifer's saccharin voice came on the line.

"Uh, yes. Hello, Jennifer, this is Kate. Could I speak to Molly, please?"

"Why, of course. She just tried to call you. She's watching cartoons with the boys right now. I'll get her."

There was a pause, followed by a jarring "MOLLY! IT'S YOUR

MOM!"

Molly said she yells a lot. Keith always liked things quiet and orderly. How does he stand that?

"She'll be here in a sec," Jennifer said, returning once again to her saccharine-sweet persona.

"How's she doing?"

"Oh, she's having the time of her life. We're just getting ready to do our nails."

"Good. Molly should have fun with that. She's always begging me to let her paint her nails."

"Well, you should do it more often. I say you're only as good as your last manicure. Here she is now."

"Hi, Mom," Molly said

"Hi, pumpkin, what's up?"

"Nothing. I just wanted to say goodbye and tell you I miss you."

"I miss you, too. I'm sorry I couldn't pick up the phone when you called."

"That's okay. I know you're not supposed to talk on the phone when you're driving. Like Daddy says, drive now, talk later." Molly laughed as she said this, which made Kate feel very relieved.

"Jennifer says you're going to paint your nails in a little bit."

"Yeah, she's got lots of different colors of nail polish, and she says I can choose whatever one I want. It's going to be so cool."

"Well, I'm glad to hear you're having fun. Don't forget what we talked about, okay? You got your necklace?"

"Right here. Oh, Jennifer's got the nail polish out. I love you Mom, see you when you get home."

"I love you, too, sweetie."

The phone line clicked, and the dial tone came on. Although she was glad Molly was having a good time with Jennifer, she couldn't help feeling a little jealous, like Jennifer was trying to take her daughter along with her husband.

Don't be silly, she told herself. It's just a little nail polish. It comes off.

"Everything okay?"

"Yes, everything's fine."

"I remember you said your daughter was having a hard time getting along with her dad's girlfriend and her kids. Is that still a problem?"

"Apparently not now. She's watching cartoons with the boys and having her nails done with Jennifer. But I don't expect it to last."

"It's not easy getting along with someone else's kids. When my dad remarried, I just hated my stepsisters. Still don't like them much, but we do manage to get through Thanksgiving dinner. By the way, when am I going to get to meet your daughter?"

Kate didn't know what to say. There were lots of reasons why she hadn't introduced Molly to Bryan. Chief among them was that it was just so much easier to maintain the relationship when her daughter wasn't involved. Molly was a wonderful kid, but she was going through a lot and this was one can of worms Kate wanted to leave unopened.

"I don't know. I'd like to hold off for a while. You know, let her get used to Jennifer and her boys, that whole 'blended family' thing. I'm not sure if seeing me with another man is exactly what she needs right now."

"You have told her about me, haven't you?"

"Yes, of course, she knows about you. And it doesn't seem to be a problem for her. I just don't want to do it right this moment. So, let's wait a while, okay?"

"Okay, I can wait. But honestly, I really do want to meet Molly."

"And you will. Soon."

"Well, let's get started," Bryan said, pointing to the door. "Your suitcase in your car?"

"Yes, it seemed kind of tacky to show up at your office with a suitcase in hand."

"Oh, Lori wouldn't mind. She's seen everything and done a lot of it herself. Not with me, though. I can't handle those twenty-somethings, don't have the money or the stamina."

This was so easy, Kate thought, laughing at Bryan's last remark as she followed him down the hallway, ready to start the four-hour drive to Asheville.

Life is good.

Travel North Carolina

Ellis Grove Inn Has It All

The *Beacon* travel editor gives four stars to the Ellis Grove Inn, located in Asheville. This recently refurbished Victorian hotel is stunning. The amenities are sumptuous, including whirlpool baths, king-size beds and wood-burning fireplaces in all the rooms. In addition, the hotel offers a workout room, a sauna and an indoor heated swimming pool. The restaurant boasts a celebrated gourmet chef, serving truly excellent food. The Biltmore Estate is five minutes away and nature lovers will enjoy the hiking trails at nearby Pisgah National Forest.

But who in their right mind would want to leave this type of luxury for a walk in the woods? If you're planning a weekend retreat, Ellis Grove Inn is your best bet.

24. ROOM WITH A VIEW

KATE AND BRYAN WERE DELIGHTED TO FIND THEIR TWO NIGHTS AT THE Ellis Grove Inn would be spent not in an ordinary hotel room but in the Presidential Suite. It was nearly as big as her house. The stone fireplace was lit when they arrived, making for a cozy, romantic atmosphere, and they had a beautiful view of the mountains. Even Bryan, who was normally unimpressed by anything, seemed taken aback by the extravagant surroundings, but like her, he managed to adjust.

The only problem Kate was having with the weekend was that the weekend was going way too fast.

They ate, they drank, they slept. They took a long hot bath in the whirlpool tub and made love five times in a row. Then they slept some more and went back to eating, drinking and making love, followed by a tour of the Biltmore Estate.

It was like a honeymoon without going to the trouble of actually getting married.

Too soon, it was Sunday morning and time to check out. Kate made one last foray around the suite, looking for any errant belongings. Finally satisfied that everything she'd brought was leaving with her, she zipped up her suitcase and followed Bryan out the door.

"Say goodbye to the high life, Kate," he said as he shut the door behind them.

"I don't want to," she said. "I like the high life. I want to keep it."

He picked up her suitcase, and they started down the long carpeted hallway. Kate loved the thick pile, and it was the exact shade of burgundy she wanted for the rug in her living room; the pseudo-oriental from Big Lots wasn't even close.

"You get soft and lazy if you live this way too long," Bryan said, interrupting her carpet envy. "And after a while you don't even notice it."

"Yes, you're right," she agreed with a sigh. "Maybe we enjoyed it so much because we never get to do stuff like this. And because someone else was paying for it. Which reminds me, you need to give a great big thank-you to that wonderful volunteer who gave us her prize. What sort of raffle was it?"

"A benefit for the local public radio station, I think. You know, make a pledge and get entered in the drawing for a weekend getaway. Lil said she wasn't up to driving from Raleigh to Asheville and couldn't think of anyone she'd care to spend that much time with all at once. Lil's one hell of a nice lady. She's past seventy and puts in near as many hours as you used to. Says it keeps her off the streets."

"In that case, give her a great big hug and a kiss, too."

They descended the grand staircase and headed for the front desk to check out. Kate watched wistfully as Bryan handed over the white plastic card that had gained them entry to the Presidential Suite. He picked up the suitcases again, and they headed for the parking garage.

"How 'bout we drive out to Mt. Mitchell State Park and go hiking?" asked Bryan after he'd loaded up the car. "We've spent enough time indoors. And it's a great day for it. The sun's out, and it's not too cold."

"Yes, we did come all this way. We should take a look at the mountains up close."

They drove up the Blue Ridge Parkway. The pine trees towered above them, majestic and green, even in mid November. Once they saw two deer poke their heads up from the brush then disappear into the woods.

Soon they had left the parkway and were making their way up a winding two lane blacktop towards Mt. Mitchell. Kate saw a sign proclaiming it to be the "highest peak east of the Mississippi."

That made her nervous.

"Bryan, how are we getting to the top?"

"We'll drive. Unless you want me to stop now and we can hike the rest of the way."

"No, driving's fine," she said, wondering if choosing the highest peak east of the Mississippi for a leisurely afternoon hike was such a good idea.

They climbed higher and higher up the twisting road until they reached a large, oval shaped parking lot. There was no need to search for a space, the lot was nearly empty.

Bryan parked the car next to the string of wooden cabins that formed the visitor's center exhibit hall and they both got out. Bryan reached into the backseat and pulled out a small daypack. Kate took her camera.

She intended to stroll over to the visitor's center and take a look at maps of hiking trails, but she was stopped in her tracks by the panorama before her. The mountains stretched out forever, deep green and blue, enveloped in clouds and covered with trees like moss.

Then Kate saw that not all the mountains were covered with trees. Here and there, she could see patches of dead gray tree trunks, sticking up like tombstones on the mountain.

"Bryan, what happened to all those trees? Was it a fire? Or some kind of disease?"

"Not a fire. Fraser firs like these can recover from a fire. In fact, fires are good for them. No, that's damage from acid rain. It could also be from the balsam woolly adelgid. It's been wiping out spruces and firs since the fifties."

"The balsam woolly whatsis?"

"Adelgid – it's an insect pest from Europe."

"How do you remember all this stuff?"

"It's my job. But I wish there weren't so many invasive species to remember. Seems like most of it was brought over on purpose."

"Like the starlings."

"Yeah, like the starlings. And honeysuckle. And the phragmites. And whatever else is coming in right now on a tanker from China." He cinched up the straps on his backpack. "Well, let's get to it."

"Aren't we going to look at the trail map?"

"No, I know where we're going. Over this way to the Balsam trail. Don't worry, it's marked easy."

They walked to the end of the parking lot to the trail's beginning. It may have been marked easy, but it did not look all that easy to Kate, who was used to doing all her walking on flat sidewalks. The trail was barely more than a narrow path, with rocks jutting out. And while not steep, it was an uphill climb.

Bryan was scrambling up the trail like a mountain goat. Within minutes he was so far ahead, she could barely see him.

195

"Hey, wait up!" she called. She shimmied over a pile of moss covered rocks, terrified she might slip and go tumbling down the side of the mountain. At more than a mile above sea level, it was a long way down. She wished she'd given her camera to Bryan to carry in his backpack. Having it slung across her shoulder where it bounced against her hip was awkward.

It took a minute or two before she managed to reach him. He was waiting for her by a grove of small spruce trees.

"What's your hurry?" she asked, a bit out of breath. "We're still on vacation. We can still take things slow."

"Well, not really," Bryan answered, and he began walking again, still maintaining a quick pace. "Remember, you have to be back in Wilmington at a decent hour."

"Don't remind me," she replied. "But can't we slow down a bit? I'm having a hard time with all these rocks."

"Little wimpy girl, working in an office all day, can't handle a little bitty old mountain trail," he teased in a high-pitched voice. "Don't worry, we're almost there.'

"Almost where?"

"You'll see."

He kept up his breakneck pace for the next ten minutes, which caused Kate no end of irritation. She would have preferred to take in the scenery. For all the good it was doing her, she might as well have left her camera in the car. In the time it would take her to stop and take a photograph, Bryan would be miles ahead.

Then Kate saw a large sign blocking the path, announcing "Trail Closed."

"This must be it," he said, ignoring the sign and continuing on.

"Bryan!" Kate shouted from her side of the sign. "You can't do that. The trail's closed. We need to turn around and go back."

"Relax, Kate. It's perfectly safe."

"But you're not allowed to go past the sign!"

Bryan laughed at her.

"You're worried about getting into trouble, aren't you?"

"Well, sort of," she admitted.

Even though it seemed silly, Kate was indeed worried about getting into trouble. She didn't know what sort of trouble it might be, possibly both of them hauled off by burly park rangers followed by an order forever banning them from every state park in North Carolina. Whatever it was, she wanted to avoid it. She was never comfortable about breaking rules.

"Trust me on this, Kate." He held out his hand to her. Kate walked past the sign and joined him on the other side.

"Look, you can see the waterfall from here," he said, pointing through the fir trees, where the water cascaded down a bare rock face. "Why don't you take a few pictures?"

"I'll do that."

While she focused her camera on the waterfall, Bryan took a bottle of water out of his backpack.

"Like some water? Maybe some trail mix?"

Kate clicked her shutter for a gorgeous shot, then pointed the camera at him.

"Oh, no, you don't!" he said, shielding his face with his hands.

"Come on. As the chapter director, you must have had hundreds of photos taken."

"Yes, and they're all bad. Don't know why they have to take so many. Nothing more useless than standing with a bunch of idiots so the development director can have photos for the newsletter. Or the chapter magazine. Or the local newspaper."

"Sorry." She put her camera down. "I wanted a picture of you to show Molly."

"Your camera has one of those delay features on it, right? How about we take a picture of the two of us, sitting here?" He pointed to a fallen tree trunk that lay on the side of the trail.

"Sure." She handed it to him, and he carried it over to one of the dead trees on the side of the trail. He looped the strap around one of the broken branches.

"Okay, you sit right here," he said, pointing to a spot on the log. He looked through the viewfinder then set the shutter. He ran over, sat down next to her and draped his arm around her. For thirty seconds, they held their self-conscious smiles, watching the small red light flashing until the camera clicked.

"Sure hope that turns out," Kate said.

A rustling came from the trees. She jumped to her feet.

"What was that?"

Bryan got up and looked toward the woods.

"I don't know. A deer or a fox, I think. Maybe a bear."

"If it's a bear, maybe we should get out of here."

"It's not a bear," said a strange voice.

Kate looked up to see a mountain man standing beside them. In a panic, she turned around, hoping to follow the path back to civilization, but Bryan grabbed her arm in a tight grip.

This man just came out of nowhere. Had he been following them the whole time?

Tall and craggy with a shock of white hair and a long scraggly beard, the intruder smiled and held out his hand to Bryan. He seemed friendly enough, but he carried a seven-inch hunting knife on his belt and a large backpack on his shoulder, possibly holding more weapons, and that made Kate nervous.

She was not about to trust him.

"No one can resist the Forces of Nature," Bryan said as he shook the stranger's hand.

Radical Group Keeps Its Secrets

Oct. 29 — What is this group called the Forces of Nature (FON)? What do they do besides set things on fire?

At the *Beacon*, we've been doing a little digging, and here's what we've found out. They're a loosely organized group of individual cells, each with no knowledge of any of the others. They believe that by destroying buildings under construction in environmentally fragile areas, the developers will eventually give up and build elsewhere.

Although it can't be verified, (in fact not much about this group can be) the group is believed to be the brainchild of a biology professor at Antioch College in Ohio. However, the name of this professor remains a mystery. Also, not one member of the Forces of Nature has ever given an interview to the press.

25. ANYBODY GOT A PEN?

ENOUGH WITH THAT STUPID CATCH PHRASE!" THE MYSTERIOUS mountain man told him. "No one can resist the Forces of Nature...sounds like that old Monty Python sketch about the Spanish Inquisition. If it were up to me, I'd have banned all members from using that years ago. Let's move on to something more interesting, like introducing me to your lovely lady friend, here."

Kate had tried to disappear, hiding as best she could behind Bryan's back. She poked her head out to take a look at the man, who with his long beard reminded her of a tall, skinny Santa Claus dressed as a lumberjack.

He smiled. She looked up at Bryan, then looked over at the mountain man. Deciding she was in no immediate danger, she emerged from Bryan's shadow.

"Bob, this is Kate Dennison. She's a reporter for the *Winslow Beach Beacon* in Wilmington."

Bob took her hand and gave a firm shake. His hand was hard and calloused; she wondered what sort of work he'd been doing with them. Chopping wood? Plowing fields? Hauling gas cans?

"Kate, this is my old biology professor Bob — "

"Let's just say Bob for now. That okay with you, Miss Kate?"

She nodded.

"Guess you've figured out that the Forces of Nature is my doing. I'm the legendary former biology professor from Antioch College who went nuts one day and started a group that got him on the FBI's Most Wanted list. And I'm here to set a few things straight."

"But you guys never do interviews. You always speak through that spokesman guy, Mike Lohrman."

"In point of fact, none of us has ever done an interview, but there's a first time for everything. And what I have to say I want to say myself, not through a spokesman. Especially Mike Lohrman. Biggest horse's ass you'd ever want to meet. But he serves his purpose. Oh, by the way, would anyone like some coffee? And for God's sake, can't we all sit down? My feet are killing me."

Following Bob's lead, Bryan and Kate sat on down on the fallen log, while Bob reached into his backpack. He pulled out a battered Thermos and a stack of grungy-looking cardboard cups from Starbucks.

"Don't worry, I washed them out," he said handing the cups around. "Don't want to bother carrying china mugs around. Too heavy, and like as not, you end up with a pack full of broken china bits. And I just can't abide plastic. These things hold up pretty well. They're made of all recycled materials, too."

He opened up his Thermos and filled the cups with steaming coffee. Kate was feeling the mountain chill, and a nice hot cup of coffee seemed like a great idea. He must have just made it. It smelled wonderful.

"Thank you." She took a sip. "This is great."

"Grind my own beans by hand, not with those fool battery-operated grinders. Only way to do it. So, little lady, let's get started."

Kate reached for her notebook and realized she didn't have one with her. Or a pen, for that matter. She hadn't expected to be covering any stories at the Ellis Grove Inn.

Typical, here was her biggest story ever, and she couldn't write it down.

"Um, anybody got a pen?"

"Some reporter you are," Bryan said. "I thought you were always prepared."

"That's the Boy Scouts."

He dug into his backpack and pulled out a pen as well as the notebook he used for recording bird sightings.

"Will this do?" he asked, handing them to her.

"Yes, thanks, Bryan. I owe you one. All right, Bob, what do you have to tell me?"

"First off, I want to say I've been reading your stories. Mike sends me clippings of any news stories about FON, and you have done one hell of a job on this thing. A lot of the other papers have already declared that poor kid guilty. Your story made him seem human. I appreciate that."

"Thank you. Some of our readers thought it was a load of crap and told me so. Someone went so far as to send me a dead rat."

"Well, they're idiots. The country's full of them," Bob said. "And we had nothing to do with firebombing your office, either. But here's what I really came to say. That boy — what's his name?"

"Timothy Kessler."

"Yes, Timothy Kessler. The memory's the first thing to go, you know. Anyway, he's not one of us. Aside from checking out the website — which I have nothing to do with, by the way — he's had no contact with anyone in FON. He's not in a cell. He's never attended any meetings. He's not connected with FON in any way, shape or form."

"Do you think it's possible he could have taken your positions and acted on his own in your name?"

"Our position is that we harm no living things. Including humans. Now, I don't know this boy, but I've met more than my share of starry-eyed idealists. One of 'em is sitting right next to you."

He looked over at Bryan and gave him a wide grin. Kate smiled at him, too, trying to imagine Bryan as a naive young college student, out to change the world.

"I've matured some in the last twenty-four years," Bryan protested.

"Sure you have, Haas, sure you have. Anyway, as I said, I don't know this kid, but it's my guess someone set him up. Someone found out he'd been to our website or heard him talk about our organization and decided it was an excellent cover for burning down a house with two people trapped inside."

Kate scribbled his words, hoping she'd be able to read her chicken scratches when it came time to write the story. If she worked at it, she could have it done in time for tomorrow's deadline.

She paused to think of something to ask. In every other interview she'd done, she'd always had a list of questions prepared. Here was her chance to find out firsthand about a secret organization. Think.

"Bob, could I ask you some questions?"

"Sure you can, but I reserve the right not to answer."

"Fair enough. Why did you start the Forces of Nature?"

"I felt I had to. Habitats were being destroyed every day. Developers are a sneaky lot. They know a hundred different ways to get around the environmental protection laws. Suing them wasn't making a dent. But if you hit them in the wallet they take notice. My idea was that we would be the flies in the ointment. We would knock down everything they built, and sooner or later, they'd have to scrap the project because they couldn't afford it."

"Like that mansion in the Florida Everglades?"

"Yes, that's one of our successes."

"Why do you call it a success?"

"That developer found someplace else to build. He knew we'd burn it down again if he tried to rebuild it. The land's been untouched since then."

"Okay. How do you keep track of your organization?"

"I don't. I check in with the members and I know what everyone's doing – which is why I can tell you with absolute certainty that the fire in Wilmington was not set by a FON member. But as far as running it, the organization pretty much runs itself. Small cells, unaware of each other, that kind of thing."

"But do you tell the members what to do? Do you have any authority over them?"

"Nope. If I did, this joker here wouldn't be greeting me with 'no one can resist the Forces of Nature.' Mostly, I advise them. I am their elder statesman. A father figure. Or more accurately, a grandfather figure. I don't have a bunch of lunatics at my beck and call, if that's what you think. These are serious, concerned people from all walks of life. And they're a fine bunch, too."

What else to ask? Kate could feel her head starting to ache from the strain.

"Any other questions, Miss Kate? Because I need to get going and so do you two."

"Okay, last one. Do you have any regrets? Is there anything you'd do differently?"

"That was two questions. Haas, you have to teach this woman how to count. Regrets, no. I'm happy to say I have none. I've done what I've done and I'm not ashamed. Or proud, for that matter. I saw a need and took care of it the best way I knew how. But I'm not so keen on this whole internet thing. I know that's how people come to us these days, but I miss the actual contact. And seems like we're encouraging people to sit in front of their computers in their nice warm three-bedroom-two-bathroom houses instead of going outside and getting their hands dirty.

"Well, that's it for me. I'll be on my way."

He gathered up the Thermos and the empty cups and put them in his backpack.

"No, wait," Kate said as he stood up to leave. "Can I take your picture? When I come back with a story about having interviewed the elusive head of the Forces of Nature, I'm going to have to have something to show my editor that I just didn't make it up."

"Are you in the habit of making stories up?" Bob asked.

"No, but I'd still like a picture."

"Kate, I don't think you should. Bob's got the FBI after him," Bryan reminded her.

"Not a problem. They'll never recognize me under all this facial hair. And I'm due for a shave and a haircut anyway. So, try to get my good side."

Bob stood tall, smiling for the camera. To be on the safe side, she took three shots from three different angles.

"Here, let me take one of the two of you. That one you took with the automatic timer is going to look ridiculous."

She gave camera to him. Then she and Bryan stood together, arms around each other.

"That should do it. Even got the waterfall in there."

"Well, Bob, it was a pleasure to see you," Bryan said.

"Likewise," Bob replied. "Do me justice, young woman."

"I'll do my best."

"That's all I ask," he said and disappeared into the woods.

"Will he be okay?"

"That man wrote the book on trailblazing. Literally. I've still got my copy. Anyway, he'll be fine. It's getting late, let's go."

They gathered up their things and headed back down the trail. Kate began forming the story lead in her head.

Kessler Has No Ties to FON

Nov. 5 — Timothy Kessler is not a member of the Forces of Nature (FON).

The group's founder, known only as Professor Bob, confirmed that in the only interview ever given by a member of this radical environmentalist group.

"Aside from checking out the website, he's had no contact with anyone in FON," Professor Bob said. "He's not in a cell. He's never attended any meetings. He's not connected with FON in any way, shape or form."

Winslow Beach Beacon

26. REPERCUSSIONS

KATE WAS ON HER LAST VERIFICATION CALL FOR HER FORCES OF Nature story. Even though she was under the gun to get it done by deadline, she wanted to be absolutely sure every word was confirmed by an independent source.

She'd already spoken to an Antioch administration official, who had informed her that a biology professor named Robert Stimson had taught there from 1977 to 1995. His departure coincided with the beginning of the Forces of Nature.

She went over all her information on the Forces of Nature, looking for names of people she could contact, and there were precious few. However, she did manage to track down a former member living in Nebraska who had never met Professor Bob but knew who he was and agreed that the man she described was probably him.

Finally, she inundated the Forces of Nature website with e-mails requesting an interview with Mike Lohrman. She was just about to hand her story in when Lohrman called.

Kate couldn't remember the last time she had spoken to anyone so condescending and full of himself.

"Well, I'd really advise against you running this story," he began. "I don't see any relevance to our mission. I'm only calling you out of respect for our founder."

"So, I did speak to Bob Stimson then?"

"Yes, you did, and I certainly hope you don't use his last name. Due to our concerted efforts to maintain secrecy, the FBI has no idea as to his true identity, and we want to keep it that way. If Bob is captured, he could be sent to prison for the rest of his life. Or even get the death penalty. Do you want that on your conscience? I don't know what possessed him to talk to a reporter, especially one from a rinky-dink little newspaper in some Southern backwater. You know, none of our members has ever spoken to a reporter before."

Professor Bob was right, this guy was a horse's ass and an idiot. The FBI had to know Bob's true identity. If she could find it out, they certainly could.

"There's a first time for everything," Kate said, tactfully ignoring the insult to her paper and her hometown. "And I doubt if he'd get the death penalty or life in prison. It's my understanding that he's only been charged with arson."

"Hey, it could happen. The polluters and defilers are out for Bob's blood. I know for a fact that they have a lot of power over the judicial system and if he's caught, they'll fix things so he goes away for good."

Kate said nothing, hoping to avoid a fruitless discussion over the integrity of judicial system and whether the polluters and defilers were really out for Bob Stimson's blood.

"Anyway, Bob has instructed me to tell you that everything he said is true."

Good, Lohrman had returned to his spokesman mode.

"The Forces of Nature had nothing to do with the fire out there, and while the FON supports the idea of destroying structures that are harmful to the environment, it does not harm living beings. And that includes humans. The young man on trial for murder is definitely not a member, and aside from one e-mail and a download, he's had no contact with the organization."

"Then why has there been no statement from the Forces of Nature on the Timothy Kessler trial?"

There was a long, theatrical sigh at the end of the line. Professor Bob had said Mike Lohrman served his purpose, but at the moment Kate believed his only purpose was annoying her no end.

"I thought I'd made myself clear on this," he said. "Timothy Kessler is not a member of the Forces of Nature. The fire at that place — what's it called? Brittany Beach?"

"Normandy Sands."

"Whatever. Anyway, as I said, the Forces of Nature had nothing to do with that event, and therefore, it was decided that no comment should be made. Let me spell it out for you. The Forces of Nature has no association whatsoever with Timothy Kessler. It has neither offered support nor condemnation for his actions. While I'm confirming that Professor Bob, as he is known, did, indeed, speak to you, as the spokesman for the Forces of Nature, I want to emphasize that the organization has nothing to say about the destruction of the house in Normandy Sands, and nothing to say about the ongoing trial of Timothy Kessler. Have you got that?"

"Yes, you know nothing."

"No, I'm saying nothing. There's a difference."

"Whatever. Thank you for getting back to me, Mr. Lohrman."

"Yes, yes, of course," he said and hung up.

Quickly, she filled in the quotes from Lohrman.

"Roger! I'm finished. You can edit the FON story now."

Roger ran out of his office and stood over her chair.

"I'll just eyeball it from here. Your copy is generally clean, and we really don't have the time to go over it with a fine tooth comb." He leaned over and read off the terminal. "Holy smokes, this is one hell of a story, Kate. I couldn't believe it when you told me about meeting this guy in the woods, and I can't believe it now."

"It's true. I spent most of the morning verifying my facts. Including Bob's identity, which I'm not printing. He didn't want me to use his last name, and I'm respecting that."

"Yes, I can see it. Fine case of solid reporting."

"Yeah, not bad for a reporter from a rinky-dink newspaper in some Southern backwater," she said. "That's what Mike Lohrman called us. I left that out."

"Thank you, I appreciate that. Listen, Kate, I do have to warn you. At the very least, this story is going to cause you some major headaches. The FBI will want to talk to you, and probably the district attorney as well. Do you think you can handle that without compromising your source?"

"Yeah, I think so." She knew she didn't sound entirely confident.

"We will back you up one-hundred percent, but remember our resources are limited. You'll probably be out there on your own."

"I'll be okay. All I have to do is quote the First Amendment and leave it at that, right?"

"Well, yes, but it's not as easy as it sounds. If it's any comfort, North

Carolina has a shield law. You can't be compelled to reveal a source."

"I can handle it, Roger. Really."

"I hope so. Well, the printer is waiting. Hit the send button, and let's go. Let me buy you lunch."

"That sounds good, considering it's almost one o'clock."

An hour later, Kate was enjoying an overstuffed chicken salad sandwich at the deli down the block, still basking in the glory of her exclusive interview with the fugitive Professor Bob. She didn't see the three men in suits and dark glasses as they came in the door, but she did notice the uniformed Wilmington police officer with them. She was about to make a lame joke to Roger about no doughnuts for sale here when they all headed toward her table.

"Are you Kate Dennison?" the uniformed officer asked.

Smith Fundraiser Slated

Nov. 5 — The Committee to Re-Elect Claybourne Smith District Attorney will hold a fundraising dinner this Thursday at the Pirate's Cove Restaurant in Wrightsville Beach. Cocktails at 6 p.m., followed by dinner at 7.

"Mr. Smith has taken a firm stand against crime in New Hanover County," said Committee spokesman Chuck Abbot. "All concerned citizens are urged to attend."

Winslow Beach Beacon

25. WE HAVE WAYS OF MAKING
YOU TALK

WOULD YOU LIKE SOME COFFEE?" ASKED ASSISTANT DISTRICT
Attorney Jeffrey Kellogg. Tall and blond with a round boyish face,
the young lawyer smiled politely at Kate, who fidgeted in her chair.

The motley group of law enforcement agents had brought her to a
conference room in the district attorney's office. Looking around the
long table, she might have been attending a city council committee
meeting. The uniformed officer had left so it was just her, Jeffrey
Kellogg, the FBI agent who'd been introduced as Agent Clarkson, and
one other man dressed in a dark suit who had yet to identify himself.

At least she wasn't in some dirty basement with a bare light bulb
hanging in her face.

Kellogg was unfailingly polite. She hadn't expected her interrogator
to be so civil. This was the third time he had offered her coffee. She
wasn't going to have any, though. She'd read somewhere that a common
ploy during an interrogation was to ply the subject with liquids and then
deny permission to use the bathroom.

She was willing to die for the First Amendment, but she wasn't so
sure about wetting her pants.

"No, thank you."

"It's a fresh pot. I made it myself. Are you sure you wouldn't like
something to drink?"

"I'd really like to check on my daughter. Don't I get a phone call?"

"Your daughter is fine. Just answer our questions, and you can walk
out of here."

"I'm sorry. I told you all I can. Under the First Amendment, I have
the right to protect my source."

"Even when that source is responsible for murder?" Kellogg asked.

"Responsible for murder? The only reason he talked to me is because..." She cut herself off, realizing she was about to say more than she should.

"Because what, Kate?" Clarkson asked in a voice so loud it made her jump. Handsome, polite young Kellogg retired into the shadows as the FBI agent took over.

"Tell us why Bob Stimson talked to you," Clarkson continued. "Yes, we know his last name. We know a lot about that group of wackos. And you're going to tell us more."

He loomed over her even though he was not a physically imposing man. He was barely an inch or two taller than she was, with thinning brown hair and pale and oily skin, but she found him very intimidating. She had the feeling he could attack like a Rottweiler, and that in the course of the afternoon, he probably would.

Just stay calm, she told herself. You'll get through this.

"I've told you all I can. I met Professor Bob in the western part of the state. If you want to know what he told me, buy a copy of the *Beacon* tomorrow."

"We've already read your story, Ms. Dennison," Clarkson said.

"But the paper's not out yet. They've just started printing it."

"We have our own sources, just like you," Clarkson said. "By the way, I'd watch my back at the paper of yours. You've made some serious enemies."

"Serious enemies?" Kate gave a nervous laugh. "I'm not important enough to have enemies, let alone serious ones."

Clarkson's red face darkened to purple. She could see the pit bull rising.

"Let me set you straight on this, Ms. Dennison. You are important. You are very important to our investigation into the Forces of Nature and the murder of John Cochran and Warren Owens. And you have made enemies, starting right here with me. Where is Bob Stimson?"

"I can't tell you that."

"How did you get in contact with him?"

"I can't tell you that."

"Who set up the meeting for you?"

"I can't tell you that."

"Tell us, or you'll never see your daughter again!" Clarkson screamed.

Kate felt her stomach wrenching. To save her daughter, she was ready to tell them everything she knew. She could tell them how Bryan set it all up, the exact spot where the meeting took place and which direction she saw Bob heading when he left. She was ready to make up a few things as well.

No, Bryan could lose his job. Besides, she was a journalist. She had to protect her sources, despite the threats of an apoplectic FBI agent. She'd made her decision when she wrote that story.

"I'm sorry," she said in a shaky voice. "I can't tell you."

"You can tell us now or tell us later," drawled the unidentified man in the corner. "But you will tell us. Or face the consequences."

The man stood up. He was a good deal older than the others with a much nicer suit and a bit of a paunch. He walked over to Kate.

"Let me introduce myself, Ms. Dennison. I'm Claybourne Smith, District Attorney of New Hanover County. We're mighty interested in what you have to say, as we believe our boy Timmy Kessler wasn't acting alone when he set that house on fire. We think he's protecting Bob Stimson, just the way you're protecting Bob Stimson. Don't know what spell this man has put on the two of you, but it's got to stop now. Tell us what you know and you can go home now and see that little girl of yours."

"And if I don't?" Kate asked, not sure if she wanted to hear the answer.

"Well, I happen to have a subpoena with your name on it, ordering you to appear before a grand jury."

He reached into his pocket and pulled out an envelope and handed it to Kate. She opened it up.

> You are hereby commanded to appear and testify
> before the Grand Jury of the New Hanover County
> District Court at the date and time specified below:

Kate saw that today's date and the time "11:00 AM" had been scribbled in the space. She was already four and a half hours late.

"The grand jury's right down the hall. At this very moment sixteen residents of New Hanover County are waiting for you to walk in and testify under oath about Robert Stimson. I'd be happy to walk you down to the courtroom. You can be in and out in half an hour, forty-five minutes tops. So what do you say, Miss Dennison?"

"I can't reveal my source."

"Does that mean you're refusing to testify?"

"Yes," she said in voice that was barely above a whisper.

"Then I will have no choice but to have you cited for contempt of court. When you walk out that door, you're either going to the grand jury room or the county jail."

He had to be bluffing. There was a law protecting journalists from being forced to reveal their sources. Roger had said so.

"You can't do that. North Carolina has a shield law."

"And you're welcome to cite that in your appeal, Ms. Dennison. You're still going to jail if you refuse to testify."

Jail.

Kate had always known there was a possibility of going to jail, but she never believed it would come to that. She was just a reporter for a rinky-dink newspaper in some Southern backwater. She was supposed to be covering deadly dull council meetings and photographing school plays. She couldn't go to jail. She was someone's mom.

"That's it, Ms. Dennison," Smith said quietly. "You just think on it for a while, and when you're ready, the grand jury will be too. We're in no hurry. Course, pretty soon it's going to be your little girl's bedtime. She's gonna be missin' her mama about now, don't you think?"

Despite her best effort, Kate felt tears welling in her eyes. The thought of Molly getting ready for bed without her was too much to bear. She hoped Marlene remembered to read her a story and kiss her goodnight.

But who would tell her that she was the best kid in the whole world?

She took a deep breath.

"I'm sorry. I won't testify. I have to protect my source."

"I'm sorry too, Ms. Dennison," Smith said, walking over to the door. He opened it, and two uniformed police officers entered.

"Boys, come on in here and take Ms. Dennison over to the county jail," he said. "Now, none of that rough stuff. And Ms. Dennison, any time you're ready to talk let one of the guards know. We'll be waitin' for you."

As the police officers placed the handcuffs on her and led her out of the conference room, Kate wondered how in the hell she'd get out of this mess.

New Jail Still Overcrowded

Nov. 5 — Despite its new facility opened in 2004, the New Hanover County Jail continues to have problems with overcrowding. Located in Castle Hayne, the jail has enough beds for 648 inmates, with 88 of those beds set aside for females. Plans are underway to create more beds without adding space to the building.

Winslow Beach Beacon

27. THE BIG HOUSE

THE NEW HANOVER COUNTY JAIL COULD DO WITH A GOOD SCRUBBING, Kate thought as the two police officers escorted her down the hall to prisoner processing. Of course, it didn't help that there were no windows in the cinder block walls. The fluorescent lights overhead were unforgivingly harsh; every speck of dirt and grime showed.

There was a strong disinfectant smell in the air, but it wasn't strong enough to mask the unpleasant odors created by six hundred people crammed together in small spaces. Although she could hear the furnace running full blast, she felt cold and wished she'd brought a sweater with her. Then again, they'd probably confiscate it.

They reached their destination, a large open area with a bank of computers behind a semi-circular white wooden counter. There were three guards stationed there, two men and a large, heavy-set woman.

"Here's the contempt charge," one of the escorting officers said placing a stack of papers on the counter.

"Thanks, boys. See you 'round."

The female guard took Kate by the arm and led her through a door into a storage area lined with metal shelves floor to ceiling. She handed her a large zippered plastic bag, a towel and an orange jumpsuit.

"Take off your clothes and put them in here," she instructed.

Kate said nothing, just stared at the jumpsuit.

This can't be happening to me, she thought.

"Don't worry, honey," the woman said. "I've seen enough naked bodies, I don't notice no more."

Despite her shaking fingers, Kate managed to undress herself. Blouse, skirt, pantyhose all dropped into the bag. Standing in her underwear, under the scowl of a uniformed stranger, she had never felt so humiliated in her life. And then it got worse.

"Take off your undies, girl. We'll be doing a body cavity search."

Kate obliged.

The guard pulled a pair of surgical rubber gloves out of a box on the desk and snapped them on.

"You ain't allergic to latex, are you, hon?"

"No, I'm not," Kate said, her voice hoarse and croaking.

"That's good. We had a gal in here a while back who got one hell of a rash down there cuz she was allergic. You may not think so, but we don't want your stay here to be any harder than it has to be."

And the county doesn't want to get sued, either, Kate thought.

"Okay, let's get started. Bend over, please."

Kate leaned forward and took a deep breath. She tried to imagine herself separate from her body, floating blissfully carefree at the ceiling, but she couldn't help feeling the guard's fingers probing her. She closed her eyes and gritted her teeth.

"Nothing in here. Okay, hon, you can stand up and get dressed." The guard snapped off her gloves and put them in a white trash can marked with a large orange bio-hazard logo.

"That wasn't so bad now, was it?" she said as Kate straightened up.

Kate nodded her head and gave the woman a weak smile. All in all, it had been no more uncomfortable than her last pelvic exam, although she would have preferred to have had the paper gown.

She pulled on the jumpsuit and chafed at the stiff, scratchy material. There were brown stains on the front left by the previous wearer. Kate hoped it was from food.

"Now, you only get one suit a week, so you'll want to try to keep yourself clean," the guard advised. "Make a mess on it, and you wear it."

The thought of staying in here for a week terrified her, but she was well aware that contempt-of-court charges were open-ended. She would stay here until she decided to talk to the District Attorney. It was quite possible she'd be in jail for months.

Don't think about it, she told herself.

"Sign this, honey. It's a list of all your belongings. You'll get them back when you leave."

She signed the form, her hands shaking so much her signature was barely legible. The guard put her clothes in a file box with a number on it and shoved it onto one of the shelves.

"Okay, hon, it's time to go to your cell."

Outside the storage room, to where the two male guards were waiting for her. One of them held a set of chains.

"I'm sorry, honey, we're going to have to shackle you. County policy. I promise you they won't be too tight and you'll still be able to walk."

Meekly, Kate put her hands out and her wrists and ankles were enclosed in the chains.

This was the worst moment of her life, bar none.

Each of the male guards took her by an arm, and she shuffled down the hall to a barred gate, her chains jingling as she walked. It reminded her of sleigh bells, but Christmas seemed a thousand years ago and a million miles away from here.

What was she doing in this place? Jail was for criminals. She'd never broken a law in her life. She'd never had a speeding ticket, she always returned her library books by the due date, she paid her bills on time, she didn't even litter. And here she was, a shackled prisoner, being escorted to her cell like a murderer or a thief, about to be thrown into a cage full of hardened criminals who'd probably beat her to a pulp.

They unlocked the gate and escorted her into the women's section.

All around her women yelled. They called the guards names. They called her names. Besides the yelling, she could hear women screaming, and a few crying. It sounded like she'd walked into the depths of hell. It took every ounce of strength she had to put one foot in front of the other.

"Here we are. Meet your new roommates."

One guard unlocked the shackles while the other opened the cell. Inside were two women and two bunks containing black vinyl pads that served as beds. Against the middle of the opposite wall was a metal toilet

"Sorry you don't get a bed," the officer added. "There was a big prostitution bust this morning and we have a full house. We'll be bringing a blanket for you later."

Kate promised herself that when she was released, she would never take privacy for granted again.

They locked the door behind her and walked away.

Her cell-mates clustered around her.

"What did a rich white woman like you do to get yourself in here? Beat the maid?" the bigger one demanded. She was African American and built like an Amazon, more than six feet tall and muscular. Kate did not want to tangle with her.

"Uh, I'm in here for contempt of court."

"What, you call the judge names? Shame on you," the second inmate taunted. This one was white, with greasy brown hair and tattoos on her arms.

"I'm a reporter. I wouldn't reveal where I got my information, so the judge put me in jail."

She could feel her lip quivering. She prayed she didn't cry. She could tell these women were testing her, and if she failed the test they would skin her alive.

"Like, they wanted you to rat someone out, right?" the Amazon said.

"Yes, they wanted me to rat someone out. But I didn't do it."

Amazon Woman slapped her on the back and gave her a broad smile.

"That takes a lot of guts. 'Specially if they puttin' you in here. Ain't that right, Crystal?"

The other woman gave loud assent.

"So, whatcha do? Work for the television?" Crystal wanted to know.

"No, I work for a newspaper; the *Winslow Beach Beacon*."

"Winslow Beach? That where you from?" Amazon Woman asked.

"No, I live in Sunset Park. Can't afford to live in Winslow Beach."

"Hey, my sister live near there. She take care of my kids, and they go to school at Sunset Park. You got any kids, Miss Reporter?"

"Yes, I have a little girl in second grade. And she goes to Sunset Park."

"Get outta here. My little girl in second grade, too. Who's her teacher?"

"Mrs. Gibson."

"My baby in Miss Harrell's class."

"That's Molly's reading teacher. She's very nice. I've talked to her lots of times."

"She a good teacher?"

"Excellent. It's a great school. I'm so glad Molly goes there."

"I got me two little girls, Ta'Quisha and Moquia. Ta'Quisha the one in second grade. Moquia go to kindergarten. My sister is doing all right with them. They good kids."

Amazon Woman smiled, but there was a deep sadness in her eyes. Kate couldn't imagine how horrible it would be to have your children raised by someone else, even if it was your sister.

"By the way, my name's Kate. What's yours?"

"My name Shalonda, and this is Crystal," she said, introducing the other woman.

It wasn't exactly like a slumber party, and Kate knew they wouldn't be friends; but she was no longer in fear of her life and, as the women talked wistfully about their own children, Kate realized what she'd always known: that mothers can always find common ground.

Giving out a grateful prayer, she knew she'd be all right.

TODAY'S BIBLE VERSE

I was hungry and you fed me, thirsty and you gave me drink; I was a stranger and you received me in your homes, naked and you clothed me. I was sick and you took care of me, in prison and you visited me.

Matthew 25:35-36

28. SINGING LIKE A CANARY

KATE WAS ALREADY AWAKE WHEN THE GUARDS GAVE THE SIGNAL FOR the prisoners to get up. All the beds had been taken, so as the newest occupant she'd had to sleep on the floor. Her body was stiff and aching from eight hours on solid concrete.

Even if she'd gotten a bed, though, she doubted if she'd have gotten any sleep. The jail was a very noisy place, with the sounds of the women snoring and moaning and one inmate who yelled obscenities nonstop until well after midnight. And there was no such thing as "lights out," the lights stayed on all night.

She got to her feet and folded up her blanket, careful not to get in anybody else's way. Shalonda had warned her the night before to watch herself at all times, as there were women here who would kill her as soon as look at her.

The guards arrived to escort them to breakfast. Judging from the dinner she had received the night before, Kate was not expecting much in the way of variety when she got to the prison cafeteria. They had their choice of boxed cereal with a carton of milk or a generic-looking frosted toaster pastry, but most of those were gone by the time she got to the front of the line. She picked up a box of cornflakes and followed the guard to her selected seat.

Sitting with all the woman at the long table reminded her of the social hierarchy at her high school. Apparently, there was no "in-crowd" table in jail; the guards made sure of that. She took her cue from her fellow prisoners, who quietly ate their breakfast, looking neither left nor right.

When the meal was over, they were taken back to their cells.

Kate soon realized that the hardest thing to take in jail was not the fear or the discomfort or the separation from her daughter, or even the loss of her freedom. It was boredom. The minutes crawled by with absolutely nothing to fill them. In time, they would go to the jail's common room where they would be allowed to cluster around the tiny black-and-white television set to watch The Montel Williams Show. Right now, that wait seemed like an eternity.

A guard arrived at the cell door.

"Visitors for Dennison and Jones!" he announced.

She and Shalonda were led down the corridor to a room with orange plastic seats along a thick Plexiglas wall. Small partitions separated the seats, and there was a telephone handset in each booth.

Sitting on the other side of the Plexiglas wall was the minister of her church, the Reverend Teresa Baird. She'd never been so glad to see another living soul in her life.

She sat down across from Teresa and picked up the phone.

"Hello, Kate, is there anything I can get for you?"

"No, I'm fine. Okay, I'm not fine, but I have everything I need. But you could check on Molly for me. She's at Roger and Marlene's house; they live next door to me. Roger's my boss, did I tell you that? Call the *Beacon* and ask for Roger Hoffman. If you could visit Molly this afternoon, that would be great. I don't know how long I'll be in here."

"The Presbyterian Women's Group is praying for you, and you know God never says no to those ladies. You should be out of here in no time."

Kate remembered the sweet group of old ladies in the Women's Group and smiled at the thought of their generosity of spirit.

"I never thought I'd be in jail. I don't suppose you spend a lot of time visiting church members here."

"You'd be surprised. Even the best of us runs afoul of the law sometimes. And you're here because you kept a promise. We're all very proud of you for that."

Kate laid her head on her crossed arms and began to cry, still clutching the phone receiver in her hand.

"Kate, Kate, it's all right." Teresa's voice seemed to come from miles away, even though they were inches apart.

"Teresa, I can't do this," she sobbed. "I hate it in here! I don't care about keeping my promises or the First Amendment. I just want to go home and see my little girl. Would I be a horrible person if I told them what they wanted to know?"

She sat up, looking straight at the minister through the glass.

Teresa smiled and placed her left hand on the glass.

"You are a good person, and we will all stand by you no matter what you decide to do," she said.

"So, what should I do?" Kate asked, placing her hand on the glass opposite Teresa's.

"Whatever you think is best."

"But I don't know what's best! Contempt of court means if I don't cooperate I stay here as long as the judge wants me to. That could be weeks or months or even years. I can't stand to be away from Molly for that long."

"Honestly, Kate, I can't tell you what to do. All I can say is that we love you and God loves you no matter what your decision is."

Kate was still for a minute, then said quietly, "Whispers in my heart."

"What was that?"

"Your last sermon. Instead of a looking for a neon sign or a burning bush, listen to the whispers in your heart. Guess if I stop and listen, I'll figure out what to do."

Teresa gave a broad smile.

"It sure is nice to know someone actually paid attention to one of my sermons. Would you like me to pray with you?"

Kate never much cared for praying in public places, aside from church where it was expected. She looked around nervously. Oh, well, if ever there was a time in her life when she needed the power of prayer, this was it.

"Yes," she replied and bowed her head.

"Dear Heavenly Father, please be with Kate in her hour of need. Help her hear the whispers in her heart and give her peace. Give her the strength to get through this difficult time. And please watch over her daughter Molly, keeping her safe and happy. In Jesus' name we pray. Amen."

A feeling of peace washed over Kate. She knew she would not be saying a word to the district attorney. At least, not today.

"I'll come back again tomorrow. And I'll check on Molly for you."

"Thanks, Teresa."

Their goodbyes were interrupted by a guard.

"Come with me, Ms. Dennison."

"But visiting hours aren't over yet," Kate protested. Still she stood up and allowed him to escort her out the door.

"I wouldn't complain if I were you," he said. "You're getting out."

Hulick Announces Retirement

Nov. 5 — Superior Court Judge Keenan P. Hulick has announced his retirement at the end of this year. With his tough-as-nails, no-nonsense attitude, Judge Hulick has presided over many important criminal cases through his thirty years on the bench. Currently, he is hearing the case against Timothy Kessler in the murder of John Cochran and Warren Owens.

Winslow Beach Beacon

29. SEE ME IN CHAMBERS

THE GUARDS TOOK KATE BACK TO THE SAME PROCESSING AREA WHERE her ordeal began the day before.

"Dennison, Katherine," one read from his clipboard. "To be released on her own recognizance, it says here."

There was a different set of personnel behind the desk, but it was still the same gender mix — two men and a woman. The woman looked over the paperwork then came out from behind the desk and took Kate's arm.

"Come with me, Ms. Dennison," she said and escorted Kate back to the storage room where she'd been strip searched, not something she particularly wanted to remember.

"Wait right there while I get your things." She disappeared behind the shelves.

Kate wondered why there were no guards to keep an eye on her for the minute and a half it took to retrieve the plastic bag with her clothes in it. She could possibly escape. But then again, they were in the process of releasing her, and who in their right mind would want to wander down Blue Clay Road in a bright-orange prison-issue jumpsuit?

"Here you go, Ms. Dennison. And remember, we're like the restaurants — we're not responsible for lost articles, so if something's missing you're out of luck."

Kate took the plastic bag and checked the contents. Everything was there, including the seven dollars and change she'd had in her wallet, along with her credit cards.

"You can get dressed now," the guard said.

Although thankfully there was no strip search, Kate still had to endure the indignity of once again taking off her clothes in front of a total stranger. Her skirt and blouse were limp and wrinkled, having been stuffed none too gently into the plastic bag. She was glad there were no mirrors. She knew she looked a mess, her hair needed combing, and more than anything she wanted a hot shower and clean clothes. She couldn't wait to get home.

When she was dressed and ready to go, the guard took her back to the processing desk, where she signed a number of forms.

"I can go home now?" she asked tentatively after the last of the papers was signed.

"No, Judge Hulick wants to see you," the guard informed her. "We'll give you a ride down there. Ordinarily, you'd be on your own as far as getting home, but what Judge Hulick wants, Judge Hulick gets."

"Shouldn't he be in the courtroom, presiding over the Kessler trial?"

"The jury went into deliberations last night, so don't worry, he's got plenty of time. Hey, Bill! Take the lady to Judge Hulick's office."

The man sitting behind the counter looked up from his computer terminal in the back got up and came over to the desk.

"Sure thing."

Bill was the youngest of the three on duty; he looked to be in his late twenties, tall with thinning blond hair and a friendly smile. Kate wondered how he managed to stay so cheerful working in a jail.

"This way, Ms. Dennison," he said, escorting her down the hall to freedom.

"What's the judge going to do?" Kate asked.

"Beats me. We just got a call saying someone else told them what they needed to know and we were supposed to let you out, but the judge wanted to talk to you."

"What would happen if I just left and didn't talk to him at all?"

"Maybe nothing, but if I were you I wouldn't risk it. Mind you, I'm not a lawyer, but I'd say chances are he'd see that as another act of contempt and you'd be back in jail. Besides it's a free ride downtown, where I'm assuming you left your car."

"Good point," she said.

She said nothing more to the officer as they walked outside. She was too tired to make conversation. She concentrated on walking, which was a lot easier without the shackles. Officer Bill took her to a cruiser and opened the door for her. Once again she'd be riding through Wilmington in the back of a police cruiser, which she expected to be just as humiliating as it was the first time. But at least she got a ride downtown where her car was parked.

The sound of the engine lolled her to sleep. She awoke with a start when the car came to a halt.

"We're here," he announced. Quickly, he got out of the driver's seat and opened her door. Kate appreciated the chivalry, then remembered that the doors to the backseat of a police car don't open from the inside.

Still she thanked him for the effort.

He escorted her into the court house and down the crowded corridor to a large door that said "Judge Hulick, Superior Court." Bill opened the door for her and she entered the outer office. A middle-aged woman sat behind the desk, a nameplate proclaiming her to be Margaret Kleiman, Clerk to Judge Hulick.

"This is Kate Dennison," Bill said. "Judge wanted to see her."

Kate was painfully aware of the wrinkles in her clothes. She probably smelled, too, not having had a shower since yesterday morning. And her hair was tangled. Couldn't the judge reschedule?

Ms. Kleiman picked up the phone and punched a button.

"Ms. Dennison is here, Judge...Yes, I'll send her back." She looked at Kate.

"Judge Hulick will see you now. Go through that door right there."

"Well, I'll see you later, Ms. Dennison. Good luck," Bill said.

"Thank you. Good luck to you, too," Kate told him, deciding it couldn't hurt to be pleasant even to one's jailers. Then, taking a deep breath, she walked into the judge's office. Ready to face the lions waiting for her beyond the door.

Judge Hulick sat behind an immense mahogany desk that should have dwarfed him, but even outside of the courtroom, he still had that aura of power and authority. He was not wearing his robes but a dark blue suit and an old-fashioned bow tie.

Then Kate noticed there was someone else in the room, sitting in the chair in front of the judge's desk. He turned and smiled at her.

"Thank you for your help in this matter, Mr. Haas," the judge said. "You can wait outside for your friend, while I talk to her."

Bryan and Judge Hulick? Was it Bryan who told them what they wanted to know?

He passed her, briefly touching her hand.

"Don't worry," he whispered. "See you outside."

The door closed behind him, and Kate stood alone before the judge. She trembled, feeling like a kid in front of the principal, only ten times worse, as this man could throw her back in jail.

"Have a seat, Ms. Dennison," he said, pointing to the chair Bryan had just vacated.

She sat, locking her hands together in her lap so the judge couldn't see them shaking. She didn't want the judge to know how afraid she was. Then again, he probably already knew.

"I suppose you want to know why you're here," he continued. "I wanted to get a few things straightened out. First, you may think you were upholding your First Amendment principles when you refused to cooperate with Claybourne Smith, but you were mistaken. In reality, you provided protection for a ruthless criminal, and in my book that makes you just as guilty as he is."

"But – "

"Let me finish. As I said, I found absolutely no merit to your First Amendment defense, but as you see, Mr. Haas came forward and provided the investigation with the needed information. So, there was no reason to keep you in custody any longer. And I believe one night in jail is enough for anybody. Now, Ms. Dennison, you may speak."

Kate couldn't think of anything to say at first. The judge was probably expecting an apology, but she wasn't sorry. Anything she said to justify her actions would fall on deaf ears. His opinion was clear and unshakable.

"I did what was right," she said firmly. "I did my job."

"Very well, Ms. Dennison, you may go. But just remember, if this happens again, if any reporter or newsperson tries this again under my jurisdiction, I will act exactly as I did this time."

"I'll pass that along." She got up to leave. She didn't say goodbye, and neither did the judge.

She hurried past Ms. Kleiman's desk and outside, where she found Bryan waiting for her. Standing there, smiling, he was the one person she most wanted to see at that moment. He wrapped his arms around her, and she clung to him like a child. All around, the courthouse population swarmed past, but she didn't notice. She finally felt safe. And she felt connected to Bryan in a way she'd never known.

He had come all this way to get her out of jail. Never again would she refer to him as the tall skinny guy who couldn't commit.

Beacon Reporter
Cited for Contempt

Nov. 12 — *Winslow Beach Beacon* Reporter Kate Dennison was released Tuesday morning from New Hanover County Jail after being charged with contempt of court by Judge Keenan Hulick. Ms. Dennison refused to reveal information as to the whereabouts of her source for a recent story on the Forces of Nature, a controversial environmental group known for their militant tactics.

Winslow Beach Beacon

30. OUT OF THE JOINT

KATE? ARE YOU ALL RIGHT?"

No one paid attention to the disheveled woman having a crying jag outside the judge's door as she sobbed into his shirt. Apparently, that type of behavior was commonplace in the courthouse. They probably assumed she'd been charged with drunk-and-disorderly coming off of a three-day bender.

"Yuh-yes. I'm fine," she said, sniffling. Great. She was stinky and unkempt and now her face was puffy and tear-streaked. She was still at the stage where she wanted to look her best for her boyfriend, and here she was crying like a schoolgirl. Guys hated that.

"I'm sorry. I-I didn't get much sleep last night," she said.

"Why don't we go somewhere for coffee? I expect you'd like to get out of here."

"I could use some coffee, but I don't want to go anywhere looking like this."

"Like what? You look great," he said, smiling that goofy grin she loved so much.

"Have I told you lately how wonderful you are?"

"Actually, you've never said a word about how wonderful I am, but that's okay. I already know."

With his arm around her, they walked out onto Princess Street. It was a clear sunny day, and Kate wanted to drink in the air. It felt so great to be outside.

"Beautiful day, isn't it? Is it always this warm in November?"

"Mostly. It does get cold here in the winter. Last January they had a record cold of seventeen degrees."

"Seventeen degrees in January is a big deal? You're kidding. We wouldn't give that a second thought in Ohio."

They crossed Second Street, heading toward the Cape Fear River.

"That looks like a good place to get coffee." He pointed to a storefront restaurant called PJ's Cafe.

"Looks okay to me," Kate said. "I think I'll stay out here, if you don't mind." After spending the night in a tiny cell, she preferred staying outside in the open air.

"You take your coffee black, right?"

"Black with sweetener," she corrected.

"Comin' up."

A little bell rang on the door as he went in. She watched him through the window. He chatted easily with the woman behind the counter, probably talking about the weather. Just like they'd been doing.

How silly. Here she was, full of questions, and all they could talk about was the temperature in January.

Bryan collected his change and picked up two Styrofoam cups. She opened the door for him. Then she took the lid off the cup he handed her and sipped the steaming hot liquid. After the coffee in the jail, this was heaven. As good as anything she'd ever had at Starbucks or Port City Java.

"There's a bench over there. How about we sit down and talk?"

"Fine with me," she said.

They settled on one of the benches lining Front Street. Kate said nothing for a minute, watching the cars going past.

"So, what brings you to Wilmington so soon?" she asked.

"Damage control. Getting you out of the mess I made when I took Bob up on his offer to meet with you."

"It was my choice," she reminded him then added, "and I'd do it again." Although she was not entirely sure she would want to spend another night at the New Hanover County Jail.

"Frank Wells called me last night, said he'd heard on the news you'd gone to jail for refusing to reveal your source. Right away, I was sure the FBI would want to know how you hooked up with Bob. I could tell them everything they wanted to get from you, and I wouldn't be violating any confidences. Bob has always been careful about keeping his whereabouts secret. I hear from him by email, and it's a different address every time. He doesn't tell me where he is, and I don't ask.

"I called the FBI field office in Raleigh and told them I had information about Bob Stimson I wanted to share. It wasn't easy. You'd think all the guy had to do was call someone in Wilmington and let them know I was ready to spill my guts, but first they had to talk to me in Raleigh, then they wanted me to come to Wilmington. I told them everything: how I communicate with Bob, where we met him, what he had to say. I even printed up all the emails so they could take a look."

"But you were handing Bob over to the FBI," she protested.

"No, Bob's too smart for that. He knows how to hide in plain sight. They've been looking for him for years, and they've never come close to finding him. So, I was a hell of a lot more worried about you than about him. Everything you could tell them I could tell them just as well, and I figured once they had what they wanted, they'd have no reason to keep you in jail. And that's exactly how it worked out. The only bad part was having to sit through a lecture about law and order from that old coot judge."

"I could have handled it myself," Kate said.

"Okay, if that's the way you feel, I'll see if I can get you back in jail so you can keep handling it yourself." There was a sarcastic edge to his voice.

"Bryan, don't be like that!" she cried. "I just meant you didn't have to do that. And the fact that you did just amazes me. I don't think I've ever felt so grateful to another human being in my entire life. Thank you, thank you, thank you."

Putting her coffee on the ground, she threw her arms around him and hugged him as tight as she could.

"Thank you," she whispered.

"You're welcome," he whispered back. He bent down and met her lips in a long, sweet kiss. "I'd do it again, too," he said. "Wouldn't want the woman I love to be locked up for the rest of her life."

My God, Kate thought. He just said the L word.

"The woman you love?"

"Yes, the woman I love. Always have, always will. Just never knew it until now. But don't expect me to say it all the time." He slurped the last of his coffee then threw the empty cup into a nearby trash can. "Kate, I'd really like to stay here with you, but I've got to get back to Raleigh. I know I've got a load of voice mails, all of 'em wanting to know where the hell I've been and what am I doing with that radical from the Forces of Nature. I'll call you tonight."

"That's okay. I just want to go home and get some sleep. I'm exhausted."

"Come on, I'll take you to your car," he said. Hand-in-hand, they walked up to Fifth Street, where she had parked her car the day before.

Law Firm Hires Tremont

Nov. 12 — Attorney Jennifer Tremont has joined the law firm of Hensley and McCormick.

"We're so pleased to have Jennifer on board," said Senior Partner Carl Hensley. "We specialize in family law, and she is definitely the best in the field. There's no one better in collecting delinquent child support."

Winslow Beach Beacon

31. MISSING

DAMN, IT FELT GOOD TO BE BACK IN HER OWN HOUSE.

Kate was having a hard time staying awake. She dragged herself over to the phone, deciding it best to check in with Marlene to see how Molly was doing. She had intended to call hours ago, but the battery on her cell phone had died during its overnight sojourn in the jail property department and she'd had no way to recharge it.

The call light on the answer machine was flashing wildly. She pressed the play button and the familiar mechanical voice said, "You have twenty-seven messages. Your mailbox is full."

She hit the stop button, not having the patience to listen to twenty-seven phone messages. She was surprised so many people had called her. Or perhaps it was just one person. Anyone that anxious to talk to her would certainly call back.

She hit the speed dial for Marlene and waited for her to answer. When the recorded greeting came on, her heart sank. She really wanted to talk to Marlene. Of course, it was past eleven o'clock, and Molly was in school now. She would just have to wait.

"Marlene, this is Kate. I'm out of jail now and I'm at home. Send Molly over here when she comes back from school, okay? And thanks so much for keeping her overnight. I owe you."

Now it was time to let the *Beacon* know she had been released into the general population. She called the office and punched in Roger's extension.

"Voice mail again?" she complained out loud. "Doesn't anyone answer the phone? Roger, it's Kate. They let me out. I'm home now getting some sleep and I won't be in to work today. Come on over tonight, and I'll tell you all about it. Bye."

Hanging up the phone, she headed for the bathroom, where she peeled off her clothes and threw them into the hamper. Maybe she should burn that skirt and blouse, or at least give them to charity. She had no desire to wear that particular outfit again or even have it in the house.

Kate turned on the hot water and stepped into the shower, letting the stream of water cascade over her. This was paradise. All her trials and tribulations were scrubbed off with a large green cake of mountain fresh deodorant soap. She could stay in here forever.

But eventually the hot water ran out, and she knew she was not going to get any cleaner standing there in the tepid spray. She climbed out and dried herself with a towel, noting how soft and fluffy it was compared to the prison jumpsuit she'd had to wear. She'd never take showers and bath towels for granted again. Or, for that matter, clean underwear, comfortable T-shirts, warm sweat pants and, most of all, the firm queen-size mattress that was all hers.

Kate crawled under the covers and fell asleep.

After several delicious hours of deep sleep, she woke to find it was well past five o'clock and getting dark outside. Her first thought was of her daughter. Molly had gotten home from school hours ago and was waiting for her next door. She had to get a move on, as she knew how upset she must be. She got out of bed and changed into a pair of jeans and a sweater as fast as she could.

Minutes later she stood impatiently at Marlene and Roger's front door, listening to Marlene's footsteps coming to the door and straining her ears to hear Molly's voice. That's odd for her to be so quiet, she thought. Maybe she was in the bathroom.

The door opened. Marlene didn't look nearly as cheerful as she had expected. A night with Molly must have taken the cheeriness right out of her.

She reached out and gave Kate a big hug.

"I'm so glad to see you," she said.

She certainly doesn't look glad, Kate thought. What's she so worried about?

"I'm glad to see you, too, Marlene." She pushed her way past Marlene, straining to hear Molly's voice. Anxiously, she surveyed the room for signs of her daughter and found none. No discarded toys on the couch, no rugs in disarray, no cartoons on the television. Something was terribly wrong here.

"Where's Molly?"

"Come on into the kitchen where we can talk," Marlene said.

Kate didn't like the serious tone of her voice. Nothing good ever started with "Let's talk."

"Marlene, what's going on? Has something happened to Molly? Tell me where she is."

"Sit down, Kate," Marlene said, holding out the kitchen chair. "Molly is fine. She's with her father."

"What's she doing with Keith? Monday isn't one of his visiting days. I talked to you yesterday, you said she was fine."

"And she was. Keith showed up half an hour later. He heard you were in jail, and he wanted Molly to stay with him."

"How did he know I'd gone to jail? It was the middle of the afternoon, and he doesn't listen to the radio at work. They could drop a bomb on Wilmington, and he'd never know."

"You're forgetting Jennifer is a lawyer. One of her cronies down at the courthouse tipped her off, and she called."

Tears of frustration cascaded down Kate's cheeks.

"He's supposed to let me know when he takes her," she cried. "We've got a court agreement, for God's sake! And why did you let her go with him? I trusted you with my daughter, and you really let me down, Marlene."

"Now, hold on a second here, Kate," Marlene said. "Molly wasn't kidnapped. She's with her father who, under the circumstances, had every right to take her. I'm just the babysitter, not a legal guardian. I don't know what's in your custody agreement, but I'm willing to bet Keith is permitted to take care of her when you can't. And it's damn hard to care for your daughter from the inside of the New Hanover County Jail."

She reached over and patted her arm.

"It was only for one night, Kate. He just wanted her to be safe. He's a good father, you've said so yourself. And I couldn't get in touch with you at the jail. I called, and they said under no circumstances would they pass messages along to prisoners. I'd just have to wait until visiting hours. I called the jail this morning to say I was coming in and they told me you'd already been released. There was no way to reach you."

Kate knew she was right, but the disappointment was just too much to bear. No longer able to keep up any semblance of the brave front she'd been clinging to, she buried her face in her hands and sobbed.

Marlene got up from her chair and picked up a box of tissues from the kitchen counter. She pulled one out and handed it to her.

"Here, darlin', dry your eyes," she said. "Then call Keith and tell him you're coming to pick Molly up."

Kate took the tissue, wiped the tears from her face and blew her nose.

"How did you get to be so smart?"

"Age and experience. Mostly age, I think." She smiled.

"I'm sorry for dumping on you, Marlene."

"Don't mention it. To tell you the truth, I was surprised at how well you took it. After a night in jail, I was expecting you to bite my head off."

Kate wadded up the tissue and stuffed it in her jeans pocket, with the intention of tossing it in the first wastebasket she saw. She stood up.

"Don't get up. I can find my way out."

Marlene heaved herself up out of her chair anyway.

"No, I need the exercise," she said, smiling.

Opening the door for her, Marlene gave Kate another warm hug.

"Forget the budget. We've got to give you combat pay."

"I'd settle for features and business shorts for the rest of my career," Kate said. "I still owe you, Marlene."

"Give Molly a kiss for me."

Kate jogged back to her house. Impatient to see Molly, she decided to skip calling Keith and just get going. She opened her front door and grabbed her purse and car keys from the rack.

Feeling that the worst was behind her, she got behind the wheel, put the keys in the ignition and started her car. Her baby would be with her soon and all would be right with the world.

Avoid Custody Battles

Custody battles are very traumatic for children. Often, divorced parents use custody issues as a way to get back at an ex-spouse. The *Beacon* Family Advisor strongly recommends that before any parent embarks on taking legal action to change a custody agreement, he or she is absolutely certain it is in the best interest of the child.

Winslow Beach Beacon

32. Dennison v. Dennison

BEHIND THE WHEEL OF HER CAR, KATE WAS TRYING FOR CALM AND serene, but all she achieved was anxious and tense. It didn't help that the traffic was crawling up Market Street and it seemed like it would be hours before she made it to Middlesound.

She inched her way to the corner of Market and Middlesound Loop Road, and turned right. Within minutes, she was driving through the two large posts of brick and flagstone that marked the entrance to Carrington Downs. As usual, each house looked absolutely perfect: huge brick Tudors alongside classic wooden Colonials. No vinyl siding here. And each home was surrounded by the thousands of dollars of impeccably designed landscaping.

She had lived in this neighborhood for three years and never felt she belonged here. The neighbors were nice enough, but she couldn't shake the belief she'd missed the orientation meeting on how to live among the almost-wealthy. She was not one of them and never would be.

Jennifer's house was at the end of a cul-de-sac, a large lemon-yellow Neo-Classical revival with a huge pillared front porch. Next door was the house Kate and Keith had once owned. It was dark, so Kate couldn't see it very well, but she didn't have to. The imposing three stories of brick towers and pointed rooftops were all too familiar. It hadn't changed too much, although it was apparent the new owners had put some serious money into improving the curb appeal. The front yard was a tangle of shrubbery, and they'd put some kind of abstract metal statue in the middle of the lawn.

She wondered if the house's bad karma had gotten them yet.

She paused on Jennifer's front porch, looking in through the windows. She could see the boys sprawled out in front of the widescreen television, but Molly was nowhere in sight. Then the front door opened and she burst out, flying down the steps and into Kate's outstretched arms. Kate lifted her up and held her as tightly as she could.

Molly's words tumbled out in an excited torrent.

"Mommy, Jennifer said you went to jail and I told her she was wrong, because only bad people go to jail and you're a good person, and she got really mad at me, but then Daddy said it was true and I had to tell Jennifer I was sorry. But you can't go to jail, you're a good person. How could you go to jail, Mommy?"

"I spent last night in jail, but I didn't do anything wrong. I wrote a story about a man and I promised him I wouldn't tell anyone where he is. But a judge said I had to tell or go to jail. I decided it was more important to keep my promise, so I went to jail."

"Then that judge was a bad person."

"No, he thought he was doing the right thing, too," Kate said. "Listen, pumpkin, I've got to put you down, you're just getting too big. Besides it's cold out here and you don't have a sweater on."

She extricated herself from Molly's bear hug and placed her daughter's feet on the floor.

"Okay, Molly, let's get your stuff and go home," she said, opening the heavy oak-and-glass door.

"Can I, Mom? Daddy and Jennifer said I have to stay here for a while."

"They didn't know when I'd be getting out. I didn't know when I'd get out."

They entered Jennifer's foyer. An antique drop-leaf table stood by the stairway. Kate couldn't help cringing whenever she saw it. Jennifer had placed a very expensive antique vase on the table. How she managed to keep it in one piece with her two boys tearing through the hallway was anyone's guess.

At the end of the hallway, she saw Keith and Jennifer sitting at the kitchen table. Empty carry-out bags from an upscale restaurant covered the table. Once again Jennifer was too tired to use her gourmet kitchen to make dinner. Did that woman ever cook at all?

They looked up from their dinner. Judging from the look of surprise on Jennifer's face, her cronies at the courthouse hadn't bothered to leak the news of Kate's release.

"Kate, it's good to see you," Keith said. "Are you all right? Molly was so worried about you. Weren't you, sweetie?"

"Yes, I was really really worried, Mom. I couldn't sleep or eat or anything."

"Molly, why don't you go watch television with the boys?" Jennifer suggested. "Your daddy and I want to talk to Mommy."

"But I want to stay with Mommy," Molly protested, hanging on to Kate's hand.

"Go on, Molly!" Keith said in his stern Daddy voice.

Kate wanted her to stay as well and was about to say so, but she and Keith never contradicted each other in front of Molly.

"Do what Daddy says, pumpkin. I won't be long," she said.

Realizing she was outnumbered, Molly turned and went back into the family room to join Matt and Austin.

"You're very lucky, Kate," Jennifer said. "Judge Hulick's a real hardass. He's held people on contempt charges for months at a time. I was sure you'd be locked up for at least a week."

"That's why I picked Molly up from Marlene's," Keith added. "You know I think the world of Marlene, but Jennifer and I felt it was best if Molly stayed with us. Under the circumstances, she needed to be with family."

"Yes, I understand. Thank you. Now, if you don't mind, I'd like to take Molly home now. It's a school night, and she needs to go to bed soon."

Keith let out a nervous cough.

He's up to something. Something he doesn't feel good about.

"You can't take her home, Kate," Jennifer said.

"What? Of course I can take her home. I'm out of jail. I'm the custodial parent. I'm perfectly able to take care of her now. There's no reason for her to stay here any longer."

"We've been thinking," Keith began.

"It's like this, Kate," Jennifer interrupted. "Since you've taken that job at the paper, you've received death threats, you nearly got yourself blown up and now you've just gotten out of jail. And Frankly, Keith and I have some serious concerns about Molly's safety. It doesn't help that the woman you leave her with has a criminal record."

Kate was flabbergasted.

"Marlene was arrested for marching against the Vietnam War!" she cried. "That's hardly a criminal record. And in any case, that was forty years ago."

"She pleaded guilty to disorderly conduct. That's a crime," Jennifer said.

"But I have custody of Molly. It's in our divorce decree." She looked over to Keith, frantically hoping he'd see reason and set Jennifer straight. Instead he just gave a weak shrug, helpless against Jennifer's steamrolling.

'In light of recent events, your decree definitely needs to be revised," Jennifer announced. "In fact, we've got an order from family court to take emergency custody of Molly. You're free to protest it, and I can recommend any number of fine attorneys who would be willing to take your case. Some of them even do pro bono work."

Kate couldn't help noticing the look of disdain the woman gave her as she delivered her last remark.

"But this is so disruptive for Molly. She lives with me. She's happy with me. Keith, we promised we'd never do this to her. What's going on?"

"You'll still be able to see her," he said. "Don't you think it would be better for her to live here, in a nice neighborhood with a great school?"

"But we already live in a nice neighborhood with a great school. We just don't have topiaries and water features out the ying-yang!"

"Of course, if you quit your job, that might go a long way toward helping family court see things your way," Jennifer suggested. "In fact, there's a researcher's job at my firm you could do. I'm sure you'd have no problem with it. A trained monkey can handle that sort of thing. And it pays much better than that reporter's job you've got. I'd be willing to put in a good word for you. You could even move into Keith's old condo."

The idea of working right under Jennifer's nose and living in Keith's old condo was too much for Kate to stomach. She was just about to say so when Keith intervened.

"Jennifer, let me talk to Kate alone, okay?"

"Sure, fine, it's time for the kids to get ready for bed anyway."

She stalked away toward the sound of the blaring television set.

"What the hell are you doing?" Kate hissed, trying to keep her voice down so Molly wouldn't hear. "How can you let her do this to me?"

"I admit she's been blunt about this, but that's just how she is. I agree with her. You have received death threats, and your office was firebombed. Anyone can find you in the phonebook and attack your house. For now, I think Molly is safer with us. And I really think you should take Jennifer up on that job. You could use the money."

"I hate your condo," Kate said.

"You don't have to live in it. But maybe you should think about moving. For your own safety."

"You can't take Molly away from me," she protested, in tears.

"I don't want to, but for now, I have to. We both want her to be safe. She's safe here. You know it and I know it. Jennifer's right; if you move and get another job, Molly can go back to you. Here, let me get you a tissue."

Keith took the box of Kleenex from the granite counter and handed her one.

Everyone's giving me tissues these days, Kate thought as she blew her nose and wiped her eyes.

Awkwardly, Keith put his arms around her.

"It will be all right, Kate. I promise."

"I guess I'd better go say goodbye to Molly."

"I'll come with you."

Suddenly, Molly came running down the hallway, narrowly missing the drop leaf table in the foyer.

"Mommy!" she screamed. "Jennifer says I can't come with you. I don't want to stay here. I want to go with you!"

She clung to Kate with a vise-like grip.

"I'm sorry, pumpkin. You'll get to come home soon. It's just for a while," Kate assured her.

"Mommy and I think it's good for you to stay here with us, sweetie," Keith added. "You'll get to see her very soon. I promise."

He reached down and pried Molly loose. She continued her hysterics, crying and wriggling and reaching out to Kate.

"I don't want to stay here. I hate it here! I want to go with Mommy!"

Keith held on to his daughter, attempting to calm her down.

"I think you'd better go," Jennifer said.

Kate left the house, her daughter's cries echoing in her ears.

Dennison Stands By Her Principles

By Roger Hoffman

All reporters like to talk about how much they support the First Amendment. But this week, the *Beacon*'s Kate Dennison put her support to the test this week, when she chose to spend a night in the New Hanover County Jail rather than reveal her source. As editor, I have to say I am privileged to have Kate working at this paper. When she took this job, she was told she'd cover the school board and write features. The possibility of jail time was never discussed. Here at the *Beacon*, we're all proud of Kate, and we hope our readers are, too.

33. BETWEEN A ROCK
AND A HARD PLACE

THAT'S ONE POWERFUL REASON FOR QUITTING."

Kate sat across from Roger, wedged into the closet-sized room that served as his office in their temporary headquarters. The office had an excellent view of the Cape Fear River, which cut down on Kate's claustrophobia, but it still reminded her of her jail cell.

She was giving her notice, having explained Keith and Jennifer's ultimatum to him.

"Yes, they didn't leave me much of a choice. Quit my job or lose custody of my daughter. Roger, I love what I do, but I'm not willing to give Molly up to keep working here."

"You think Jennifer might be bluffing?" He leaned back in his chair, and bumping his head on the wall.

"Could be. She's always been pretty sneaky, even though Keith never could see it. She is a lawyer, after all. And you know why sharks don't eat lawyers, don't you?"

"Professional courtesy," Roger said, chuckling. "At least you haven't lost your sense of humor."

"I bet Jennifer could come up with the right forms to take that away, too. 'We have hereby decreed that Katherine Reid Dennison shall never laugh again, smile again or tell another lawyer joke as long as she lives.' Which reminds me, how many lawyers does it take to change a light bulb?"

"How many can you afford?"

Kate laughed, out of desperation more than anything else. It was better than crying.

"Ohh, I got another one," she said. "What's the difference between a lawyer and a prostitute?"

"Now, that one I don't know, Kate. What is the difference between a lawyer and a prostitute?"

"A prostitute will stop screwing you once you're dead."

A steady supply of lawyer jokes and maybe she could keep it together to make it through the day.

"Seriously, Kate, I understand perfectly why you need to leave," Roger said. "I will give you the best reference letter ever written. I'd still like for you give it some time before making your final decision, though. I don't know Keith very well, but I've always thought he was a good father. Good fathers don't do this to their kids."

"Yeah, I'm hoping that eventually cooler heads will prevail. But you never know with Jennifer. She seems to live in a state of perpetual agitation. I don't believe she's ever experienced a cooler head in her life."

"Everything will work out. I know it will. In the meantime, if there's anything Marlene and I can do to help out, let us know. The door's always open, here in this fancy tenement and, of course, back at the house."

"Thanks, Roger. I'm getting plenty of support. It's really amazing. I was on the phone with Bryan for an hour last night. My sisters have all called, and just about everyone in my church has promised they'll swear to the fact that I'm the best mother this side of June Cleaver. Our choir director Gary McClain said he'd be glad to represent me for a greatly reduced fee."

"I'm assuming Mr. McClain is a lawyer in addition to being a choir director."

"Where do you think I learned all those lawyer jokes?"

"It's good to hear you've got that taken care of. Anyway, there are other matters to discuss." He opened his desk drawer and pulled out a long white envelope. Kate's name had been written on the front in a loopy handwriting she didn't recognize.

"This is to you from our former business editor," he said and handed it to her.

"Former business editor? Are you kidding me? Janie's always said Clarisse would be here long after the rest of us were gone. What happened?"

"She crossed over the line this time. Actually, she's crossed over so many lines for so many years, we finally reached a breaking point."

She ripped the envelope open and looked at the contents. The note had been written with an old typewriter; Clarisse never did care much for computers.

Dear Kate,

I apologize for alerting the authorities to your story. It was a thoughtless gesture on my part and I am sorry for any inconvenience my decision may have caused you.

Sincerely yours,

Clarisse Hopper

"Inconvenience? A night in jail is an inconvenience? Interrogation? Losing my daughter? I'd hate to see what she would call suffering and pain."

"It was hard enough to get her to write that. She insisted that turning you in was her civic duty. I pointed out that once the paper was out, everyone would have known anyway so, as far as I was concerned, it was a blatant act of backstabbing."

Kate read the letter once more, trying to imagine Clarisse sputtering in protest as Roger questioned her motives.

"You know, I've never cared for forced apologies, but I am relishing the fact you made her write it. How'd you get her to do it, at gunpoint?"

"No, I simply informed her she was getting close to retirement age, and I offered her the chance to enjoy her golden years without the shame of having been fired from a job she's held for thirty-seven years. Also, I told her we'd continue to run her travel stories, so at least she can keep on making those lavish trips of hers and deduct them as business expenses."

"She was right about the Ellis Grove Inn. That place was incredible. Wish I had the money to go back there."

"Maybe you'll get another chance to go. Like on your honeymoon."

"Why is everyone in such a hurry to marry me off?"

There was a knock at the door.

"Hey, boss, it's me. You ready for the meeting?" Barry called from outside. "I'd come in there, but I don't want to take up the last of your usable oxygen."

"Guess it's time to meet with the troops," Roger said.

They stood up and headed for the door.

"Yes, all two of them. With Clarisse gone, it's just Barry and me."

"All the more reason for you to stay. Barry's good, but he's already doing the work of three people. Come to think of it, so are you."

Outside, Barry was bowing and waving his arms in mock adulation.

"I'm not worthy, I'm not worthy," he chanted over and over. "Seriously, you're both awesome," he said, standing up straight. "Kate paid the ultimate price for the First Amendment and Roger got rid of Clarisse. You are an inspiration to me, and I promise to name all my children after you, if I ever have any. You guys rock."

"Thank you, Barry. It's been a while since I was an inspiration to anyone," Roger said. "But we've still got a paper to put out. Pull up the chairs, and let's get started."

Kate and Barry scrambled for the chairs and pulled them to the middle of the room. Notes in hand, they all sat down.

"Guess the meetings at Port City Java are history now, right?" Barry asked

"Not enough time or money to cover that luxury for now, Barry," Roger answered. "Although I think it would be a nice idea for you and me to treat Kate to lunch at the restaurant of her choice. She needs to get the taste of prison food out of her mouth."

"Actually, prison food is not that bad," Kate said. "It's kind of bland but it's filling. It's the atmosphere that's so hard to take."

"Speaking of your jail time, Kate, would you be interested in writing a column about it? I'm assuming most of our readers have never been to jail, and they'd be interested to know."

Kate paused before she answered, contemplating whether or not she was ready to write about her ordeal.

"Not sure if I want to do that, Roger. I really don't want to call attention to the fact I've been to jail, even if it was for a noble cause. I'd like to put some distance between myself and the experience. It's not something I really want to advertise, if you know what I mean."

"Fair enough. Do you have any objection if I write an editorial about it?"

"No, that's fine."

"We will be running a news story about it, which Barry will do. You will talk to him about it, right?"

"It's news after all, Kate," Barry added.

"I'd rather not, but I suppose if I want my side out there I'll have to talk about it."

"I promise I'll be gentle with you."

"Thanks. I appreciate that."

"So, we've got Kate on page one. What else have you got on for this week, Barry?"

"Oh, it's been busy. Number one with a bullet is the Kessler murder trial. The case has gone to the jury, and it looks like they'll be out for a while. Timmy's lawyer put up one hell of a defense, definitely some reasonable doubt there. Also, we've got some good stuff going on with the city council. They're talking about annexing Winslow Beach again."

"They might as well get it over with and take over the entire county," Roger said.

"What else, what else?" Barry continued. "Oh, the television series that films here is going to be doing a remote at that doughnut shop on the Winslow Beach boardwalk. Kind of a last hurrah before they take the show up to Canada. And I've got an interview with a guy who's training for the Winter Olympics in bobsledding."

"That in itself is newsworthy, considering there's hardly any snow and not a hill worth mentioning in Wilmington," Roger noted.

"Yeah, you really got to admire the guy. He gets around it by going up to Lake Placid."

"Anything else?"

"Aside from the usual stuff, no, that about covers it."

"Kate, what have you got?"

"Not much, really. I missed a planning and zoning meeting yesterday, but I'll call the administrator today. Joe Vining's a good guy, I'm sure he'll fill me in on what, if anything, happened. I've got a few school pageants lined up. It's that time of year again, you know, all those cute little gap-toothed first graders dressed up like Pilgrims."

"Including your own first grader?" Barry asked.

"Excuse me, Molly is in second grade, thank you. And I'll have you know her two front teeth came in months ago. She — " Suddenly, Kate felt the tears were coming. For just a second, she'd forgotten that Molly was with Keith and Jennifer. Embarrassed, she quickly wiped her face and tried to smile.

"Oh, God, Kate I'm sorry, I completely forgot. I heard about your ex-husband taking Molly, but I figured you didn't want to talk about it. And here I go bringing it up."

"It's okay. It's not like she's gone for good. For now, Keith wants her with him because he thinks she's safer there. And I guess he has a point, with the firebombing and the death threats. I'm handling it."

"Well, if there's anything I can do, let me know."

"Know any good lawyer jokes?" she asked with a smile.

"Uhh, what do you call a lawyer gone bad?"

"I don't know."

"Senator."

"Good one, I'll have to remember it. Thanks, Barry." She went back to her notes. "Now, where was I? School pageants, planning and zoning. Yes, here it is. I'm working on a feature about Abigail's Attic, the charity that Warren Owens volunteered for. His widow took over for him. She's trying to get funding to help secure childcare and drug rehab programs. I think she'll do it, too. That's a woman on a mission if there ever was on. And for tomorrow, I've got that Young Entrepreneurs' Fair at Cape Fear Community College."

"Oh, Kate, that's going on today," Roger said. "Clarisse told me she got the date wrong. You don't have to cover it if it's a problem."

"Why does that not surprise me? Today's not a problem; the college is just down the street. I'll go as soon as I get that call in to Joe Vining at the planning commission."

"Thanks, Kate," Roger said. "Well, that about wraps it up. Clarisse was kind enough to hand over enough business stories to keep us going for a few weeks. This time of year, things are a bit slow, so I'm not worried. And next month I'll be bringing in an intern from the university."

"Oooh, can we have a pretty one? Please, Roger?" Barry asked.

"I'm just hoping for one that can spell. Okay, back to work, everyone."

Technology Stars at CFCC Expo

Nov. 12 — The future is now at Cape Fear Community College. The CFCC Entrepreneurs Expo is a showcase of the state-of-the art technology embraced by these talented young business owners. Security, web design, custom entertainment systems and landscape architecture using computer animation are just some of the successful ventures on display. Come on down to the Schwartz Center and see what the future holds for you.

Winslow Beach Beacon

34. NERD-O-RAMA

THE BASKETBALL COURT AT THE SCHWARZ CENTER WAS CRAMMED WITH booths. This bastion of athletics had been invaded by rows and rows of techno-nerds armed with laptops and tri-cornered display boards. Wires snaked across the polished gymnasium floor, powering countless computer monitors offering countless video presentations. With no need for spectators at this event, the bleachers were pushed against the wall. Beneath one of the basketball hoops was a small platform with a podium and a microphone and a number of folding chairs, the site of the upcoming awards ceremony.

Wandering through the crowded displays, Kate was amazed at how many college kids were running their own businesses, and making money at it. According to the Expo program, there were two hundred participants. There had to be at least three times that many attendees and they all were congregated around the same eight or nine exhibits.

The sound of the crowd bounced off the walls and ceiling, making it difficult for Kate to understand what people were saying, even when she was standing right beside them. She wondered if her ears would ever stop ringing.

Kate stopped in front of the display for Lawrence Turf Unlimited. Standing behind the rickety card table was the owner, Chase Lawrence. Tall, bronzed, with a muscular body the maintenance of which must have required permanent residence in a gym, he was more than happy to talk about his business exploits.

"Oh, yeah, we grossed over eighty thousand last year."

He rattled off some more figures as she watched the computer slide show depicting more muscular young men operating lawnmowers and weed trimmers. Definitely some fine-looking guys on the payroll, she noted. Worth the price just to watch.

"But aren't you just mowing lawns?"

"Oh, there's way more to it than that," Chase explained. "We use twenty-first century technology to meet and exceed our clients' needs and wants. We do testing for each of our clients, and we keep extensive records, which are continuously updated. We know exactly when we need to re-service, and exactly what products are needed. We've got that extra edge that keeps us competitive. By the way, Ms. Dennison, do you do your own lawn care?"

"More or less, but my front yard is all ground cover. Creeping phlox and ivy, with a few crape myrtles. And a garden gnome."

"Lawn ornaments are pretty hot these days. We get a lot of demand for that type of thing. Especially the retro ones. Ms. Dennison, I'm sure you're a busy woman. Wouldn't you like to add some curb appeal to your house without the hassle? We can make it happen for you."

"No, thanks," she said. "But I appreciate you taking the time to talk with me. Mind if I take your picture?"

"No, go right ahead."

Chase gave a practiced smile, and Kate clicked away. She felt a little guilty about all the attention she was lavishing on glorified lawn care, and she knew it wasn't fair to the rest of the entrants, but Chase was by far the best-looking entrepreneur in the room, with everyone else being the "great personality" guys. They were either overweight or rail-thin, wearing ill-fitting clothes with no style whatsoever.

Two such gawky young men were glaring at her from the next table. Embarrassed, she smiled at the them, thanked Chase again and moved over to their table.

"Hi," she said, "I'm Kate Dennison with the *Winslow Beacon*. I'd like to talk to you about your business."

"Uh, sure, go right ahead," the taller one said.

"First, could I have your names, please?"

"Right. I'm Theo Shelton and this knucklehead here is Ryan Coulter." He pointed to his partner, who grinned sheepishly and tugged at his tight T-shirt.

"Pleased to meet you," Ryan mumbled.

"So, Theo and Ryan, could you tell me something about your business? What exactly does..." She paused and read the name off the banner. "CyberClops? That's an interesting name. What does CyberClops do?"

"Oh, it does just about anything you want," Theo replied, his enthusiasm obvious. "It is absolutely the best tool out there for web security and investigation. Nothing gets by CyberClops. It protects against all worms and viruses, disabling them instantly. For companies who want to eliminate unauthorized web surfing, it monitors everything employees do online, the sites they go to and who they email. You can even get copies of every single email message sent on the company system. They're automatically sent to a special file every day. A great way to weed out the bad apples and malcontents."

"Sounds a bit harsh," Kate said. "I'm not sure if I care for the idea of my boss looking over my shoulder at every email I write."

"Hey, who's paying for the system?" Ryan chimed in. "The company, right? People are there to make money for the company, not play Fantasy Football online, right? It's all about productivity, right? You know, time is money and no one's making money if everyone's fooling around on eBay, right?"

"The sellers on eBay are," she pointed out.

Ryan and Theo both gave her a scathing look.

"This is a serious business," Theo said, full of indignation. "Lost productivity is the single greatest drain on a company's profits. A good server costs money, and a good company would want to use it to their best advantage."

"Theo, tell her about the investigation package," Ryan urged.

"Investigation package? Who do you investigate?"

"Whoever you want," Theo replied. "Employees, nannies, girlfriends – give us a name and you'll know more about that person than their own mother does. And that's not all. We offer a special spy feature whereby the company can monitor an employee's online activity from his own computer. It's really ingenious. The company sends out an email to the employee's home address and our tracking system embeds itself in the software, sending out daily reports on sites visited."

"Now, that's an invasion of privacy," Kate said, shocked that such technology was even legal. "Where you go online on your own time should be your own business, and your employer has no right to know what you're doing."

"Not if you're sharing company secrets," argued Ryan. "Or breaking the law. We had one client who found an employee running a child porn site. Because of our system, a dangerous pervert is off the net."

"Very commendable," she said.

"We can do the same thing with a website," Theo continued. "Visit a website, send them an email and you can track all the people who visit it. You can contact potential clients that way. Or find out if your employees have been in touch with the competition."

"Yeah, that client I was talking about — you know, the one with the dude into kiddie porn? They took that package, too," Ryan said "They picked out this tree-hugging save-the-earth wacko site and wanted to know everyone who visited it. Then they had us investigate the only local guy who did. So, you see, we're, like, really versatile."

A tree-hugging save-the-earth wacko site? Investigating the one local guy who visited it? Kate's interest in CyberClops increased substantially.

"Yes, you certainly are versatile," she said. "This is really fascinating. Any reason why that company wanted that particular site? Did it have anything to do with their business?"

"We don't ask questions," Theo said. "We just do what the client wants."

"I always kind of wondered about this company, though," Ryan went on. "I mean, this site didn't have anything to do with them. Kominsky Builders sold these big houses by the beach."

Theo went pale, dropping his jaw in shock.

"Client confidentiality, you idiot!" he hissed into Ryan's ear as he punched him hard in the arm. "Can't you keep you big mouth shut for one second? The woman's a reporter, for God's sake!"

"Did you say Kominsky Builders?" Kate asked.

"No, it wasn't Kominsky Builders," Ryan said, rubbing his arm. "Not them."

"You aren't going to print that, are you? We could be sued. We signed a contract that all our work would remain confidential. And you have no proof, anyway."

Kate stood there, putting it all together. Someone at Kominsky Builders set Timmy Kessler up, using CyberClops spyware to identify him as a local Forces of Nature sympathizer. It had to be Shane Cochran.

He had the motive, and as Kominsky's assistant, he certainly had access to the Cyberclops files. She needed to get back to the paper and do some digging.

"Don't worry, it's off the record. I won't mention it when I write this story."

Ryan and Theo both relaxed, heaving audible sighs of relief.

"Hey, are you going to take our picture?" Ryan asked.

"Okay."

They posed self-consciously, and she took several shots, even though she was itching to get back to the office.

"Thanks, guys," she said as she turned to leave.

"Sure thing," said Theo. "When's this going to appear?"

"Next Tuesday."

"Cool," they said in unison.

Glad to be finished with this pair of Wilmington spies, Kate hurried past the displays, pushing her way to the exit.

"Ms. Dennison!"

Who could be calling after her now?

She turned, and standing behind her, big as life, was Ed Kominsky. In seconds, he was practically on top of her, shaking her hand like a polished politician.

"Aren't these kids amazing?" he asked. "I can't believe the things they come up with. Lots of talent here. Lots of talent. You're covering this, I assume?"

"Yes, I am. Just on my way out to write it up."

"Fantastic! Do you have a minute you can spare?"

"Maybe a minute, but not much longer than that."

"Well, I have to admit, I've got a bit of a bone to pick with you."

"Oh?" Kate braced herself for another rant about her story on the Forces of Nature. Hadn't she suffered enough for that one?

"I'd like to have equal time with that criminal you put on the front page of that newspaper of yours."

"Absolutely, Mr. Kominsky. I'd be glad to interview you anytime."

"Great, we'll do it right now."

"Um, now's not a good time for me, Mr. Kominsky," she protested. "I need to get back to the office. And I need a little time to prepare questions."

"Nonsense, you're a great reporter. And you can always call me later if you think of anything we don't cover. I'm here. You're here. Let's do it."

"Well, all right." She pulled her pen and notebook out of her purse.

Kominsky grabbed her arm and started toward the stage.

"Not here. Way too noisy. I wouldn't want to be misquoted. As it happens, I have access to an office in this building, great place. We won't be disturbed there. Besides, I have my speech to make in half an hour, so I promise you, you'll be on your way in twenty minutes."

Kate followed along, not sure what was going on. Kominsky led her through the rows of displays, turning left at the bleachers and stopping in front of a door marked Custodian.

"The janitor's office?"

"Yes, total privacy."

They entered, and he shut the door

Great, more small places. The room was not much larger than a broom closet. They weren't exactly alone, either. A very large man stood silently by the desk, his eyes trained on Kate.

"This is Gordon, my assistant."

"I thought Shane Cochran was your assistant."

"I'm a busy man. I need lots of help. Gordon doesn't say much, but he's very helpful. Have a seat, Ms. Dennison. Let's get started."

FBI: Violence Against Women Increasing

According to the latest report from the FBI, violent crimes against women increased substantially. The majority are committed by persons known to the victims. The *Beacon* is offering a pamphlet on self-defense for women and encourages all women to take classes in self-defense.

Winslow Beach Beacon

35. WOMAN IN JEOPARDY

S HE WAS IN TROUBLE.
Gordon was well over six feet tall and must have weighed at least two hundred and fifty pounds, probably all muscle. He sneered at her over Kominsky's shoulder, as if daring her to step one toe out of line.

Kominsky was all smiles, but Kate sensed a sharp edge to his joviality. The walls of the tiny office were closing in on her, and all she could think of was how many steps it was to the door.

"Go ahead, Ms. Dennison. Sit down," Kominsky said, pointing to a folding chair shoved against the wall. "I realize it's a bit small, but it's so much quieter in here than out on the floor."

She remained where she was.

"If you don't mind, I think I'll stand. You had something to say about the Forces of Nature?" she prompted.

"Well, Ms. Dennison, it's like this," Kominsky began. "Those damn tree-huggers are ruining our city, and your paper puts them on the front page."

"I see. Go on," she said, scribbling furiously. Looking at her chicken scratches, she wasn't sure she'd be able to decipher them later, but she figured that she'd humor him by at least appearing to take notes.

Hoping he wouldn't notice, she quietly slid one foot over then the other, inching toward the door. The closer she was to the exit, the safer she felt.

"It's not just the nutjobs that burned down the house at Normandy Sands," he ranted. "It's all of them. Those little twerps whining about sea turtles and water quality, spouting EPA regulations and filing those damn motions. They didn't realize that Normandy Sands is good for the whole county. It brought in jobs, good jobs like construction and sales.

It will attract wealthy people, who'll spend lots of money and boost the economy. Who gives a damn about a bunch of turtles when you can make the community a better place for everyone?"

"I've never thought of it that way, Mr. Kominsky," Kate said. "So, how would you deal with the environmental groups who oppose your development?"

"What needs to be done is to expose them for the hopelessly misguided morons they are, and that's damn near impossible, what with the liberal media. A bunch of little old ladies lie down in front of one of my bulldozers, and the people on the TV news call them heroes for risking their lives to save the turtles. No one says anything about how much money I had to pay the driver, or how the delays in building hurt all the people who work for me. There are plenty of turtles in Wilmington. Just take a look in Greenfield Lake."

"Mr. Kominsky, those are snapping turtles. They're not endangered."

"A turtle is a turtle. Same thing with the damn pine trees. I've heard it enough times. The long-leaf's endangered, and the whatcha-call-it, the loblolly, grows around here like a weed. I say if you can't tell the difference, why bother protecting one over the other? We've got enough pine trees in North Carolina. For the life of me, I can't see why these people have to make so much trouble for me over these damn long-leaf pines. I'd really like to just rip every last one of them out. Then they'd have nothing left to bug me about."

Kominsky balled his right hand into a fist and smacked it hard into his left hand, the violence in the gesture not lost on her. With much relief, she saw she was by the door. She reached out and touched it with her left hand.

"Thank you so much, Mr. Kominsky. I'll just go back to the office and write this up. And I'll make sure it appears on page one, just like the Forces of Nature story."

"Ms. Dennison, you're not going anywhere."

She made a grab for the doorknob, twisted it and opened the door, coming face-to-face with an old man dressed in dirty coveralls.

"Can I help you, ma'am?" he said, looking confused to see so many people in his office.

Kominsky stood up, hurried over to the janitor with his hand outstretched.

"Hello, I'm Ed Kominsky, featured speaker for the Expo. I apologize for taking your office. Ms. Dennison wanted to interview me for her paper, and we needed a little privacy. So noisy out there on the floor, you know. She's got just a few more questions, so I'd be much obliged if you could let us stay here just a bit longer."

"No problem, Mr. Kominsky. Take your time." He shut the door and was gone, along with Kate's chance to get out of the room safely.

Gordon and Kominsky were now practically on top of her. Her back was against the door, and there was no way for her to open it and get away.

"Now, Ms. Dennison," Kominsky said, "you and your damn paper have caused me enough trouble. The papers were supposed to see my company as the victim. Everyone was supposed to see what maniacs these environmentalists are, burning down houses. But your little rag kept telling everyone otherwise. You guys just wouldn't give up, even after we had your place torched."

With the revelation of the *Beacon* firebombing, Kate knew without a doubt the two men were going to kill her. She fought back the terror, and managed to remember the advice of a self-defense pamphlet she read years ago.

If you're cornered by the bad guys, make sure you breathe.

Kate took in a deep breath and with the much needed oxygen, came a plan — keep the man talking. As long as he was talking, she was living.

"You're the one who set Kessler up," she said, her voice cracking.

"Give the lady a cigar," Kominsky said.

"You burned down your own house?"

"Had to. We were losing money, and the house was falling apart; one of the subcontractors cheaped out on the cement in the foundation. There was no way to fix it. And wiping out John Cochran was my only chance to get his land. I knew Shane would sell it to me in a heartbeat. I saw a story about the Forces of Nature on the news and figured hanging the arson on them was just the ticket."

"What about Warren Owens? He was your friend. You went to his funeral."

"My friend?" Kominsky sneered. "In my business, I can't afford friends. Owens was no friend of mine. In fact, he'd been getting a little too nosy for his own good, if you know what I mean. So, I figured I could solve all my problems with a lit match. Those little computer geeks you were talking to found me the perfect guy to blame it on, and Brandon Fawkes was more than happy to make the accusation. It was either that or have his nasty little side business exposed. I know from experience that a pretty boy like that wouldn't last long in prison. Especially for a kiddie porn conviction."

Gordon grabbed Kate's right arm and pulled her away from the door.

"Should we do her now, boss?"

"No, Gordon, that janitor knows we're here. Ms. Dennison, if you know what's good for you, you won't make any trouble for us."

Kominsky opened the door.

"Let's go."

Gordon reached into his suit jacket and pulled out a gun. He grabbed Kate's left arm and pushed the barrel firmly between Kate's shoulder blades. She was frozen to the spot.

"Walk, bitch!" Gordon snapped.

Her feet seemed to be made of lead, but she managed to put one in front of the other as they returned to the expo. Gordon had his arm around her, and the gun concealed behind her back. Kominsky walked directly behind her, blocking Gordon's gun from sight.

"Isn't there any other way out of here?" Gordon asked. "Look at all these people."

"No, we have to walk through the gym to get outside," Kominsky said. "There's an exit to the parking lot over there." He pointed to the other side of the gym floor and there was a sign marked Exit. "A couple of minutes and we'll be home free."

With so many people, Kate thought somebody would be able to tell she was in trouble. But nobody noticed her — not the students clicking through their computer presentations, not the men in business suits clustered around the popular booths, not the young women hunched over their cell phones furiously texting. Everyone's attention was elsewhere.

"Don't try anything," warned Gordon.

Screaming seemed like a good idea, but she couldn't find her voice. She was having a hard time moving. Although it was not her intention, she dragged her feet like a petulant child.

Out of nowhere, she recalled an episode with Molly in a department store, just after her second birthday. Molly refused to leave the toy department. Kate had taken her by the hand, but she wouldn't budge. She flopped down on the floor, kicking and screaming. What a scene that was.

Every step Kate took brought her closer to death. Just like Molly, she was not going to cooperate.

She went completely limp, collapsing on the floor in a heap.

Gordon was holding on to her arm so tightly, she nearly wrenched it out of the socket as she fell, but she didn't care.

People were looking at her now.

She lay face down on the floor, immobile, covering her head with her arms. If these guys were going to take her away, they'd have to drag her out of the Schwartz Center by her ankles. Either that or shoot her in front of five hundred witnesses.

"Hey, lady, are you all right?" she heard a voice say over her.

"Look, he's got a gun!" someone else shouted.

Kate looked up to see Kominsky and Gordon sprinting toward the exit, but a dozen young entrepreneurs jumped them before they could make it. Kate waited another minute to make sure they were out of commission then stood up, noting that another work outfit was now covered with dirt and grime. Several hundred pairs of feet can leave a lot of dirt on a floor.

"Can I get you anything?" a young man asked her.

"No, I'm fine," she said, although still a bit shaky.

"What was that all about?"

"A long story," she answered. "Thanks for your help."

"You probably should stick around. I think the police will want to talk to you."

"I expect they will. Seems like that's all I do these days is talk to police. Hey, I could sure use a cup of coffee. Could you get me some? They've got it set up by the door."

"Sure."

"Black with sweetener," she called after him. She found an empty chair by an abandoned display and sat down to wait for the police.

This was going to be one hell of a story.

POLICE NEWS

Nov. 17 — Several alert students at Cape Fear Community College thwarted an attempted abduction during the college's Young Entrepreneurs' Expo. Witnesses reported seeing a woman held at gunpoint. There were no injuries, and two men were arrested.

Winslow Beach Beacon

36. LOOSE ENDS

KATE WAS EXHAUSTED. SITTING IN THE CRAMPED, WINDOWLESS ROOM at the Law Enforcement Center, she was nearly finished with her eighth recounting of how Ed Kominsky had lured her into the janitor's office, admitted to burning down the Normandy Sands house and then ordered his burly "assistant" to take her at gunpoint. She was ready to go home now, but no one seemed interested in letting her go.

"So, you just fell on the floor?" Detective Garrett Loftin asked. He was an older man, gray-haired and paunchy. "Pretty smart thing to do. Where'd you get that idea?"

"Ever try to make a two-year-old leave the toy department?"

"I know what you mean." He gave her a wide grin. "When my son was small, he about drove my wife crazy. If you just looked at him cross-eyed, he'd be down on the floor, screamin' like a banshee. Thank God, he grew out of it."

"How old is your son?" Kate asked, much preferring to discuss child-rearing than go over her latest ordeal one more time.

"Let's see, Jesse's thirty – no, thirty-one. Has a nice job at the Wachovia Bank. Course, there were times we didn't think he'd get past ten. He was a real daredevil, that boy."

They both chuckled. Loftin looked over his notes, clicking his tongue.

"Well, that about wraps it up for me, Ms. Dennison. You're free to go. Thanks for all your help," he said.

Heaving a great sigh of relief, Kate picked up her purse and stood up.

"Oh, what's happened to Ed Kominsky?"

"Don't you worry about him," Loftin said, also getting to his feet. "We got him in jail without bond. We ran his prints, and it turns out he's

285

got a prison record and he's wanted on three counts of fraud in Illinois and two counts of extortion in Iowa. He won't be going anywhere for a long time."

"So, that story he always told about turning away from the gangs in Chicago was all a lie."

"Yup, he had us all hoodwinked, that's for sure." He opened the door for her.

She paused outside the door, not sure which way to go.

"Looking for the exit?" he asked. "See that door down there? Go through there, turn left, take the elevator to the ground floor and you'll be on Princess Street."

"Thank you so much. I probably would have wandered around here for hours."

"No problem." He waved and walked toward one of the desks, while Kate headed for the door. The elevator was exactly where he'd said it would be. She pressed the down button.

"Kate! Hey, Kate, wait up!"

She turned to see Barry, disheveled and running down the hall. He skidded to a stop at the elevator, panting and sweaty.

"I've been looking all over for you," he said. "Where have you been?"

"Answering police questions," she said.

"Wow, is this some story or what? Did you know it was Kominsky who killed Cochran and Owens? It was him all along: he had the fire set, he got Brandon Fawkes to frame Timothy Kessler and he even firebombed our building. Not to mention sending you that dead rat."

"Yes, I know. Well, not about the dead rat, but everything else. He told me just before he was about to kill me."

"And here I've been doing all this fine investigative reporting, while you knew it all along."

The bell rang to announce the elevator's arrival. They got in, and Kate pressed the ground floor button.

Kate stared at the dirty floor of the elevator car.

"Barry," she said, "you don't know how weird it is to have someone actually want to kill you. They'd have shot me right there if the janitor hadn't decided to come to his office."

"Yeah, you sure were lucky. When the police questioned Kominsky's goon, he told them the plan was to drug you, rape you and strangle you. They wanted to draw attention away from the trial and have the city in an uproar about a dangerous killer-rapist on the loose."

"What were these guys thinking, anyway? How could they possibly get away with it?"

"He very nearly got away with the Cochran-Owens murders. But the jury just found Kessler innocent, even without Kominsky's confession."

"They found him innocent?"

"Yes, the verdict came down this afternoon. It was really emotional. Kessler's grandma cried and hugged the lawyer. You should have seen it. That lawyer had the right idea, but pinned it on the wrong guy. Shane Cochran had nothing to do with his father's death."

The elevator door opened, and they continued out to Princess Street.

It was dark now; the sun had set long ago. If Molly were home with her, Kate knew she would be worried about getting home to fix her dinner. A real dinner, not fast food take-out, either.

"You going home, Kate?"

"No, I think I'll head back to the office. Might as well write my story on all this, while it's still fresh."

"Well, I'll walk with you. There's a lot of crazies out."

"Tell me about it."

In minutes, they entered the *Beacon*'s temporary office. Kate was expecting it to be dark and deserted at this hour, but the lights were still on and the door was unlocked.

"Guess Roger must be staying late as well," Barry said.

They passed Roger's door, which was closed tightly, and went into press room. Kate sat down at her desk and found a sheaf of pink phone messages.

"Look at all these," she said, sifting through them.

"Poor Janie," Barry said. "I bet she really misses the voice mail. Can't understand why they couldn't get it to work in this building."

"Good Lord, Keith must have called a dozen times. Oh my God, this is from Children's Services! Damn, they're closed now. Don't these people have pagers or cell phones?"

"Calm down, Kate. Don't jump to conclusions. If anything's happened to Molly, someone would tell us."

"Maybe that's what Keith was trying to do when he was calling every half-hour," she pointed out. "She could be in the hospital, she could have run away, she could be — "

"Don't go borrowing trouble, Kate. You know as well as I do that Children's Services can be called in for minor stuff. Maybe one of the neighbors didn't like the way Jennifer was talking to Molly and reported her. Happens all the time."

"Keith's got his cell phone number on all these calls. I guess he knows what's going on."

She dialed and got a message: the number she was dialing was not available. Obviously, Keith had let his battery run down again.

"Great," she said, slamming down the receiver. "What's the good of having cell phones if you can't get hold of people when you need them? I don't want to talk to Jennifer, but I guess I'll have to."

"Kate? I thought I heard you in here." Roger came into the pressroom. "I've been waiting for you to get back from the police station."

"Roger, do you know what's going on with Molly?" she asked. "I've got all these messages from Keith and from Children's Services."

"Molly is fine."

"How do you know?"

"Because she and Keith are at my house right now, waiting for you. Marlene's been calling every fifteen minutes for hours. Get out of here."

"Wait a second, I'll walk you to your car," Barry said.

"Well, get a move on. My baby's waiting for me."

FAMILY TALK

What To Do When You Suspect Child Abuse

If you suspect a child you know is being abused, The *Beacon* urges you to immediately contact the New Hanover County Department of Children's Services. Your call will remain anonymous, and the information you supply could very well save a child's life. Remember, a child's safety is your business.

Winslow Beach Beacon

37. HOME AT LAST

ALL THE LIGHTS WERE ON IN ROGER AND MARLENE'S HOUSE. IT seemed almost festive, like Christmas. In her rush to see Molly, Kate nearly ran over one of Marlene's shrubs by the driveway. Before she turned off the car engine, Marlene was outside the door and on the porch.

"Where the hell have you been?" she shouted.

"Talking to the police," Kate yelled back. "Didn't Roger tell you? Ed Kominsky tried to..." She stopped herself. If Molly were listening, she didn't want to scare her by saying that someone had tried to kill her today.

What a week this has been, she thought. I went to jail on Monday, lost my daughter on Tuesday, nearly got myself killed on Wednesday. God knows what misery I'll suffer on Thursday.

"Yes, I know," Marlene said. "Always thought that man was on the wrong side of the law. You were lucky to get away from him."

"Luck had nothing to do with it. I just refused to cooperate."

She was on the porch now. She tried to get a look inside the house, over Marlene's shoulder. She thought she saw Keith sitting at the kitchen table, but she couldn't see Molly anywhere.

"Good thinking on your part," Marlene went on. "Now get in here. Your husband needs to talk to you."

"Ex-husband, Marlene, don't ever forget that."

Keith stood up when she entered. He was wearing a pair of jeans and a blue polo shirt instead of his usual work clothes of a suit and tie. He must have taken the day off. Hell must have frozen over, she thought. Keith never took days off on the spur of the moment.

"Where's Molly?"

"She fell asleep about half an hour ago," he said.

"We put her in the spare room," Marlene added. "You weren't the only one who had a hard day today."

Kate rushed down the hall. The guestroom was dark, but with the light in the hallway, she could make out her daughter's small body curled up on the antique coverlet. Molly's hands twitched, and Kate smiled when she mumbled something unintelligible.

She and Keith often joked about how Molly talked in her sleep.

She could have stood there forever, just gazing at her sleeping daughter. Keith had brought her back. Nothing else mattered.

She heard footsteps behind her and turned to find him right behind her.

"Amazing how soundly she sleeps, isn't it?" he said.

"Yes, it is," she murmured.

"Bet you're wondering what's going on."

"Well, between going to jail on Monday and the attempt on my life today, I've been kind of preoccupied."

"Marlene told me about Kominsky holding you hostage. It must have been terrible."

"Keith, you're not going to use that against me, are you? It was him all along, you know. The death threats, the office fire, everything. He's in jail now, so it's all over. And I doubt if I'll be cited for contempt of court again anytime soon."

"No, I understand that. I'm sorry you had to go through it."

"Thank you," she said.

"Have you had anything to eat? Molly had dinner but I wasn't hungry. Now I'm famished. We could go to Elizabeth's Pizza and talk. We have a lot to talk about."

"Thanks for the offer, Keith, but I'm too tired to manage dinner out. I just want to take Molly home. I've got about a gallon of chili in the refrigerator. You're welcome to share some with me."

"Uhh, I've had your chili. It nearly killed me."

"Don't worry. It's not spicy at all. I made it mild so Molly would eat it, and I just add some hot sauce to mine."

"Molly eats chili?"

"Yes, if you give her lots of oyster crackers and put cheese on it, she does."

"All right, let's go to your house, then."

He went into the room and scooped Molly into his arms. He groaned a bit as he straightened up.

"She's a lot heavier than she used to be," he said as he carried his burden down the hallway.

"Remember, Molly's always been big for her age and she's grown a lot in the last year. Did you bring her things with her?"

"All at your house. Marlene let us in."

Marlene was waiting at the front door, holding it open for them.

"I gather you're taking our baby home?" she asked.

"Yes. She's going to sleep in her own bed tonight," Keith replied.

Her own bed. Molly was home.

🌿 🌿 🌿

"You know, this is pretty good," Keith said, spooning more chili into his mouth. They sat together at Kate's claw foot dining room table, accented by the red and blue laminated construction paper place mats Molly had made in first grade.

"Well, you put enough cheese and oyster crackers on it, it should be," Kate said, taking a swig of beer.

"No, I meant I can eat it. I remember the first time you made me chili, it nearly set my mouth on fire."

"How was I to know you didn't like spicy food? You never told me."

"How was I to know you liked your food so hot your nose runs, your eyes water and steam comes out of your ears?"

"We should have talked about that stuff before we got married," she said, smiling. "So, how about filling me in on why you're not living happily ever after in Jennifer's big house in Carrington Downs?"

Keith set his spoon down and said nothing. Tears welled up in his eyes.

"I really screwed things up. I didn't know what Jennifer was like and I – oh, Kate, I'm so sorry," he sobbed.

Although Keith had always been prone to weepiness, Kate was surprised at the intensity of his outburst. She reached across the table and put a comforting hand on his shoulder.

"It can't be as bad as all that," she said in a soothing voice. "Molly's back home safe and sound, and you escaped from Godzilla. I'm not in jail and I'm not dead. We should be considering ourselves lucky."

She left the table and came back with the box of tissues she kept on the end table next to the couch. She pulled out a handful and gave them to Keith.

"Here you go," she said, leaving the box on the table.

"Thanks," he sniffled, wiping his eyes and blowing his nose.

Kate said nothing for a minute, sitting quietly while Keith pulled himself together.

"So what happened after I left?" she asked when his tears subsided.

"Molly was hysterical and it took me nearly an hour to calm her down. Jennifer didn't help at all. She kept telling her to stop. Like she expected Molly to adjust to leaving her mother just like that."

"Well, you know Jennifer is not known for her patience with children, her own or anyone else's."

"I know," Keith said. "Anyway, I figured things would be better in the morning. Of course, mornings are a zoo over there. Jennifer gets up at five to get herself ready for work. The boys get up then, too, but they watch cartoons on television. I was up at six and so was Molly. She was fine, back to normal, I thought. We both got dressed, she had her books ready for school, and we came down for breakfast.

"Jennifer barely says two words to us. She was busy ironing her clothes and screaming at the boys. I fixed Molly a bowl of cereal and poured myself some coffee. Then Molly said something about knowing all her spelling words for the pre-test in Mrs. Gibson's class, and Jennifer yelled across the room that she wasn't going to that school anymore, she'd be going to Ogden and she starts today.

"Just as I was about to tell Jennifer I thought it was better for Molly to keep going to school at Sunset Park, Molly burst into tears. Jennifer ran over to the table and just went off on the poor thing, screaming that she lives with us now and we don't have time to take her to her old school, that she better get used to it if she knows what's good for her.

"By this time, the boys heard all the commotion and they came in to see what was going on. Molly was beside herself. She looked up at Jennifer and said, 'I don't want to go to Ogden and I don't want to live here. I want to go home.' Jennifer said, 'This is your home, you ungrateful little brat,' and she slapped her hard across the face."

"Oh, my God!" Kate said. "How could she?"

"I couldn't believe it myself. Molly was so stunned she didn't say anything. She just got out of her chair and ran upstairs as fast as she could. Then Austin said, 'That's nothing. Wait till Mom goes after her with the belt. Then she'll have something to cry about.'

"Your mother hits you with a belt?" I asked, and they both nodded. I looked over at Jennifer, and all she could say was, 'As a parent, I have every right to discipline my children as I see fit, especially when they deserve it.' That absolutely floored me. No kid, not even Matt and Austin, deserves to be beaten with a belt."

Kate shook her head in disbelief.

"I never thought Jennifer was very good with those boys, but my take was that she only screamed at them while they did whatever they wanted. I never imagined she beat them. And I certainly never thought she'd go after Molly. So, what did you do?"

"I went upstairs and told Molly we were leaving. I'll never forget the look of relief on that little girl's face. Oh God, Kate, do you think she'll ever forgive me for putting her through that?"

Tears streamed down his face again. Kate's heart went out to him. Even though she thought he was misguided in the attempt, she knew how much he'd wanted to create a happy family with Jennifer and the boys, and that he really believed he'd be able to do it. Having to see it all go so horribly wrong so quickly must be painful.

"I'm sure Molly already has forgiven you," she said. "You can do no wrong as far as she's concerned. She thinks you make the sun shine in the morning and the stars shine at night. She loves you. You're the best daddy in the whole world."

"You think so?" Keith said, wiping his eyes.

"Molly thinks you are. And I do too."

"Thank you," he said, squeezing her hand. "That means a lot."

"So what happened next?"

"You know the rest. Molly and I packed up our stuff, and we were out the door in about fifteen minutes. By this time, Jennifer was acting terribly sorry and begging me to stay, but I ignored her. I'd had enough."

"Aren't you just a little bit sad about losing that happy family you were so excited about a couple weeks ago?"

"That happy family never existed," Keith admitted. "You were right. I didn't want to be alone, and after you and Molly moved out. Jennifer was right there, inviting me to dinner, listening to my troubles and helping me with all the stuff you used to do for me. Women like Jennifer never showed any interest in me, and it was flattering."

"What do you mean, women like Jennifer?"

"You know — beautiful, strong, confident. I used to think rich until I got a look at her finances. The woman spends money like there's no tomorrow. With her income as a lawyer, plus the huge amount of child support she gets from her ex-husband, she shouldn't have any problem making ends meet. She makes a hell of a lot more money than I do. But she's on the brink of bankruptcy. I suspect that's the reason she wanted me to move in. She was hoping my credit rating would bail her out."

"Sounds like you got out just in time," Kate said. "So where did you and Molly go once you left Jennifer's house?"

"We went out for breakfast. After that we went to Children's Services and then to Fort Fisher Aquarium. I decided we both needed the day off. Anyway, at breakfast, we had a nice long talk. I was really worried about her when we left. I thought Jennifer had scarred her for life, but she took it all in stride."

"What did you say to her about it?"

"That it's never okay to hit, especially for grown-ups to hit children. That Jennifer has a hard time being a mom and sometimes she gets things wrong. She needs somebody to show her what she's supposed to do. And I told her we had to report Jennifer to the Department of Children's Services so she could get help."

"You handled that very well. It's hard to explain something like that to a child without laying blame. That was exactly the right thing to say. I'm proud of you, Keith. "

"Thank you."

"So what's going to happen to Jennifer? It's got to be difficult for her, considering she works within the family law system."

"Well, the social worker said it would be kept confidential and that there wouldn't be any charges brought against her. She'd probably just have to go to parenting classes and counseling. I tried a dozen times to call you and explain what was going on, so you didn't freak when the social worker called you."

"All I saw was a stack of messages when I got back, including one from Children's Services. My first thought was that Molly had tried to run away."

Keith laughed.

"She did run away, and she took her daddy with her."

"Keith, I'm so glad you brought her home."

"I don't know why Jennifer was so intent on taking her away from you. My guess is she thought that if she managed to get Molly for me I'd stay with her. Or maybe she can't resist a good custody fight. I don't know. That woman has me completely baffled. Of course, I've never claimed to understand women."

"It works both ways, dear," she told him.

He scraped his empty bowl with his spoon.

"Like some more?"

"No, thanks."

He said nothing for a moment.

"Uh, Kate?"

"Yes?"

"Do you ever wish we could have stayed married?"

Kate was not expecting that question and didn't know what to say.

"I wish we could have stayed happily married, but that was impossible," she said finally.

"Nothing's impossible. We could have tried harder. I know I could have tried harder."

"No one could have worked harder at saving the marriage than you did," she said. "Keith, do you remember the day I told you I wanted a divorce and really meant it? We were having dinner together, and everything we said seemed so forced, so unnatural. We were trying so hard to follow the rules of communication that we couldn't even talk to each other. At that moment, I knew that I'd never be able to keep it up and we had to end it. It wasn't fair to you or me or Molly."

"I guess you're right. But we did have some great times together."

"Yes, we did."

"Well, it's late, and I have to go to work tomorrow."

He got up and took his plate back to the sink. He was always so good about keeping things neat and tidy.

"Do you mind if I go check on Molly one more time?"

"I'll go with you," she said. They tiptoed down the hall, even though they knew Molly could sleep through thunderstorms and hurricanes. Opening the door a crack, they peeked in.

"We got this right, didn't we?" Keith commented.

"We sure did."

Dennison Honored

April 14 — The Reporter's Association of North Carolina (RPANC) has announced that the *Beacon*'s own Kate Dennison is the winner of this year's First Amendment Award. In November, Ms. Dennison was cited for contempt of court for refusing to reveal a source and was sent to the New Hanover County Jail. Ms. Dennison will receive her award at the RPANC to be held in Raleigh this summer.

Winslow Beach Beacon

38. RESTING ON LAURELS

THAT'S IT, MOLLY! YOU GOT IT!"
The red-and-gold Phoenix kite dipped and soared in the wind along Wrightsville Beach, its long tails streaming behind it. Molly gripped the kite's plastic string holder, dancing excitedly. Bryan stood by, ready to take over in case of any mishaps. Kate watched them both from her beach chair, marveling at how well they were getting along.

"Now, don't touch the string while it's going out like that," he instructed. "You could cut your fingers really bad. Just hang on to the handle, okay?"

"Okay, Bryan." Just then a gust nearly yanked the kite away. Molly squealed but managed to hold on to it.

"Whoa, you are good at this," Bryan said. "You sure you never flew a kite before?"

"Nope, this is my very first time."

"I'd have never guessed it."

After about ten minutes, the novelty of flying the kite wore off, and Molly said she would like to play with the group of children building a sand castle nearby. She handed the holder back to Bryan and was off in a flash.

He reeled the kite in and carried it to where they'd set up their beach chairs. He slid it under the cooler so it wouldn't blow away then flopped down in the chair next to Kate.

"Hello, award-winning journalist," he said. "Is this seat taken?"

She laughed as he leaned over and kissed her lightly on the cheek.

"Will you stop with that award thing?" she asked. "It's not that big a deal. Roger nominated me for it, figuring I was a shoo-in. I was the only reporter in North Carolina to go to jail for refusing to reveal a source this year. No competition whatsoever."

"Hey, you get a free dinner out of it. You wouldn't happen to know if there's an open bar, do you?"

"Probably. Reporters are notorious drinkers. It's part of the mystique. Although I expect I'll have a glass of wine and stop at that. I never was much of a hard drinker."

"Well, I'm looking forward to it. Should I rent a tux?"

"Definitely not. A suit and tie will be fine."

"Darn, I had my heart set on this powder blue suit with ruffles. I understand the lounge singer look is coming back."

"Don't even think about it."

"Not to change the subject, but you've really got a great kid. Real steady with that kite," he said. "I tried flying a kite with my nephew once but he lost patience with it long before we got it airborne. Molly's a natural."

"Did she thank you for the kite?"

"Yes, she did. And for the record, I said 'You're welcome.'"

"Good. Manners are important. You'll find that out if you spend a lot of time with kids. By the way, that was a wonderful present for her. I'm surprised at how taken she is with you. She's normally shy around strangers."

"We're going to get along just fine," Bryan assured her.

"I wouldn't count on it. There's bound to be a few rough spots. It's the nature of the beast."

"I think Molly and I can handle it. We'll have to. Because we're going to be seeing a lot of each other."

"We see a lot of each other now," Kate pointed out. "You're down here practically every weekend."

Bryan dug his long toes into the sand, looking at the ocean.

"I'm talking about moving down here."

"But you're the chapter director. You've been with the Nature Trust for years. You can't just leave."

"As a matter of fact, I can. I've been demoted, although the top brass is calling it a lateral move. And that's fine with me."

"So, what are you doing?"

"I'll be in charge of the John Cochran Memorial Preserve at Piney Point."

"I didn't know there was one."

"There is now. After some lengthy negotiations with Shane Cochran and what's left of Kominsky Builders, the Nature Trust has acquired a huge tract of land for a preserve. All of John's property and all of the Normandy Sands development. We'll be opening a field office here, and I'm in charge. They're announcing it on Monday."

She felt her stomach lurch a bit. Bryan living here? This was getting complicated.

"I thought you'd be happy about this," he said. "I know I am. I could use a break from the traffic on I-40."

"I am, really."

"You don't sound like it."

Now, it was her turn to dig her toes into the sand.

"It's so easy now," she said after a long pause. "I just see you on weekends and have my life to myself the rest of the time. After my divorce, I swore I'd never get married again. It's just too hard. Trying to stay together was awful and breaking up was even worse. I just can't do it again."

"First, let me point out that you only know what it's like to be married to Keith Dennison. You can't generalize the experience to all men. And who said anything about getting married? I'm just going to live in Wilmington. In my own place."

"Relationships have to go somewhere. They're like sharks. They have to keep moving forward or they die."

"Now that's an interesting analogy. Didn't Woody Allen say that? Look. I love you, and I want to spend my life with you. I missed out once, I'm not letting that happen again."

"But – "

"No buts, Kate. For once in your life, just sit back and let things happen."

Let things happen.

A formation of pelicans dive-bombed the ocean. Seagulls called and scolded to each other. Molly and the other children had abandoned their sand castle and were chasing each other in the waves. Bryan reached over and held her hand.

Kate smiled and squeezed his hand affectionately in return.

"Need any help finding a place?"

Winning Essay

The *Beacon* is proud to publish this prize-winning essay by Ta'Quisha Jones, a third grader at Sunset Park Elementary School. Ta'Quisha won the New Hanover County Schools Essay Contest for "Why My Mother is the Greatest."

EPILOGUE

Why My Mother Is The Greatest
By Ta'Quisha Jones

My mother made mistakes. She did some really bad things. Last year she even went to jail for a while and Miss Willis, the lady at Children's Services say my sister Moquia and me have to live with Auntie Rose because Mama can't take care of us.

My auntie say that Mama is not a bad person. She just made some bad choices. Auntie tell me to remember that my mother always love me and always love Moquia.

Sometimes we visited Mama in jail. It is not a nice place. It smelled bad and Mama had to sit behind a glass wall to talk to us.

We were very very sad.

Mama promised us she would never go back to jail again.

She kept her promise. She got out of jail and went to a place called Abigail's Attic. It's not really an attic. It's a big building with lots of rooms in it. The people there told my mama they would help her find a job so Moquia and I could live with her again.

There was a really nice lady there. Her name is Caroline Owens and she is so pretty. She wears lots of sparkly jewels and fancy clothes. She smiles all the time. Miss Caroline tell me that my Mama is the best worker ever.

Miss Caroline picked out some beautiful clothes for my Mama to wear on job interviews. Other people there help Mama learn new things, like how to type and work the computer.

Then one day Mama called Auntie Rose and say she got a good job. After that, she got a nice apartment close to our school. There is a upstairs and a downstairs and she got bunkbeds for me and Moquia.

Next, Miss Willis from Children's Services say my mama did such a good job that Moquia and me can go live with her in her apartment.

Every day before she go to work, Mama walks with Moquia and me to school. She give us both a big hug. We still go to Auntie Rose's house after school, but we live with Mama now.

My mama work very hard. She say that

Just because you make mistakes you can't give up. That is why she is the greatest mother ever.

ABOUT THE AUTHOR

JUDY NICHOLS grew up in a Batavia, Ohio, a small town twenty miles east of Cincinnati. She holds a bachelor's degree in journalism from Kent State University and even managed to find a paying job as a journalist but didn't have the stomach for asking the hard-hitting questions. After a long stint of temporary office work in Cincinnati, she decided to go into elementary education and spent three wretched years as a substitute teacher in the Columbus, Ohio, public schools.

Eventually, she moved back to Cincinnati and found work as a customer service representative, which was far less stressful than teaching and paid the bills. And she didn't have to deal with all those surly fourth graders just itching for a fight.

At this time, Ms. Nichols met Nigel, a British national who lived in an old farmhouse outside of Aurora, Indiana, a small town 20 miles west of Cincinnati. It was in that farmhouse, one day in 1996 while her baby daughter Alysoun slept, she decided it was time to get started on the book she'd always intended to write. She fired up the word processor, and five years later, her first book, Caviar Dreams, was finished. In August of 2003, it was published by Zumaya Publications.

She would still be living in Aurora if GE Aircraft hadn't made Nigel an offer he couldn't refuse — a chance to live near the ocean with GE footing the bill for moving expenses. So, now, the family lives in Wilmington, North Carolina.

ABOUT THE ARTIST

APRIL MARTINEZ was born in the Philippines and raised in San Diego, California, daughter to a US Navy chef and a US postal worker, sibling to one younger sister. From as far back as she can remember, she has always doodled and loved art, but her parents never encouraged her to consider it as a career path, suggesting instead that she work for the county. So, she attended the University of California in San Diego, earned a cum laude bachelor's degree in literature/writing and entered the workplace as a regular office worker.

For years, she went from job to job, dissatisfied that she couldn't make use of her creative tendencies, until she started working as an imaging specialist for a big book and magazine publishing house in Irvine and began learning the trade of graphic design. From that point on, she worked as a graphic designer and webmaster at subsequent day jobs while doing freelance art and illustration at night.

In 2003, April discovered the e-publishing industry. She responded to an ad looking for e-book cover artists and was soon in the business of cover art and art direction. Since then, she has created hundreds of book covers, both electronic and print, for several publishing houses, earning awards and recognition in the process. Two years into it, she was able to give up the day job and work from home. April Martinez now lives with her cat in Orange County, California, as a full-time freelance artist/illustrator and graphic designer.

CPSIA information can be obtained at www.ICGtesting.com
Printed in the USA
LVOW070042180412

277943LV00001B/164/P